HER VENGEFUL SCOT

THE HIGHLAND WARRIOR CHRONICLES
BOOK TWO

CHRISTINA PHILLIPS

PHOENIX 18 PUBLISHING

Cover Art by Kim Killion Publishing
5/26

ISBN 978-0-6487568-7-3

For Peggy and Frank, with love

CHAPTER 1

THE KINGDOM OF CE, PICTLAND.
SUMMER, 843

*E*lise, Princess Clodrah of Circinn, stood by the side of the queen of Ce and watched her cousin, Aila, ride into the distance. She tried to quell the bubbling resentment for not being allowed to accompany Aila to Dal Riada but couldn't quite manage it.

She needed to travel to Dal Riada, land of the cursed Scots. It was the only way she would discover if her dearest friend Droston was still alive.

Was he held hostage in the royal stronghold of Dunadd? Or had he, along with so many other noble Picts, been slaughtered in the massacre that had claimed the life of the king of Ce?

The pit of her stomach churned. Droston, whom she loved like a brother, couldn't be dead. He was alive and it was up to her to find a way to secure his release.

Because nobody else would.

Aila and her husband Connor MacKenzie disappeared with their band of warriors into the mist-swathed glen. Elise felt the queen give a barely discernible shiver. Elise glanced at her and saw the stricken look in her aunt's eyes and the brief tremble of her lower lip.

"Come," the queen said, no hint of her inner turmoil clouding her voice, and she abruptly turned and headed back to the palace. Elise's grandmother gripped her fingers as if she would never let her go, and Elise smothered a sigh.

She knew why she had been forbidden to accompany Aila into Dal Riada. It had little to do with the wishes of Elise's absent husband, Ferelei mac Uurguist, and everything to do with her aunt and her grandmother not wishing to lose another of their kin.

"But Aila will be back soon," Finella, not yet eleven, said, staring at the rigid back of her mother. She turned to Elise and curled her fingers around her arm. "Won't she, Elise? Before her babe is born? She promised."

"Yes, of course she will." But even as Elise comforted her small cousin, she wondered at the truth of her words. Would that Scots' devil, MacAlpin, allow Aila to leave his realm after she willingly entered Dal Riada again?

From the corner of her eye, she saw the warriors Connor had instructed to remain behind in Ce. Officially they were here as protection since so many of their own warriors were held hostage in Dal Riada. But it didn't matter how Connor tried to sweeten the situation with half-truths and platitudes. Their presence served as a constant reminder that their treacherous king sought utter domination across the land.

As the warriors bowed their heads in recognition of the women's royal status, the glimmering of an idea began to form. Before the massacre, Pict and visiting Scot had mingled freely. Liaisons had bloomed and tears had been shed from several noblewomen at the Scots' departure.

But that had been months ago, in the spring. Before the bloodied alliance to join Pict and Scot against their common enemy, the Viking. Before MacAlpin had gone back on his word.

Before Aila had taken Connor as her husband.

During this last week, relations had been strained. The Scots were their enemy. How could they be anything else? And yet Aila, the eldest Princess Devorgilla of Ce, had fallen in love and married a Scot. A Scot who had disobeyed his king by bringing Aila back to her homeland.

For that, the queen welcomed Connor MacKenzie and, to a lesser degree, his personal band of warriors. They were of the enemy, and yet were not responsible for the murder of the king of Ce. Extending a cautious friendship would not be seen as treason.

Aila had known nothing of Droston's fate. And because Elise had been so certain she was to accompany her cousin into Dal Riada she hadn't thought to question Connor on the matter.

But surely one of these Scots would know? Or at the very least, possess the means to discover the truth. Now that a Scot held such a powerful position in Ce, messengers would be sent at regular intervals between Ce and Dal Riada. She was under no illusion that a message from her, a minor princess of the neighboring Kingdom of Circinn, would even reach its destination. A Scot messenger would not bother. And no messenger from Ce would travel into Dal Riada without the queen's personal authority.

Heart thudding, Elise surreptitiously shifted her focus from the queen to the crowd that lined the path back to the palace. She would place her faith in her beloved goddess, Bride, and befriend the warrior whose glance she snared. It wasn't as if any of them were strangers. Before the upstart MacAlpin's betrayal, she had enjoyed their company, had flirted with them just as her fellow noblewomen had. Circumstances had changed and the fragile tendrils of trust had shattered, yet fundamentally, nothing about these warriors had altered. She knew, as did her grandmother, that none of the Scots in Ce had known anything of their king's true plans.

Drawn by an invisible thread—except she knew it was the benevolent power of her goddess guiding her—Elise looked up.

Eyes so dark they appeared black bored into her. Eyes that held no respect for her status, no regret for the way his people had so brutally betrayed hers. Eyes that held nothing but undisguised contempt.

Disbelief clutched low in her gut. Denial tumbled through her panicked mind. *Not him.*

There was a mistake. Of all the Scots warriors left in Ce, how had her glance fallen upon the only one she could scarcely stand to look at, never mind anything else? Even during the spring, before the darkness had descended over Pictland, she'd been unable to speak to him as she had spoken to all the others.

With rising desperation, she attempted to drag her gaze from his, but she was locked in a mutually distasteful enchantment with the glowering warrior. Every step she took brought her closer to where he stood. There was no deference in his stance despite the approach of her queen.

Why couldn't she break eye contact? Her stomach lurched, reminding her of the time she had been thrown from her horse as a child, and goddess help her, but her palms were sweaty. And still Cameron MacNeil glowered at her, as though he blamed her personally for the fact he had been one of those ordered to remain behind in Ce while his compatriots returned to Dal Riada.

They drew level. She dredged up every particle of pride she possessed to stop herself from wilting beneath that condemning glare. Condemnation he had no right directing her way.

Still his expression didn't alter. In her peripheral vision, she saw his fingers caress the hilt of his sword, but it was his dark eyes and his granite hard features that filled her mind and imprinted upon her brain.

With a sense of horror, she realized she was still staring, despite having passed him, and with shaming effort, she forced her attention back to reality. Her ragged breath echoed in her ears. The painful staccato of her heart thudded against her ribs.

Her legs were oddly weak, and a distressing whirlpool of sensation ignited between her thighs.

But most of all, despite how she was no longer looking in his direction, she was acutely aware that Cameron MacNeil hadn't taken his burning gaze from her.

~

CAM'S FINGERS tightened on the hilt of his broadsword as he watched the royal party enter the palace gates. Except it wasn't the royal party he watched. It was Lady Elise, with her golden hair, blue eyes, and haughty demeanor every time she deigned to glance his way.

It was clear she considered her filthy Pictish blood superior to his.

"Christ, Cam," Ross MacIntosh hissed. He hadn't even realized the other man had approached. "Why don't you draw your sword and impale the queen? It would scarcely be less subtle."

Cam loosened his grip on his hilt and shot Ross an irritated glare.

"I have no quarrel with the queen." He knew he sounded as though he meant the opposite, and yet his words were true. Six months ago—hell, as little as three months ago—such a remark would never have entered his mind, much less passed his lips.

But the killing of the nine Pictish nobles in MacAlpin's war chamber had shaken the foundations of his belief. To be sure, there were now nine less Picts in the country, which could only be a good thing. But the circumstances gnawed at his guts, an uneasy suspicion that, despite official word to the contrary, the Picts had been ruthlessly ambushed by his own king.

"Her personal guard think otherwise." Ross sounded grim and Cam dragged his thoughts back to the present and the apparent insult he had directed against the Pictish queen. "Did you not see the way they looked at you? The situation's bad enough without you making things worse."

"I'll not make things worse, MacIntosh," Cam ground the words between his teeth. "And neither will I apologize for not going around with an imbecilic grin on my face like MacGregor."

Ross glanced across the dispersing crowd to where Stuart MacGregor was engaged in charming a witless serving maid to doubtless part her thighs. As if to validate his thought, Stuart looped his arm around the girl's shoulders and led her in the direction of the town inn.

"At least he doesn't go around antagonizing the natives." Ross folded his arms and glowered at Cam. "When was the last time you had a woman?"

"None of your goddamn business."

"It's my business to keep the peace here in Ce. By my calculations, it's been more than three months. And by God, Cam, it shows."

Instinctively, Cam's hand fisted and only with the greatest effort did he manage to keep from smashing Ross' jaw. Three months? Was MacIntosh keeping a tally of every warrior's conquests? Or just his?

Three months? More like five.

The harsh realization of how long it had been since he'd enjoyed the pleasures of the flesh ripped through his groin, and brought to mind a golden-haired, blue-eyed Pictish princess. The image was so visceral his cock hardened, and his glare intensified, because a heathen Pict was the last female on God's earth he'd ever take.

"You're wrong." The words were a low growl, but Ross failed to heed the warning.

"No." Ross sounded smugly sure of himself. "You ignored all offers the last time we were in Ce, and then as soon as we returned to Dal Riada, we were dispatched to Northumbria. I don't recall you engaging in any liaisons before we accompanied Connor back to Ce."

MacIntosh had forgotten that, before their first mission into Ce, they had been fighting the Norse on the Isle of Iona. There were no women Cam would bed there, either.

Not that he intended to remind Ross of that fact.

"Unlike some," Cam deliberately glanced in Stuart MacGregor's direction, although the man had now disappeared. "I don't parade my conquests for public consumption."

Ross grunted. He obviously didn't believe a word Cam said.

"God only knows how long we'll be stationed here. Find a willing maid and take the edge off, MacNeil, before you combust. I doubt any of us will be welcomed in the noblewomen's beds again, but there are plenty of others to choose from."

Plenty of Picts to choose from. And therefore, no choice at all.

Elise's hauntingly beautiful face swam into his mind, her blue eyes deceptively innocent, her smile an invitation from hell itself. Elise, who three months ago had charmed and bedded half the Scots warriors in Ce, Stuart MacGregor included, but had scarcely acknowledged Cam's existence.

Elise, the damned Pictish princess, who invaded his nightly fantasies and left him sweating and infuriated and unimaginably frustrated.

Aye, there were plenty of Pictish women who had made it clear they were available for illicit liaisons. The death of their king, the upheaval in the land, appeared not to interfere with their lust for a tumble.

But he had no interest in such entanglements with a Pict. They were the enemy, no matter how this alliance professed otherwise, and they would remain his enemy until death claimed his soul.

And MacIntosh was wrong. Cam had seen the furtive glances the noblewomen had given the Scots during this last week. Their men were held hostage in Dal Riada, and the Scots offered fresh blood and energetic bed-sport. The liaisons with the nobility would recommence. Not as they had before, out of deference to their widowed queen, but that would only add to the Picts' love of intrigue.

He looked toward the royal palace. It was nothing more than a glorified stronghold, but there was no doubt as to its magnificent strategic position. The view of the surrounding Highlands was unparalleled. And because of the alliance, because Connor MacKenzie had somehow, despite his lack of royal blood, managed to wed the Princess of Ce, this land was now under tacit Scots rule.

In one respect, MacIntosh was right. They could be stationed here for months before being recalled to Dal Riada. He would die before confessing aloud, but he ached for the release only a woman could provide. And there was no Scotswoman within two weeks ride of Ce.

The crowd had dispersed. MacIntosh had vanished. The Highland wind molded his plaid to his thighs, his shirt to his chest, as he stared at the distant mountains, their peaks obscured by clouds.

Endless nights stretched before him, tormented by visions of a golden-haired temptress. A woman he despised by virtue of her birth and heritage. A heathen. And yet he couldn't dislodge her from his mind.

The famed Scots charm had bypassed him. He couldn't flatter and tell the pretty lies women loved to hear. He wasn't a master of the flirtatious arts he knew the princess found so irresistible.

What the hell was he thinking?

He was not a Pictish barbarian whose actions were led by his cock. No matter how despicably he desired Elise, he would never act upon it.

Not that she'd accept him, even if he offered.

His jaw clenched. He had no intention of offering, no intention of being rebuffed. Let her resume her liaison with

MacGregor or sample one of the other Scots. Her merchant husband was still absent. She would soon search out another lover with whom to pass the time.

He didn't give a shit who she favored.

With effort, he dragged his gaze from the distant mountains. He resented being left behind in Ce but knew it was a deliberate act on Connor's part. To test him. To see if he could curb his temper and cool his hatred of the Picts for an extended time, as any warrior worthy of the name could do.

Let Connor test him. He'd not disgrace the honor of his fellow warriors or himself. But he was in the heart of Pictland. Tenuous peace pervaded the land. The opportunity to hunt down the man who had raped his younger sister nine years ago was too potent to ignore.

Personal vengeance had no place in this new alliance between their peoples. Connor MacKenzie and Ross MacIntosh would force a blood oath from him to abandon retribution if they discovered the magnitude of his obsession for justice that still scorched his soul.

But MacKenzie was on his way back to Dal Riada. And MacIntosh would never know. Cam wouldn't ask questions, wouldn't draw attention to his quest. But while his fellow Scots indulged in fornicating with the enemy, he would hunt down and destroy Ferelei mac Uurguist.

CHAPTER 2

*B*y the time she entered the queen's private garden, Elise had managed to convince herself she had misinterpreted Bride's message. It was obvious her goddess had told her to approach any of the Scot warriors with her request—*except* for Cameron MacNeil.

It would be likely wise to avoid Stuart MacGregor as well. Three months ago, he hadn't been amused when she had failed to turn up in his bedchamber after an evening of harmless flirtation. It wasn't her fault if he'd read more into her conversation than she had intended. Thankfully, his rancor hadn't lasted more than a few hours. Only for as long as it took him to persuade another of the queen's ladies to share his bed.

"Well?" The queen's tense voice intruded into her thoughts and she glanced at her aunt to see her staring at the dowager. "Will Aila return before the birth of my grandchild?"

Relieved the queen hadn't directed the question at her, Elise trailed her fingers over the weathered face of the stone sundial. Her aunt so often expected definitive answers from the gods, when in truth such revelations rarely occurred.

Her grandmother sighed, her thoughts clearly mirroring

Elise's own. "Devorgilla, I can only repeat to you what I have already said. Aila will survive the birth and her child will bridge the chasm between Pict and Scot. But whether she returns to Ce before her time is upon her—is not clear."

The queen paced the length of the stone terrace, the only outward sign of her agitation. Then she stopped abruptly by the sundial and glared at Elise.

"What do you see?"

The raw desperation in her aunt's voice pierced Elise's heart. If only she could ease the queen's pain. But like her grandmother, all she knew for sure was Aila and her babe would survive.

But there was one more certainty she knew that her grandmother did not.

"I will see her again, madam. Before the birth." It was that certainty that had misled her into believing she would be allowed to accompany her cousin into Dal Riada. She had been wrong about that. But she knew she wasn't wrong in her conviction.

The queen gripped her hand. "She will return?"

Elise dearly wanted to look to her grandmother for help but knew she couldn't. This certainty was hers alone.

"I only know that I will see her again. And soon. But—I cannot say if that reunion occurs in Ce or elsewhere."

The queen's grip tightened. "Then look harder, Elise. Call on Bride. Ask her. Now."

Elise obediently closed her eyes, smothering her sigh. She knew her aunt was grieving for the king, was devastated at Aila's decision to return to Dal Riada and desperate to be at the birth of her first grandchild. But even so, the queen knew no god could be commanded. A mortal was the conduit. Those who believed could beg favor and offer sacrifice for imparted wisdom, but even for those chosen by the gods there was no guarantee their questions would be heeded.

But she loved her aunt. And so she opened her mind and her heart and sent blessing to her beloved Bride.

The distant call of birdsong faded. The summer breeze stilled. Her breathing slowed and her heartbeat echoed in her ears. And into her mind flowed the vision of…

Cameron MacNeil.

Shock punched through her and she gasped in disbelief. Her eyes snapped open, to be confronted by the unblinking gaze of the queen.

Goddess. Why had she thought of Cameron MacNeil? Now of all times when she was trying to help her aunt? And why hadn't she managed to hide her reaction, the way she had learned to hide her true feelings so well over the last few years?

"Yes?" The queen's voice was scarcely above a whisper.

Again, Elise closed her eyes and attempted to reach the plateau of calm required. But the Scot was still there, invading her mind, preventing her from communicating with Bride.

Panic snaked through her, coiling in the pit of her stomach. Bride didn't always answer her call, that was true enough. But never had anyone slid into her mind and severed the connection. It was—outrageous.

"Elise?" Her grandmother's voice was mild and yet there was a distinct undercurrent of curiosity. As if, goddess forbid, her grandmother sensed what had occurred.

"I only see," her voice faltered. She couldn't lie to her grandmother, but she certainly couldn't tell the absolute truth. "The Scots."

Her aunt made a noise of disgust and released her hand.

"The Scots encroach everywhere. I don't need the gods to tell me this. I want to know if I will ever see my daughter and son again."

"Madam," Elise was compelled to say. "My lord Talargan is well. Connor MacKenzie gave his word the prince would remain unharmed." Talargan, Elise's cousin and Aila's brother, was a valuable royal hostage. His wellbeing was of paramount importance.

Unlike Droston, whose heritage, while noble, was certainly not deemed worthy enough to use as a means of negotiation.

The familiar rage at such injustice bubbled deep inside and she dragged in a deep breath in an attempt to smother it. The rage was ancient, a remnant from her younger self, and it did no good to rail against that which couldn't be changed. Droston had her love and her undying support and she wouldn't desert him when he needed her most.

One of the queen's ladies approached to inform her that a messenger had arrived. With an impatient flick of her hand, the queen motioned him forward and took the sealed parchment.

There was a silence as she read the contents. Then she looked directly at Elise and unease fluttered in her breast at the look on the queen's face. Was it bad news from Elise's mother? Had something happened to one of her four sisters or their children? Had there been word on her father, who was also held hostage to MacAlpin's greed and ambition?

"Elise." Only someone closely attuned to the queen's tightly controlled emotions could have detected the note of sympathy in her voice. Elise's unease heightened, her stomach knotting, fingers gripping together. "Your husband is returned from the Eastern Empire. He is already on his way to Ce."

The unease solidified, became a fist, and gripped her throat in a remorseless vise. She remained standing, remained perfectly still. Even managed to keep her face utterly devoid of expression.

But inside, the scream pummeled against her skull, filled her brain, and threatened to erupt from her tightly compressed lips.

Ferelei had been gone for four months. She hadn't expected his return to Pictland for another two months at least. And now he was on his way to Ce to collect his wife. And once she was back in Fib, in the stronghold Ferelei called home, she would have no chance of discovering whether Droston was still alive.

She had less than two weeks—perhaps a lot less than two weeks —before her husband arrived. It left no time in which to carry out her tenuous plan of charming a Scot into sending a message to Dal Riada. Even if a message was sent today, it would take at least two weeks to reach Dunadd, the royal stronghold of the Scots.

As the unfairness of the situation thundered through her mind, a mad, shockingly seductive idea surfaced. What if, somehow, she managed to persuade a Scot warrior into taking her to Dunadd?

Ferelei's fury would be boundless if he arrived in Ce and she wasn't there. A wild, fantastical hope illuminated the darkness in her soul. Would his anger be so great as to fatally damage his heart? Could she possibly achieve, by this one outrageous act, not only Droston's freedom but also her own?

The hope withered before it had time to fully bloom. Ferelei would never release her in so satisfactory a manner. He would ride after her, overtake her, and challenge any Scot foolish enough to voice dissent at his right to reclaim his wife.

And should his aged appearance mislead the Scot into thinking such a challenge an easy victory, he would be cruelly slaughtered. Although, thank the merciful Bride, Ferelei's cock had been nearly useless for the last five years, his sword arm was still as fearsome as it had ever been.

"Perhaps," her grandmother said, "we can persuade him to allow you to remain in Ce for the summer, Elise. It would be," she paused for a telling moment. "A kindness to us all."

Ferelei cared nothing for kindness. But he did care for the good favor of the royal houses of Pictland. It was a slender hope, but all she had.

It still didn't help with her plan to discover the fate of Droston. Unless Ferelei could be further persuaded to not only allow her to remain in Ce, but for him to return home to Fib.

She forced a smile to her lips. Pride forbade that she show her aunt or grandmother how deeply she feared her husband. Despite her pride, she knew they were aware her marriage was far from happy. But that was scarcely a revelation. Few noble marriages were based on love.

They were likely more curious as to why she had never taken a lover during Ferelei's frequent absences. But of course, they would never ask. And she would never tell.

"I will give sacrifice to the goddess for such a favor." She curtsied, suddenly desperate to be gone, to be alone with her thoughts. Although since word of the king of Ce's murder, she was never alone. Now she was tailed everywhere by a hulking bodyguard who neither smiled nor spoke, and whenever she remained within the palace confines, she was surrounded by a dozen or more of the queen's ladies.

She should be used to it. She had grown up with such strictures. And yet in Ce with Aila, she had always enjoyed a measure of freedom her own mother had never allowed her. As a Princess of Circinn, even as the youngest princess of five, she had never been allowed a moment to herself.

She had become an expert at eluding her companions.

And look at what her fierce desire for independence had cost her. Ten years ago, she had slipped on the wet rocks and tumbled down the crag into the river. Her leg had snapped like a twig, her skin and muscle ripped to shreds.

The memory rushed through her mind, as horrifying as if the events had occurred just the other day. If not for Droston, her childhood accomplice in their daring adventures, she would have drowned in those treacherous rapids.

He had saved her life. She would do everything within her power to ensure she saved his. And the first step was to ensure Ferelei didn't insist on her returning to Fib.

She lost her bodyguard with a simple maneuver she'd used many times in a variety of ways as a child. Instructing him to remain in the passageway, she entered a chamber filled with ladies embroidering and gossiping. And then she discreetly slipped into the adjoining chamber and left the palace through an alternative route.

With luck, he would never know.

~

As Cam left the monastery, located some distance from the palace and the local village, he was forced to concede it was as serviceable as any in Dal Riada. Not that its presence made any sense to him. Why would a heathen people like the Picts maintain a house dedicated to the one true God?

Of course, the monks were nothing like the ones in Dal Riada. They were irreverent and appeared far too fond of material luxuries, but he couldn't fault their knowledge. Damned if he'd confess any of his sins to them, though.

A mirthless grin twisted his lips at the thought of confiding his murderous intentions against one of their premier warriors. But, without asking direct questions or mentioning a particular name, he had learned one thing—no warrior with origins in Fib was currently within the boundaries of the royal Kingdom of Ceeviot. Ferelei mac Uurguist, the bastard, was likely still at sea plundering any ship unfortunate enough to cross his path.

Unwilling to return to camp—unlike last time, no offer of palace chambers had been extended to the Scots—he tramped up the slope where he knew, beyond, was a secluded copse. It would be a welcome relief to be rid of the constant presence of Picts. He'd be in peace to consider strategies as to how to persuade MacIntosh to let him travel to the southern Pictish Kingdom of Fib, where Ferelei would return sooner or later.

He eyed the massive boulder that sat on the rim of the slope. Its ancient pagan carvings caused an eerie shiver to scuttle over his arms. Wasn't it sacrilegious to build a monastery in the center of such a stone circle? Without thinking, he reached out and brushed his palm across the surface of the rock. It was warm and oddly soothing. Unnerved by such errant thoughts, he snatched his hand away, took another step and nearly collided into the crouched form of Lady Elise.

Heart pounding, he glared down at her. She'd been completely hidden by the boulder until he'd almost fallen over her. And the way she was staring up at him, her blue eyes wide with shock, gave the impression she imagined he'd crept up on her unawares on purpose.

The thought irked him.

"What are you doing there?" His voice was harsh, his Pictish raw. She was fortunate he hadn't crushed her delicate hand under his boot. It was sheer chance that he had not.

She sat back on her heels, her hand now safely clasped by her other on her lap. Her jaw was tilted at an angle as she looked up at him, and her sky-blue gown, so unlike a Scotswoman's gown, hugged her curves and gave an unobstructed view of her tempting cleavage.

Lust gripped low in his groin, twisting like a serpent. His shaft thickened and it was all he could do to prevent a groan from escaping his dried throat. He couldn't even look at her for a moment without wanting to lift her skirts and thrust himself into her. Despite her heritage. Despite the fact she had never given him the slightest indication she was interested in him.

With damning reluctance, he dragged his hot gaze from her creamy breasts and the illicit fantasies of burying his face in her scented flesh. He battled the urge to pull her to her feet and trap her against the boulder, and instead focused on her face. And saw only her parted pink lips, so tantalizingly on level with his damn unruly cock.

Insane images of gripping her head and ramming into her wet, willing mouth hammered in his brain. The vision burned behind his eyes, obliterating all else. The haughty Lady Elise, on her knees before him, as he pumped his hot seed down her slender, royal throat.

Infuriated by his lack of control he folded his arms across his chest. It did nothing to curb the rabid need clawing through his groin or help cool the fervid fantasy incinerating his mind. But at least he was no longer tempted to reach out and slide his fingers through her shining hair.

Much.

She still hadn't answered him. But then, why should she? She was a princess and he a foreign commoner. Doubtless, she considered his question impertinent. He should turn and walk away. Leave her.

The tip of her tongue moistened her lips and he could no sooner turn and walk away than he could summon up a witty remark on their unexpected meeting. So he did what he did best and glared at her.

She shivered, as if a breeze chilled her, but for once the wind didn't race across the mountains. Perhaps he'd imagined it because a rose blush heated her cheeks and she certainly didn't look cold.

"You startled me." She spoke in Gaelic, her voice soft, her accent enchanting. Her blue veil framed her face, giving her a deceptive air of innocence. "Scots do not normally wander so far from the delights of the village."

Was she accusing him of something?

"We haven't been confined to the village, my lady." He sounded as if he was being deliberately antagonistic when all he'd intended was to convey he was breaking no royal command. Even when he attempted to keep the peace when confronted by a Pict, he appeared incapable of conversing in a civilized manner.

Not that he'd had much practice. He avoided them whenever possible and during the last week, none had gone out of their way to speak to him. His surly reputation from three months ago had obviously lingered in the locals' minds.

Elise didn't deign to answer, but he saw her grip her fingers together on her lap. Then his glance slid from her lap to the ground. Ice stabbed through his chest. God in heaven, she was kneeling at a pagan altar in front of the standing stone.

His fists clenched as he fought the urge to make the sign of the cross. He looked at Elise and she was staring at him as though she had done nothing blasphemous.

But then, she likely didn't think she had.

The silence screeched in his ears. He couldn't fathom why he still stood there, gazing at her like a dumbstruck boy. And so he once again glowered at the glittering crystals and smoking incense arranged in a five-pointed star design she had been— what, worshipping at before his arrival?

Elise moved to stand up, her normally elegant deportment marred by a slight stagger, as if the muscles in her right leg had cramped. Only when she stood before him did it belatedly occur to him that he should have offered her assistance.

MacGregor wouldn't have missed such an opportunity to worm into her good favor.

"I'm sure you can wander wherever you please," she said. "But there is nothing of interest here, only the copse."

MacGregor, Cam knew, would have a ready response to that comment. Unfortunately, Cam couldn't think of a single word. At least, none that conveyed flattery.

God Almighty, why did he have this despicable need to flatter? His lack of social graces had never plagued him before.

"And this." He jerked his head at the ground. That she could so casually conduct pagan rituals within sight of the monastery made him feel ill. Why did the monks allow the people to continue with their ancient ways? Such practices would never be tolerated in Dal Riada.

"What of it?" There was an edge of defensiveness in her voice, as if she knew what she did was wrong. Once again, her blue eyes snared him, and once again, the urge to walk away thudded through his brain.

It was none of his concern what Elise did. Connor MacKenzie

might be the tacit king of Ce, but he hadn't outlawed the old beliefs. MacAlpin might covet all of Pictland, but he was still king of only Dal Riada.

But Cam had never possessed diplomacy. And he couldn't shake the unease that polluted his blood. An unease so potent it vied for supremacy with the lust still burning his body.

The question refused to remain locked inside his head. "Is this some kind of demon worship?"

∽

ELISE STARED at the black haired, dark eyed Scot warrior who glowered down at her, as though her very existence offended his sight. Yet if that was so why did he continue to converse with her? Why didn't he turn and go on his way? And why did his angry countenance cause her nipples to strain against her bodice and illicit desire to spiral between her thighs?

It was hard to focus on his words when his closeness caused such havoc with her senses, but *demon worship?*

"I don't believe in your demons, Cameron MacNeil." And she didn't believe this conversation, either. After steadfastly ignoring her three months ago, and during the last week, he now appeared rooted to the spot and had said more to her than she had ever heard him utter to any of the queen's ladies. "This is an offering to my goddess."

Not that Bride appeared to be listening. Surreptitiously Elise pressed her thighs together, in an effort to stifle the distressing tremors fluttering through her. *This* was the reason she couldn't speak to him. Because whenever he drew near, her body behaved like an untouched maid of thirteen. And it had been eight years since she had been thirteen and believed the touch of a man would bring her nothing but delight.

But why did she feel this way with Cameron MacNeil? None

of the other Scots warriors affected her, no matter how many pretty words they whispered in her ear.

For a moment, she thought he was going to take issue with her response. The Scots were rigid in their beliefs, but he had no right to criticize. They were in Pictland, not his barbarous Dal Riada. And what did it matter if her request to Bride teetered on the precipice of sacrilege? She would do anything her goddess demanded if, by so doing, Ferelei's arrival in Ce would be prevented. Permanently, if possible, but indefinitely would do.

Cameron MacNeil continued to glare at her, his eyes smoldering with black passion. She tried to ignore the prickles of awareness that burned her flesh beneath his gaze. But her chest constricted, and it was hard to breathe, never mind engage in conversation with him.

That he desired her was obvious. That he hated the fact he wanted her was also painfully obvious. She could only hope he had no idea of the effect he had on her.

"Why are you out here alone, my lady?" he said, still speaking in his bone-meltingly accented Pictish although it was apparent to them both, she was more fluent in his language than he was in hers.

But how did he manage to inject so much venom into such a mundane question? If he loathed conversing with her people to this degree, then why did he continue to torment her with his unwelcome presence?

As if to belie her thoughts, her treacherous gaze drank in the way his unbound hair whipped across his face in the Highland breeze. The way his white linen shirt stretched across his broad shoulders. How it molded against his powerful chest beneath the length of plaid slung over his shoulder.

His presence tormented her. But despite that, it was not unwelcome.

Fire flooded her veins, warming her cheeks. Goddess, she was blushing like a maid. No man made her blush. She was immune to their charms, no matter how much she enjoyed their company. And even if Cameron MacNeil awoke long dormant desires within her, it was nothing but a cruel contradiction—for she certainly did not enjoy his company.

Her heart hammered an erratic rhythm as she watched him step closer to her. The sky receded. The earth fell away. He filled the world and stole the air, raised the heat, and made it hard to think, to reason.

He was so close she could feel his uneven breath across her face. Could see the deep brown of his eyes, the intriguing thickness of his lashes. For a fleeting instant, his features softened, and she saw beneath the simmering hatred he appeared to hold against her people. And in that moment, the gaping chasm of want and loneliness that corroded his soul slammed through her breast.

She gasped. A shiver trickled along her spine at the eerie certainty that she had just glimpsed the true man beneath the warrior. For one brief moment, his façade had cracked. And even though now, once again, his countenance was as forbidding as it had always been, she knew the truth.

His air of fury and his curt words were not intended as a personal affront against her or her people.

It was an act of self-preservation.

CHAPTER 3

Cam heard Elise gasp, saw her eyes widen in fear and her body stiffen in preparation for flight. In the second his lust-fogged mind registered her responses, he also registered how close they were. How he loomed over her, his shadow encompassing her diminutive figure. That she felt threatened was clear. That he hadn't noticed until this moment was despicable.

With a muffled curse, he stepped back, putting distance between them. If he'd pressed any closer, she would have felt his cock digging into her belly. The thought of his cock digging into any part of her inflamed him further and his scowl intensified, even as his pulses hammered with desperate need.

"I wanted a moment by myself." Elise's voice was breathless as though terror rendered her all but incapable of coherent speech. His self-disgust deepened, twisting his gut at the notion he'd managed to intimidate a woman. A man could sink no lower. And this was why he avoided situations where charm was a requisite. The Scotswomen of his acquaintance were used to his ways. Foreigners were not. And then Elise spoke again. "To commune with my goddess."

It took him a moment to realize she was answering his question. He had forgotten he'd asked her anything. What the hell had he asked her?

He focused on the pagan symbol on the ground. Again, an eerie shiver inched along his spine, a strange unease that whatever Elise had been doing, she had been invoking the wrath of God.

"You shouldn't wander the countryside alone." He made it sound like an accusation. It was an accusation. She was a princess. She shouldn't traipse the land unattended, like a common serving girl.

"Are your fellow Scots warriors not to be trusted, then?"

He backed up another step. None of the warriors Connor had instructed to remain behind in Ce would take a woman by force. They merely had to smile at a woman, and she would open her legs for them, whether she was a serving maid or possessed royal blood in her veins.

Elise was clearly not referring to any of the other warriors. And besides, she had firsthand experience of MacGregor's charms, and who knew how many others who remained stationed in Ce.

She was questioning his integrity.

"You can trust each of us with your life." Even as the words snarled from his mouth, he recognized how she could see the hypocrisy. Whatever had occurred in MacAlpin's war chamber, no Pict believed their people had betrayed the alliance. As far as they were concerned, the Scots had attacked without provocation. Why should Elise believe Connor MacKenzie's men were any different? That *he* was any different?

Why did he give a shit what she thought?

Elise gazed at him as though he was some type of fascinating insect. "Theoretically then, I should be perfectly safe without my personal guard to watch my back."

"I don't speak for the integrity of any Pict."

Her eyes widened in clear affront, but he hadn't intended it as an insult. It was simply the truth.

God damn it, why couldn't he think before he spoke? He never saw how his comments could be taken the wrong way until it was too late. He gave her a stony stare, waiting for a counteraccusation. And whatever she said, he would accept in silence. There couldn't be any danger in maintaining silence.

"I wouldn't ask you to, Cameron MacNeil." She sounded haughty. But then, she was a princess.

He remained silent. She waited, clearly expecting a response. Her breasts rose and fell with distracting purpose, as if she had been riding.

A fractured breath escaped his clenched teeth. Too late, he tried to envisage her on a horse, but instead all he could imagine was her riding *him*. Her golden hair tangled around her shoulders, naked breasts inches from his mouth. Her fingers gripping his shoulders for leverage and, most torturously, her tight cleft hugging his thrusting cock.

Her faint scent of late spring flowers drifted on the breeze, tormenting his senses, and underlying that, he caught the evocative musky hint of woman.

His balls ached with lust, heavy with frustrated release. If he didn't get away from her soon—*now*—he feared he might drag her into his embrace and silence her horrified protests with his mouth and hands and body.

"No Pict would dare raise his hand against me." There was a sharp edge in her voice, but she still spoke in Gaelic, and the potency of her words was lost beneath her enchanting accent.

"Are no Picts starving?" Hell, he hadn't meant to answer her. But it appeared even when he kept his mouth shut, he was more than capable of annoying her.

She blinked, as if his question made no sense. "What?"

"People will do a great deal to put food in their family's bellies."

This time the look she gave him suggested she thought he might have lost his mind.

"Are you truly saying, Cameron MacNeil, that a Pict would harm me because his family was starving?" She sounded incredulous. He wished to God she would stop addressing him as *Cameron MacNeil*. Coming from her lips, wrapped around her exotic accent, it was like a sensuous slither of silk across his throbbing shaft.

"I'm saying…" What the devil was he saying? All he could see was Elise looking at him. Focusing her entire attention on him. But she wasn't smiling. Wasn't flirting. Wasn't inviting him up to her bedchamber. She was looking at him because she thought he was insane. "I'm saying that a desperate Pict wouldn't think twice about taking you for the right price."

"Taking me?" She repeated his words as if they were utterly obscene. "That may be the Scots way, but I can assure you that we Picts—"

Was he not making himself plain?

"For the Norse." He glared at her. "Do you know nothing of politics?"

She blushed, and the vision was so captivating, he clenched his fists to stop his hands from cradling her face. She didn't blush because she was attracted to him. It was because, this time, he'd managed to deeply offend her.

"Indeed." Her voice chilled the air. "I'm well versed in the political situation, MacNeil. The Vikings are not in the habit of bribing Picts to abduct royal hostages."

Aye, he'd insulted her all right.

"In Viken, the practice of stealing their neighboring kingdom's royal daughters is widespread. What makes you think they won't extend that practice here, by whatever means they can?"

Elise glared at him. It was the first time he'd ever seen a less than pleasing expression on her face. Unfortunately, it did nothing to lessen the rampant need still thundering through his blood.

"Nothing whatsoever." She tilted her head at him as though he had just emitted a particularly offensive odor. "After all, is that not precisely what the Scots have done?"

How had he managed to so thoroughly raise her ire? All he'd intended was to warn her of the danger she could face by wandering the countryside alone. No matter how well protected Ce-eviot might be, in such troubled times spies could infiltrate anywhere. After all, he knew only too well it was not only the Norse who used abduction as a way of securing a valuable foreign bride.

"And yet still you take the danger lightly."

She stepped toward him. For a second, he thought she was going to strike his face and to his disgusted disbelief, the prospect didn't anger him. But she didn't touch him. She merely gave him a look that should have withered his cock but instead caused his balls to ache with tormented denial.

"You are in my way," she said in a voice as haughty as any he had heard the queen of Ce use. He waited for her insult and tried not to notice how she only reached his shoulder. How her eyes sparkled with anger. How her breasts quivered with every uneven breath she took.

He didn't move immediately. She was of royal blood, but she wasn't his princess and he'd be damned if he'd allow her to speak to him as though he were a peasant. But that wasn't the reason he didn't obey her implied command. He was incapable of moving. As if, by stepping toward him, she had woven a pagan enchantment around him rendering him immobile.

Her eyes darkened, swallowing the blue and her lips parted in tempting invitation. Would she push him away if he reached for her? Struggle if he crushed her against the roughness of the standing stone?

Protest if he claimed her mouth with savage intent?

The moment shimmered, a glimpse of infinity, where sanity and madness hovered on the horizon. Sanity won. Barely. He pulled back and allowed her room to pass. But she didn't pass right away. She appeared immobilized by desire.

In his dreams. The notion caused a mirthless laugh to escape. Elise started, as if she'd just awoken from a trance.

"My lady." He offered her a bow but maintained eye contact and saw the way she blushed once more. He hadn't imagined her the type to blush. Couldn't recall ever seeing her do so before and yet this afternoon she had done nothing but.

Damn it, everything she did beguiled him. The sooner she was back in the palace the better.

The sooner she was out of temptation's reach, the better.

She glared at him, as if she considered his show of respect nothing but a mockery, before sweeping past him, a proud tilt to her jaw. Gritting his teeth, he fell into step beside her, hands fisted by his sides. So now, instead of fighting for his king, he was reduced to ensuring a pampered princess came to no harm.

Elise came to an abrupt halt. "There's no need for you to accompany me." She didn't look at him and for a lingering moment, he allowed himself to admire her proud profile. The remnants of her blush still stained her cheeks and he knew her eyes would likely be glinting with fury.

"I'll see you back to the palace." Did she think he'd allow her to return by herself? The chances were, she was perfectly safe here in Ce-eviot, but he wasn't going to risk it. If her self-indulgent ways caused her harm, it wouldn't be because he'd neglected his duty.

Finally, she turned to him. There was an odd expression on her face. "Why?" she said at last, and although her voice was far from friendly, it no longer held that note of regal disdain. Did she truly not know why he was duty bound to ensure she returned to the palace unmolested?

Unmolested. The irony echoed through his brain. She was

probably right. No Pict in Ce-eviot would dare accost her. He was the only one she was in danger from.

The notion irritated him, despite the fact he'd never take an unwilling woman. And she was a Pict. The reminder slid through his brain as though he might have forgotten her heritage for a few insane moments.

He would never forget her heritage.

"Because if anything happened to a precious princess of Pictland, who do you think would be blamed?" He sounded feral and couldn't help it. "Whatever our personal feelings over this alliance, we can't afford any more bloodshed between our peoples."

Her lips compressed in clear affront and with a sense of despairing inevitability, his gaze fixed on her mouth. He'd only told her the truth. Why would she take offense? Was it because his manner was too abrupt, because his words lacked the flowery phrases that fell so easily from the tongue of MacGregor?

And why the hell did he keep comparing himself unfavorably with Stuart MacGregor?

EVEN HOURS LATER, as Elise accompanied the other noblewoman to the feasting hall, her temper still simmered. It was intolerable that a man, that *Cameron MacNeil*, had so ruffled her composure. How dare he imply she was ignorant? How dare he look down his arrogant Scots nose at her? She could trace her ancestry back for a thousand years. She knew the history of her people, the stories of their gods and could trace the intricate and interwoven lineages of all the members of the royal houses in Pictland.

She knew of the practice of abduction for the purposes of maintaining tenuous peace between one clan and the next. It had happened often enough in the past in Pictland. More often than not, the abducted princess would end up marrying her captor. It was hardly a revolutionary or astounding notion, although the practice in Pictland had been abandoned some generations ago.

It was no surprise to learn the Vikings undertook a similar strategy. Indeed, it wasn't even shocking to discover that they might one day extend that practice into Pictland, although she fervently hoped not.

But the idea, the very suggestion that a Pict would assist in capturing and handing over a royal princess to their deadliest enemy—that enraged her. No doubt the Scots wouldn't think twice about betraying their own. But the Picts were not Scots and Cameron MacNeil had no right to utter such slander against her people.

What had she been thinking when she imagined his fury and curt words were not personal? Everything he said and did was personal. And none of it was unintentional.

"Did you hear," Berthe, a young noblewoman, said as they crossed the wide entrance hall. "The queen is allowing the Scots to attend the nighttime feasts once more."

"It's good political strategy," Kila, recently widowed and clearly relishing her freedom, said. "One should always keep one's enemy close."

There were a few muffled giggles at that, and Elise flashed the culprits a dark glare. Just because the queen had decided to extend hospitality to the Scots didn't mean they should instantly welcome them with open arms.

Even if it did make her plan of charming information from them somewhat easier.

"Do not frown so, Lady Elise," Kila said, slipping her arm through Elise's and giving a comforting squeeze. "How many times have you and Lady Aila told us these Scots are innocent of the crimes committed by their king?"

Too many to count. For the sake of Aila, her new husband and their unborn child it had been imperative that their people accept

Connor MacKenzie and his personal band of warriors if not entirely as friends, then at least not as their deadly foes.

But that had been before Cameron MacNeil had insulted her intelligence. Yet even that wasn't the reason she hadn't been able to get the damned Scot from her mind. What really irked was the knowledge that, when he had insisted on seeing her back to the palace, for one insane moment she thought he had been going to say something… flattering.

But it had nothing to do with him wanting to spend a few more minutes in her company. It was because he didn't want suspicion to fall upon his head, should anything happen to her while she was not chaperoned.

"I am greatly grieved that Ewan MacKinnon returned to Dal Riada," whispered Lilas, whose husband had accompanied Ferelei on his last sea voyage. "I thought—I hoped we might continue our friendship from the spring."

"Forget MacKinnon," Kila said. "Work your charms on Stuart MacGregor. I hear his performance in the bedchamber is little short of breathtaking." Kila nudged Elise in the ribs. "Is that not so, my lady?"

Another time she might have laughed and allowed the ladies to draw their own lascivious conclusions. But tonight she wasn't in the mood.

"I haven't the slightest idea, nor do I desire to know of his performance."

"Nor I." Lilas sighed heavily as they entered the feasting hall. "There was a special connection between Ewan and I. He is truly one of the noblest warriors I've ever encountered."

Elise shot Lilas an incredulous glance. But the other woman looked utterly serious and more than a little heartbroken.

"Ewan MacKinnon," she felt compelled to point out, "bedded half our friends, Lilas. Please tell me you didn't take his pretty lies and flattering ways to mean any more than they did."

"The others meant nothing." Lilas sounded defensive. "He told me I was different."

"And you believed him?" Elise could scarcely believe her ears. She had lost count of the times warriors had murmured in her ear that she was different. Special. A thousand other meaningless words, all designed to entice her to lift her skirts.

She enjoyed the banter, but none of it ever touched her. Even her friends who took lovers didn't believe any of the sweet talk. It was simply a part of the seduction ritual.

"Lilas, my poor love," Kila said. "All the Scots have silken tongues. Ewan MacKinnon took what you offered but alas, he most certainly gave you nothing but his body in return."

"Not all the Scots have silken tongues," Berthe said, and she gave a disdainful sniff that was so out of character that even Lilas stopped glaring at Kila and stared at the younger woman. "That MacNeil never attempts to charm or flatter. Indeed, I do believe he goes out of his way to deliberately insult with his foul manner."

Although Elise agreed with every word, a flicker of irritation heated her at Berthe's accusation. She couldn't imagine why. Berthe was, after all, only stating the obvious. Everyone knew Cameron MacNeil was a rude bastard who thought he was too good to socialize with Picts.

"Dear goddess." Kila sounded both scandalized and intrigued. "You didn't try to entice MacNeil into your bed last spring, did you? Of all the Scots in Ce you could have experimented on, you chose *him*?"

Elise forgot she was annoyed with Berthe and reached out to take her hand. At scarcely sixteen, and married almost a year, Berthe often still behaved like a dreamy maid of twelve. But she was a woman, and she possessed a woman's needs. Needs that her husband, with his preference for young boys, rarely bothered to address.

Berthe blushed and looked as if she wished she hadn't said anything.

"He was the only one not panting after everyone else." She smoothed down her gown in a nervous gesture. "I thought he might be agreeable to an eve of flirtation but..." She suddenly looked very young, and very inexperienced.

"It's not you." Elise squeezed Berthe's hand. How well she understood the younger girl's lack of confidence in her powers of seduction. "It's Cameron MacNeil. He's incapable of stringing two civilized words together. You had a fortunate escape, for if his manners in the bedchamber are anything like his manners in public, he likely ruts like a wild boar."

"I wouldn't be averse to such an experience," Kila murmured as they paused by the high table. "Have you seen the muscles on his arms? I certainly wouldn't say no to a night crushed against that hard chest of his."

An inexplicable flash of anger whipped through Elise's breast at the vision of Kila wrapped around Cameron MacNeil's naked body. Of MacNeil once again abandoning his grim exterior and smiling.

Somehow, the notion of him smiling at Kila, of him voluntarily dropping his permanent scowl instead of it momentarily cracking by accident, was even more potent than the image of hot, sweaty sex. Not that it would ever happen. MacNeil, to her knowledge, hadn't bedded any woman, noble or otherwise, during his stays in Ce.

Perhaps he, also, preferred men?

The thought only caused her ire to rise further. Which didn't make sense. In fact, she couldn't imagine why she was spending so much time thinking about Cameron MacNeil at all. Especially when he was the reason Berthe's already fragile self-confidence had taken another battering three months ago.

"That will never happen." She couldn't help the waspish sting in her voice as she glared at the older woman.

Kila's eyes gleamed. "Would you care to make a wager, my lady? I feel up to a challenge."

Elise offered her a tight smile. "I have no interest in taking your wager when the outcome is patently obvious."

Kila smiled and tugged at her gown so her ample cleavage was more readily exposed. If she so much as leaned over, her nipples would be on full display. A man would need to be dead not to notice such blatant invitation.

"Observe," Kila said to Berthe, who looked both resigned and forlorn. "And learn." Then she flashed another knowing smile at Elise and sauntered off.

~

WOULD THIS NIGHT NEVER END? Elise sat at the high table next to her grandmother and attempted to focus on the food and not a certain Scot warrior. Usually she sat with everyone else, but since the betrayal in Dunadd the queen had insisted she take her place at the royal table.

Unfortunately, her elevated position meant she had a clear view of the rest of the hall. And that included MacNeil whom Kila had managed to sit next to.

Every time Elise glanced their way, which was far too often, but she couldn't seem to help herself, Kila was smiling, touching MacNeil's forearm, or gazing at him in an intense manner that couldn't be mistaken for anything but raw primal lust.

While she had yet to catch MacNeil responding to Kila's overtures, she could imagine what was occurring under the table. Kila's hand sliding up beneath his plaid. Curling around his cock. His hand between her thighs, fingers exploring.

Elise shifted on the hard timber chair. No matter how she told herself she was imagining such things, the truth was pooling between her thighs. She was *damp*. With *lust*. For a man she had no intention of ever speaking to again.

She shot him another surreptitious glance. He appeared oblivious to Kila and her all but naked breasts, although he did respond to her comments in his usual monosyllabic manner. But then, Kila wasn't interested in his conversation. She merely wanted to sample his body. Simply to prove she could.

When the final platters were removed, Elise stood and prepared to follow her aunt and grandmother from the hall, as she had every eve since news of the king's murder had reached them. But tonight the queen paused and turned toward her.

"Elise." Her voice was low. "You will stay here for the entertainment. Observe the Scots. Encourage liaisons. I want to know everything they know. Do you understand?"

For a second Elise stared at her queen, not at all sure she understood.

"Madam?" She glanced at her grandmother, but the dowager said nothing. "You want me—all of us—to spy on the Scots?"

"Of course." The queen flicked a disdainful glance down the hall where the residents of Ce-eviot mingled freely with the Scots and remaining warriors of Ce.

But there was a stark lack of noble warriors of Ce. So many remained hostage in Dunadd.

"Oh." Elise knew her response was inadequate, but she was at a loss as to what she should say.

The queen gave an impatient sigh. "Open your eyes." Her voice was hard. "Already our ladies invite the Scots to their bedchambers with seductive glances and coy smiles. They think a more overt display would offend me."

Was she speaking only of Kila? With a jolt of disbelief, Elise realized she had no idea whether any other noblewoman had spent the evening flirting with the Scots. Her entire attention had been riveted in one direction only.

"But you—are not offended?"

"It doesn't matter whether I am offended or not. That won't

give me any answers. And if the goddess won't help, then I must find a way to discover information myself."

"My love." Her grandmother took her hand. "We're not suggesting you take a Scots lover. Merely let it be known that, should any lady do so, it is their duty to pass on any gossip they learn. Men will reveal a great deal more in the bedchamber, under appropriate coaxing, than they would in normal circumstances."

Elise felt her face heat. She knew it was true. Her friends often confided the most scandalous of secrets they had learned in just such a way. But she had never mastered the art herself.

Then again, the only man whose bedchamber she had shared was Ferelei's, and the less she knew about *his* secrets the better.

"Although," her aunt said, leaning in close. "You have my blessing should you decide to do so. Perhaps you could engage the interest of Ross MacIntosh since he is the leader now that Connor has departed."

Was her aunt suggesting she seduce Ross MacIntosh for information? Was she ordering her to bed a man to gain strategic advantage?

The breath tightened in her lungs, as if a band of iron wrapped around her chest, crushing her. Suffocating her. A terrifying buzzing filled her head, the noise of the hall receded, and the faces of her kin blurred.

Before she could thoroughly disgrace herself by fainting, her aunt grasped hold of her arms and gave her a quick shake.

"Goddess preserve us." The queen sounded irritated. "If the thought of bedding a Scot distresses you so, then pray do not even consider it. Perhaps you can discover another means of extracting information from MacIntosh."

Elise stared at her aunt as the full implication of her words finally sank in. The queen was commanding her to renew her friendship with Ross MacIntosh. To spend time in his company. To extract information from him.

It was exactly what she had wanted to do to discover the fate of Droston. And now that she had her aunt's permission, she wouldn't need to use subterfuge or feel she was betraying her aunt by going behind her back. It could all be out in the open.

It didn't matter that her aunt wouldn't know the full reasons for Elise's compliance.

She drew in a shaky breath. Relief thudded through her breast at this additional sign that it was Ross MacIntosh and not Cameron MacNeil who was the answer to her prayers. For one lingering second, doubt hovered, but she shoved it aside. Of course this odd sensation was relief. How could it be anything else? Because it most certainly couldn't be a strange, unformed regret.

CHAPTER 4

*E*lise made her way through the gossiping crowd under pretext of needing to speak to the musicians. In reality, she was searching for Ross MacIntosh. But the only Scot she kept catching sight of was Cameron MacNeil.

Was Kila still with him?

Distracted, she rose onto her toes to get a better look, but once again, he vanished in the throng of bodies. And really, it was none of her concern whether Kila was still with him or not. There was no need to pass on the queen's edict to the other woman. After all, in the unlikely event Kila did manage to entice MacNeil to her bedchamber, she would be only too willing to divulge all the details tomorrow.

Except they would be of the intimate and salacious kind. Of that, Elise had no doubt. Because she couldn't imagine MacNeil ever allowing an unwary word to escape his lips, no matter how skillful his lover.

"Lady Elise." The deep voice with the Scots accent wrenched her back to the present and she turned, to see Ross MacIntosh offering her a bow. His smile of welcome faltered, and it took significant effort to wipe the scowl from her face.

She, who never scowled, who never allowed her innermost emotions to show in public. She forced the irritating image of Cameron MacNeil to the back of her mind and took a calming breath. Even if she had become momentarily distracted, thankfully Bride was guiding her. The very one she was searching for had found her.

"Ross MacIntosh."

"It's very gracious of the queen to once again allow us to join the evening feasts."

For a few moments, they bantered back and forth and before long, MacIntosh's excruciatingly polite demeanor began to fade and he once again reminded her of the man who had entered Ce three months ago.

Droston hovered on the edge of her mind. She desperately wanted to ask whether MacIntosh knew anything of the fate of the less important hostages but knew the time was not yet right. She couldn't rush this. She had to let the conversation flow naturally and that might take more than a single night.

If only she knew for sure how long she had before Ferelei arrived.

Strange prickles of awareness trickled over the back of her neck, and she frowned. At the same instant, MacIntosh stopped mid-sentence and raised his eyebrows in apparent astonishment. Elise stiffened as a sudden certainty gripped her.

Heart thudding, she spun about and came face-to-face—or rather, face-to-shoulder—with Cameron MacNeil.

"Cam?" MacIntosh said. "Is everything all right?" His tone conveyed that unless there was a major crisis, he wanted the other man to disappear.

Elise fought the urge to take a step back. MacNeil was far too close. She didn't like the way she had to look up at him. But to retreat would show him that his presence bothered her. And it didn't.

At least, she didn't want him knowing it did.

"Aye." He responded to MacIntosh's question but continued staring at her. The look on his face suggested he found her proximity highly unpleasant. But since he was the one who had crept up on her, and he was the one who insisted on standing so close they were almost touching, he obviously couldn't find her that disagreeable.

The thought invaded her mind before she could prevent it. And goddess damn, she was blushing again.

In a vain attempt to distract any unwelcome attention from the heat swamping her face, she gave a dismissive flick with her hand.

"Where is Lady Kila? I thought she was with you."

As soon as the words left her mouth, she regretted them. They made her sound as if she had been watching him. *Spying* on him. And just because she had, was no reason for him to guess such a thing.

If he was surprised by her question, he didn't show it. Indeed, he showed nothing but his normal surly countenance. Anyone would think she had interrupted *him* instead of the other way around.

"No."

And he was as communicative as ever. If he had nothing to say to her, then why had he approached her?

MacIntosh slapped Cameron on the shoulder. Elise hadn't been aware that the other man had even moved. Although it was a friendly slap, there was power in it. And a message. A message that reinforced the unspoken order to leave.

"Perhaps you should find Lady Kila, Cam," MacIntosh said. "I'm sure she'll forgive your uncouth manners if you beg forgiveness."

She wanted him to leave. She needed him to leave so she could continue to charm Ross MacIntosh. But the notion of Cameron leaving so he could continue with his unorthodox seduction of Kila did not please her in the least.

"No," Cameron said. Was that the only word he intended to utter this night? He once again looked at her and it was as if molten gold trickled between her thighs. Hot and liquid and strangely heavy. "I have something to say to Lady Elise."

"Then get on with it, man." Irritation now threaded MacIntosh's voice although he still maintained a friendly demeanor. "Lady Elise and I are reacquainting ourselves with each other."

It was becoming harder to breathe. Desperately she clamped her lips together before she began to pant like a bitch in heat. Goddess, it was inconceivable that MacNeil could affect her so profoundly. He wasn't even trying to seduce her, unlike Ross MacIntosh. But MacIntosh, for all his charming words, blue eyes, and easy smile, didn't affect her in the slightest.

"What I have to say is for Lady Elise's ears only."

She couldn't imagine what he might want to say to her that was so private. That was so important he had deliberately sought her out and caused him to ignore the unspoken demand of his commanding officer.

She couldn't imagine, but she couldn't wait to find out.

Not that she intended to allow MacNeil to guess how much his odd behavior intrigued her. He still looked at her as if he wished he were anywhere but here.

"MacNeil." There was an undercurrent of iron in MacIntosh's voice now. "If you have something of such importance to convey, then see me in the morn and I'll ensure the message is relayed."

"I'll speak to no one of this matter but Lady Elise."

Elise couldn't drag her fascinated gaze from him. He was openly defying MacIntosh. From the corner of her eye, she saw the other Scot stiffen in clear affront, and before she could stop herself, she turned to him and drifted the tips of her fingertips along his forearm.

"I'm sure this matter won't take long." She offered him one of her prettiest smiles, the smile Aila used to jest about and say no man with stones could ever hope to resist. "Perhaps I can meet with you later?" After all, he was the chosen one of Bride and her queen, and she needed to rekindle their friendship as swiftly as possible.

Renewed interest flared in MacIntosh's eyes. She knew then that he would meet with her later. That if she chose her words wisely, he would answer her questions without even realizing he did so. The knowledge should have thrilled her, but instead she only wished he would make haste and leave her alone with Cameron MacNeil.

Only because she wanted to know what was so important about his message. It certainly had nothing to do with the way her stomach fluttered, and heart thundered, at the intense glare he arrowed her way. Or the hint of foreign spices that drifted from him in a tantalizing caress across her senses.

Somehow, she resisted the overpowering urge to once again look in his direction. Ross MacIntosh was the Scot she needed to charm. She couldn't afford to insult him and possibly lose the chance of discovering crucial information.

MacIntosh took her hand and brushed his lips across her knuckles. For all the impact it made on her, he might as well have been her father kissing her.

"Until later, my lady." His eyes held promise of what *later* might involve. "Do not allow my fellow Scot to detain you overlong."

Finally, he departed, and Elise stifled a relieved sigh before she once again turned to Cameron. His eyes were narrowed and the expression on his face suggested he knew exactly what MacIntosh insinuated and the thought disgusted him.

How dare he stand in judgment of her? And why did she care that he did?

"Well?" Her voice was sharp. At least that had been the intention but instead the word soundly breathy and seductive. As if she wished to entice him into her bed this night. The thought hovered with malignant promise, a tempting glimpse of an impossible liaison.

Disbelief at her errant thought stabbed through her mind. Cameron MacNeil might make her blush like a fool and her insides tremble like a virgin, but he was the last man she would consider suitable as a lover. If that man ever appeared, and she was not convinced such a man even existed, then he would need to possess a gentle demeanor and kind heart. She had no use for warriors or pirates who masqueraded as merchants. No use for a man who made it plain he thought her beneath him.

Well? The word echoed in her mind. She might not be able to control her voice, but she could certainly control her features and angled her jaw so she could give him a disdainful glance.

Except once she caught his dark gaze, she couldn't look away.

"Is there somewhere less conspicuous we can converse?"

For a second, she stared at him in blank incomprehension. Was he propositioning her? But although awareness sizzled in the air between them, although she knew lust simmered just beneath his surly exterior, she also knew he would never act on it.

Because he despised all Picts. And unlike another man who would overlook that for the chance of parting a woman's thighs, Cameron MacNeil appeared to have principles. Even if those principles were warped and, for her as a Pictish princess, highly insulting.

"Less conspicuous?" Her mind conjured up her bedchamber and just as swiftly, she crushed the image. And then she thought of the concealed staircase Aila had loved to use, between the inner and outer walls of the palace.

That would afford them a great deal of privacy, without the implications a bedchamber instantly suggested.

But perhaps it was too private.

"Aye." His dark eyes roved over her face, and suddenly she wasn't at all convinced that Cameron MacNeil's principles were as immovable as she imagined. And instead of terrifying her, the prospect… fascinated.

She flattened her hands against her thighs so she couldn't wrap her arms around her waist and prove to him, beyond doubt, just how thoroughly he unnerved her.

"If you insist on such theatrics, then we can *converse* in the time-candle nook." Oh great goddess, had she really put such emphasis on converse? As if she didn't believe that's what he had in mind? Before he could respond or worse jump to the conclusion that *she* had more on her mind than simple conversation, she swung on her heel and hastened to the alcove on the far side of the hall.

She knew he'd caught up with her before she saw him fall into step beside her. He was just a man. A Scot. He possessed nothing that other men did not, and indeed lacked a great deal that other men did have. Such as a pleasing manner, an agreeable smile, and charming words.

Why then did he affect her like no other man ever had?

She pulled up short at the alcove. If he thought she would enter the nook first, and therefore be trapped in the corner, he must think her utterly ignorant. Since that notion still stung, she thrust it from her mind and turned to give him a regal look.

He gave the nook a cursory glance. It was an ideal location for the time-candle, set back in the thickness of the wall and protected from the general bustle of the hall so its flame would not inadvertently be extinguished. It also afforded privacy without seclusion.

After a moment where he appeared to be waiting for her to enter first, he finally stepped into the recess. Refusing to glance over her shoulder to see who might be watching this bizarre performance, she followed him.

Thanks to the sturdy candle set upon its plinth, there were no shadows in the nook. But the confined space caused Cameron

MacNeil to loom over her, despite the fact he had retreated as far as possible.

She let out a measured breath between her lips and hoped he hadn't noticed. It was hard enough to maintain a semblance of detachment in the hall, but when his presence all but swallowed this tiny space, it was a major effort not to slump against the wall for additional support.

His gaze slid from her face and focused on her breasts. White-hot flame licked through her, curling with lustful disregard around her sensitive bud. Her breasts were strangely heavy and between her thighs, for the second time this night, unwanted dampness bloomed.

He had no right to look at her in such a manner. She struggled to regulate her breathing, to form a coherent sentence, but the more she struggled the more erratic her breath became. Her bodice had become so tight for a horrified moment she imagined her breasts would spill from her gown.

"What is your message?" The words tumbled from her tongue, and her voice wasn't calm or measured as befit her status. She sounded like a lust-soaked serving girl.

His eyes meshed with hers. They were almost black, and for a wild second she imagined he was going to crush her against the wall, capture her lips with his and cradle her aching breasts in his large, calloused hands.

Her fingers clawed against the fabric of her gown. If he didn't answer her instantly, she was going to leave. In fact, she was going to leave now.

If only her legs didn't feel as if they might collapse if she so much as moved a muscle.

"I don't have a message," Cameron said. His Scots accent sank into her mind, sent illicit quivers along her nape, over her shoulders and across her damn treacherous breasts. Then his words penetrated her fogged brain. He didn't have a message?

Desperately she dragged the tattered remnants of her composure together. She wasn't a commoner to be trifled with or a serving wench to tease. Despite the fact she could scarcely comprehend Cameron MacNeil was the type of man to do either, why else had he lied in order to speak to her without Ross MacIntosh being present?

"In that case"—thank the goddess she no longer sounded like a desire-drenched half-wit—"I demand to know the reason why you insisted on seeing me alone."

His gaze scorched her, and although he didn't make a move toward her, she had the insane notion that the space between them vanished. If she lifted her hand, she could trail her fingers across his broad chest. Feel the steady—erratic?—thud of his heart.

She could wind her arms around his neck. Pull him down toward her. Savor the taste of a man who didn't reek of decay. A man who was only three or four years her senior.

The image was so real, so intensely carnal, that for a second she felt his lips on hers, felt his hands span her waist. Only when he shifted did the mirage splinter and she realized she had inadvertently swayed toward him.

Mortified she froze before she could further shame herself. Perhaps he hadn't noticed. She had not, after all, *stepped* toward him.

Just swayed. As if she were about to faint. Perhaps he thought she was about to faint? And that was why he looked at her with such taut wariness?

It irked her that he might think such of her. But she would rather him think that, than ever guess the truth.

"I thought to return something to you." His voice was gruff, and a ferocious frown darkened his brow. "I didn't think you'd want MacIntosh to bear witness."

Her scattered wits attempted to make sense of his words. But he spoke in riddles. What on earth could Cameron MacNeil have in his possession that belonged to her?

"I don't know what you—" Her words lodged in her throat as he reached for his leather belt. Transfixed, she watched. *He's not removing his belt.* Logically she knew, and yet still icy terror snaked through the pit of her stomach, coiled around her heart, and froze her ability to think beyond the panicked thunder in her head.

He loosened a pouch that hung from his belt and handed it to her. She stared at it, unable to look at his face in case he saw the remnants of fear that still scudded through her blood. But neither could she reach out and take whatever it was he offered her.

Her fingers were still clutching her gown, embedded in her thigh.

With a disgruntled growl, Cameron MacNeil pulled open the pouch and balanced it on his palm before once again shoving his hand under her nose. She blinked, frowned, and peered into the leather pouch.

Her paralysis shattered with a startled gasp, and her hand clamped across her mouth as her gaze collided with his. Still he frowned, but it was not as fierce, as though her reaction was not as he'd expected.

With great effort, she forced her hand from her mouth. It was too late to hide her shock from him. Too late to pretend she had not entirely forgotten about the sacred crystals she had used by the standing stones earlier that day.

The sacred crystals that now nestled in Cameron's leather pouch.

Heat washed through her, followed instantly by feather light chills. Bride could not be any clearer. Not only had she pointed MacNeil out that very morning, but to reinforce her choice she had sent him to Elise with a message that couldn't be ignored.

It was Cameron MacNeil and not Ross MacIntosh who would help her discover the fate of Droston.

CHAPTER 5

Cam had no clear idea how he'd expected Elise to react when he returned her heathen crystals to her. He still couldn't fathom what had possessed him to return to the standing stones and gather them up after he'd ensured her safe return to the palace.

But no matter how misplaced or unwarranted it was, he couldn't shake the uneasy sensation that she was in danger. And although it was nothing to do with him, he'd still been compelled to seek her out.

He'd half expected her to slap his face for daring to touch her pagan crystals. Instead, she looked on the point of fainting.

His grasp on the pouch tightened at that alarming possibility. "Here. Take them." Once again, he shoved the pouch toward her. Much as he fantasized about holding Elise, the thought of carrying her unconscious body across the great hall wasn't something he relished. Not least because he doubted Elise would ever forgive him for such a public humiliation.

He ignored the mocking voice in his head that wanted to know why he gave a shit as to whether Elise would ever forgive him or not. He didn't need her approval. He didn't need her pretty smiles or flirtatious glances.

He didn't need anything from Elise. Except in the darkness of night while his body burned with unrequited lust, he wanted it all.

"Thank you." Her voice was breathless and for a moment, he wondered if he'd misheard. She didn't sound angry at his presumption. She sounded grateful. "It was kind of you to return them to me."

She took the pouch from his outstretched palm and twirled her finger through the crystals. Fascinated, he couldn't help staring at her averted face.

Before he'd traveled to Pictland in the spring, he'd imagined all Picts to be brutal barbarians. It had been an unpleasant revelation to discover they possessed knowledge and learning to rival that of the scholars of Dal Riada.

But even that paled into insignificance when compared to how Elise affected him. Right from the first moment he'd seen her, she had entrapped him. And she had managed it without a single seductive glance in his direction.

In the spring, it had corroded his pride. A Pict had destroyed his sister Isla and murdered his father in cold blood. For that, all Picts deserved eternal damnation. For his king, he had suffered the Picts hospitality. For the sake of peace and the treaty between Scot and Pict against the Norse, he had forcibly tethered his festering need for vengeance.

But since the massacre at Dunadd, nothing was as clear as it once had been.

"You shouldn't leave such things out where anyone might come across them." Whatever he thought of her practices, they were obviously important to her. He had no wish for her crystals to be stolen. Especially when he suspected it was his fault she'd forgotten to take them with her in the first place.

She snatched her finger from the pouch as though it

contained snakes and clasped the soft leather against her breast. He tried not to stare. Failed. Hell, why did Elise captivate him so?

"They wouldn't harm anyone." She sounded defensive and he reined his lascivious thoughts back into line. Elise wouldn't part her thighs for him this night, or any night. MacIntosh had made it clear he had set his sights on her.

Another night, perhaps?

He swallowed, his mouth dry. Elise hadn't passed two words with him in the spring. She was only speaking to him now because he had cornered her. What was wrong with him? She was only a woman, like any other.

Except she was like no other woman he'd ever met.

"I meant if someone came across them and took them." As the words hung in the air, he sensed their absurdity. Who would wish to steal a handful of crystals? The realization he'd once again made a fool of himself in front of Elise blackened his mood and despite his best intentions, he felt a scowl form.

Elise licked her lips and God damn, was she really blushing again or was it a trick of the candlelight?

"Oh. Yes." She sounded confused but he detected a trace of relief in her voice too. He couldn't imagine why she would sound relieved. An unsavory possibility surfaced. Unless she'd thought he meant something else by his remark? Had she, in reality, been casting a spell?

A chill crawled along his spine at the thought. It was one thing to know she worshipped pagan gods. It was another to suspect her of witchcraft.

He shoved the suspicion aside. Black magic entailed blood sacrifice and there had been nothing by the standing stones to suggest anything of the kind.

Elise was not a witch.

He watched her transfer her crystals into a pouch secured to her belt, before returning his to him. He crushed the soft leather in his hand. Her fingers were slender, and her nails were not square cut, but a pleasing oval shape. He smothered a groan of defeat. What man found a woman's fingers so cursed riveting?

She clasped her hands together at her waist. He waited for her to bid him farewell. For her to return to MacIntosh and lead the other man to her bedchamber.

He folded his arms across his chest. The alternative was to drag her into his arms and once he did that, he feared he might not be able to let her go.

"Would you care to have a goblet of wine with me?"

Her question was so unexpected he stared at her in disbelief.

"What?" His voice was gruff, and Elise flinched as though his response had physically wounded her. His glare darkened. Did she really want to spend more time with him or was this simply a perfunctory question, one to show her appreciation for his act but not intended to be taken seriously?

She took a deep breath. He refused to break eye contact, although every sense he possessed was vitally aware of how her breasts rose beneath her bodice, a tempting vision.

"As a small token of my thanks for returning my crystals."

He could think of another way she could show her thanks. But Elise would never offer herself to him. All the Pictish ladies of the court enjoyed flirtatious banter and Elise excelled at the art. In the spring all the Scots warriors—save for Connor—had vied for her favor.

To his knowledge, she'd taken five as her lovers, including MacGregor. Each one possessed a silken tongue when it came to seduction. Each one could charm the sourest spinster into forgoing her virtue.

That was the type of man Elise found irresistible for her fleeting liaisons.

He didn't want her gratitude. But this was likely the only time she would ever willingly offer him her company.

To hell with that. He wasn't that desperate for her company.

And knew that he was.

"Very well." The words sounded feral. As though the thought of spending more time with her filled him with disgust.

She swallowed and then offered him a smile. It wasn't one of her mesmerizing smiles that she so freely bestowed on his fellow countrymen. But it managed to paralyze him just the same. Because it was the first smile she had ever directed his way.

"Good. I wouldn't wish you to think I'm ungrateful for your thoughtfulness. These crystals once belonged to my great-grandmother. I'd be devastated if I lost them."

Unsure how he should respond to that, Cam grunted, tied his pouch to his belt, and followed her out of the alcove. Her hair rippled in golden waves to the small of her back. He imagined spreading those silken threads across his pillow and his cock hardened at the vision.

This evening was going to be torture.

As they made their way across the great hall, he realized she was still talking.

"… and then having to return to Ce so swiftly. It must have been hard leaving your homeland again so soon."

"A warrior goes where he is ordered by his king." Oddly, her words reminded him of just how long it had been since he'd set foot inside his own hillfort. Almost two years. But there was nothing there for him. Nothing but horrific memories.

"Of course." She gave him a sideways glance. "But surely you must miss your loved ones, Cameron? Do you not possess a wife in Dal Riada?"

"No." What woman would want to be mistress of Dunmar? His mother had never been happy there. Isla had died there. One day he would need to take a wife, and when that day arrived, he'd have to do something about Dunmar. But that was a problem for the future.

Elise gazed at him for a few seconds longer, but finally appeared to realize that was all he had to say on the matter. What else was there to say? He had no wife. Yet the certainty gnawed through him that, had he possessed the wit of MacGregor or MacIntosh, he could somehow have used Elise's question to his advantage.

She cleared her throat as they approached the table where wine jugs stood. No coarse ale or common mead for those of royal blood.

"Do you have no kin, Cameron?"

She no longer affixed his family name when she addressed him, but the way she said *Cameron* in her enchanting accent still managed to fire his blood. Perhaps he should insist they spoke in Pictish. But her Gaelic inflexions were too pleasing.

"No." He had no intention of saying anything more on the matter, except he caught the fleeting glance Elise shot him. There was an odd sense of despair about it. He felt his brows drawing together and forcibly halted the scowl before it could take hold of his face and cause Elise to once again retreat.

She was simply attempting to make conversation. It wouldn't kill him to try to respond in a likeminded manner.

"I had a younger sister. She died in my arms when she was eleven."

Elise's eyes widened in evident horror and she turned from the table to face him. "Oh, I'm so sorry." She gripped her fingers together at her waist and looked as though she wished she were anywhere but here. "How terrible for you."

Aye, it had been terrible. But it hadn't been his intention to upset Elise by his remark. He'd only wanted to prolong their conversation. But it seemed every time he opened his mouth, he managed to insert his considerably sized boot.

"It happened many years ago." The words emerged as a growl.

"You must have been quite young yourself." Elise appeared transfixed. He couldn't imagine why. She even appeared unaware of the servant offering her a goblet of wine.

"I'd barely reached my sixteenth year." For six months, he had watched Isla slowly lose her fight for life. Her death, and the reason for it, was scored into the fabric of his soul.

"At least," Elise hesitated as though she was unsure whether to continue or not. "You were with her at the end, Cameron. I'm sure that gave her some comfort."

He doubted his sister had even been aware of his existence at that point. The familiar acidic pain twisted through his chest at the memory.

This wasn't something he wished to discuss with anyone, least of all Elise. How had they managed to touch on such a matter? Even he, with his lack of social graces, knew this wasn't a topic fit for a princess.

"You have many sisters, I believe."

Elise blinked in clear surprise at his abrupt change in the conversation. But how else could a man change the subject? He took the goblets from the servant and handed Elise one to distract her from the frown that was, yet again, furrowing his brow.

"I—yes. I have four older sisters." Elise smoothed the fabric of her gown with her free hand and appeared unwilling to meet his gaze.

"But no brothers."

Elise's lips thinned. She clearly imagined he'd slighted her family. Silently he cursed his unwary tongue. In Dal Riada a woman craved for sons. Why would it be any different in Pictland? Yet he'd meant no insult. He had merely been stating a fact.

"I have only four royal siblings." There was an icy edge to her voice. "But in Pictland the royal succession is through the female line. A son does not necessarily inherit the kingdom."

He knew about the strange inheritance laws of the Picts. It was, after all, the reason his king had been able to seize Fortriu, the Supreme Kingdom of the Picts, due to the bloodline of his royal Pict-born mother.

The lines of inheritance were the last thing he wanted to

discuss with Elise. Because they were also the reason for the massacre at Dunadd of every Pict male noble with a claim to Fortriu.

~

ELISE TOOK a fortifying sip of wine and tried not to stare as Cameron drained his goblet in one long swallow. His manner suggested he didn't want to be with her. But she knew if that were the case, he would have refused her offer. She could only think he was simply incapable of sweet talk.

She'd never met a warrior or nobleman who lacked such a skill. Even Ferelei's tongue possessed the ability to drip honey when it suited him.

At least Cameron didn't try to blind her to his true personality by pretty lies and false promises. He despised her people and didn't try to hide it. It appeared that whatever crossed his mind came straight out of his mouth. It wasn't exactly comforting, but in an odd way, she found his bluntness... intriguing.

He glowered into his goblet. She had the strangest certainty that he was attempting to summon up another topic of conversation. Perhaps she should assist him. After all, she'd been the one who'd inadvertently caused him to recall the untimely death of his younger sister. Goddess, she'd wanted to sink through the floor when Cameron had told her. A look of such desolation had washed over his features, she'd had the frightening urge to wrap her arms around him.

Her fingers tightened around the stem of her goblet at the thought. Cameron MacNeil was nothing like the girlish fantasies of a lover she'd harbored as a maid. And yet of all the Scots warriors, he was the only one she had ever imagined touching with more than her fingertips.

The seductive image sank into her mind. Shocking darts of

pleasure attacked low, between her thighs. How would it feel if Cameron touched her *there*?

Her chest constricted and it became hard to breathe. Her lips parted in a vain effort to draw more air into her deprived lungs. But it didn't help at all. If anything, it heightened the turmoil thundering through her breast.

She knew they were surrounded by scores of ladies, warriors, and nobles. But she and Cameron might have been alone in the feasting hall, for he was all she could see. He took a deep breath, his inevitable scowl still plastered across his face, and a terrifying combination of anticipation, delight and long denied lust rippled through her.

Was he going to ask her for an illicit assignation? Unlike his compatriots, he wouldn't sweeten his words or flatter her with outrageous compliments. He would come straight to the heart of the matter.

A shiver coursed through her and she tightened her grasp on the goblet before it slipped from her nerveless fingers. For the first time since her marriage, she imagined taking a man up on his offer. Giving herself to him. Discovering for the first time how it felt not to be ridiculed and belittled the moment she stood naked and vulnerable before a man.

Goddess, how wonderful that would be. But it was only a dream. No matter how her body yearned for more, she would never succumb. And while she couldn't fathom why Cameron was the only man to have awakened her dormant desires, in the end it didn't matter.

She would refuse him, as she refused them all. Let him tell his fellow warriors he'd taken her if that would save his face. He wouldn't be the first. Except this time regret burned through her at the thought.

She didn't want him to speak of her as another Pictish conquest. She wanted… goddess, what did she want?

"And you, Lady Elise." Cameron's growl dragged her back to the present and she held her breath, every sense aware of his closeness, the aura of danger he radiated. He was... intoxicating, and she had not the first idea why.

"Yes?" Was that truly her voice? She often used sultry tones when flirting with a man, but never had her voice sounded like this.

His dark eyes mesmerized her. He appeared as ensnared in this strange, sensual cocoon as she. It took every particle of willpower she possessed not to lean toward him, to luxuriate in the primal heat of his hard, muscled body.

"Do you have sons?"

Sons? Did she have sons? Had she misheard? Why would he ask her such a thing when they'd been talking about...

What *had* they been talking about?

Her bemused senses struggled to make sense of his question. "What?" Curse her husky tone. She sounded like a fool. A desire-drugged, lust-driven fool.

He swallowed and tugged on the open neckline of his shirt as though the linen choked him. But that couldn't be, for the shirt was loosely tied and she could see a tantalizing glimpse of his bronzed chest.

Her mouth dried. Heart thundered. Blood rushed through her head and pounded against her temples. While she had been fantasizing that Cameron MacNeil harbored a secret desire to take her to bed, he had been thinking no such thing.

"Or daughters." There was an undercurrent of desperation in his voice. This conversation was clearly killing him. Mortification washed through her at her dreadful mistake and yet again, she felt her face heat. "Children," he added and offered her a thunderous glare to underscore his point.

Merciful Bride, please don't let him guess where my errant thoughts wandered. She attempted to bestow a smile his way, to show that this conversation was just like any other she shared with a Scots warrior, but the act was beyond her.

She gave up. "No." Now she sounded as monosyllabic as he did. She clutched the goblet tighter, relieved it wasn't made of delicate glass. "My husband has seven grown children from his previous two marriages and is not inclined for any more."

How she had wanted children as a young bride. But now she was glad, more than glad, that her dearest wish had not been granted. Children would have been merely one other way for Ferelei to exert his power over her.

Cameron's brows drew together in obvious incomprehension. She didn't blame him. It didn't matter how many children a man had, when he took a new bride he always desired more.

But Ferelei was not a normal man. She suppressed a shudder and tried to thrust his face from her mind. He hadn't wanted her to become pregnant because he hadn't wanted her body to swell with child.

He hadn't married her for what her womb would give him. He'd married her for her royal connections.

"Your husband must be a great deal older than you."

Elise stared at him, momentarily loss for words. She knew his manner was blunt to the point of rudeness but had expected him to remark upon the strangeness of her husband not wanting any more offspring.

But to comment on the vast age gap between them—she hadn't expected that, not even from Cameron MacNeil.

And the way he said it suggested he found the notion repugnant.

The thought stung. Even though she found her marriage repugnant, she didn't want anyone else thinking it. Especially not Cameron MacNeil.

"It was a mutually advantageous match." Her voice was haughty. She couldn't help it. Pride was all she had when it came to hiding the truth of her marriage to the outside world.

And it had been an advantageous marriage. Ferelei, thanks to his successful past as a pirate, was wealthy beyond measure. He had promised untold luxuries to the royal house of Circinn in return for the hand of their youngest princess.

"Advantageous for a merchant to marry a princess." Cameron still sounded disgusted and it scraped along her nerves. He behaved as though Scots married only for love and never for duty. And she knew that wasn't true. Her own cousin Aila had married a Scots prince out of duty when her heart had belonged to Connor.

"My husband is also a warrior of fearsome reputation." Why was she defending Ferelei's reputation to Cameron? She cared nothing for her husband's reputation, or what anyone might think of him.

But for some reason she wanted Cameron to think her husband treasured her. She didn't want him to imagine her family had virtually traded her to the highest bidder or that she'd regretted her decision to go along with their wishes every day since her wedding.

Cameron grunted. It was obvious her remark didn't impress him in the least. "A pirate, then." He sounded as though that fact gave him a measure of satisfaction.

It was true that many merchants with a warrior background had at one time or another engaged in piracy. Ferelei most certainly had. But she didn't like the way Cameron instantly jumped to that conclusion. It suggested he thought Picts capable of little else.

"Not all merchants are pirates, Cameron MacNeil." Damn, but she liked the way his name tasted on her tongue. She shoved the notion aside. Whatever she might think of the Scot, and whether he lusted after her or not, he'd made it very plain he would never act upon those base desires.

For which she was grateful. Of course she was. It meant she wouldn't need to find excuses to evade his amorous advances.

"The name Ferelei mac Uurguist is enough to halt the fool-hardiest from attacking my husband's ships."

But if only they would.

CHAPTER 6

Cameron stared at her and for one eerie moment, she imagined that he had heard her thought, and despised her for it. Of course that was impossible. He had done no such thing.

But why did he still look at her as though she'd just confessed to a heinous crime? She might daily fantasize about her husband's death, but she would never raise her hand against him. She would leave that to her beloved Bride.

"Your husband is Ferelei mac Uurguist?" There was a strangely dead sound to Cameron's words. He hadn't moved a muscle and yet she had the oddest feeling he had retreated.

"Yes." She forced herself not to squirm under Cameron's unblinking scrutiny, but it was hard. "We've been married for six years." And it often seemed more like sixty.

His jaw clenched, and his glare remained unwavering. An unpleasant thought occurred to her. Had he met Ferelei? If so, it was clear Cameron despised him.

"Six years." He ground the words between his teeth. "You must have been a child bride." His outrageous remark and the damning accusation she heard in his tone struck her like a physical blow.

"Indeed, I was not." She angled her jaw at him in a proud manner, a poor shield against the pain that squeezed her breast at his uncaring words. "I was fifteen and ripe for the marriage bed."

Let him make what he wished of that. She hoped the word *bed* caused him masculine discomfort. MacNeil might consider himself above all Picts but like all men, there were times when his cock ruled his head. And at this moment, no matter that he hated it, she knew he wanted her.

An odd expression flashed over his face. But it wasn't suppressed lust, or dark desire or any number of emotions she had half expected. With an uncanny shiver, she recognized the fleeting look as desolation. The same as when he'd told her about his sister.

Curse this Scot, why did he never behave in the way she expected? Instead of issuing a chilly good night and leaving him to his own barbarous devices, as had been her intention, she remained rooted to the spot. Unable to tear her fascinated gaze from him.

All because of her infuriating certainty that there was more to Cameron MacNeil than the surly façade he presented to the world.

"Lady Elise." The Scots accent penetrated her mind, but it wasn't Cameron's voice. He remained silent and darkly brooding, staring at her, as unmindful as she of the approach of Ross MacIntosh.

With great effort, she relaxed her fingers around the stem of the goblet and turned to the other Scot. He was smiling at her, but tension sizzled in the air. He clearly now saw Cameron as a rival for her affections.

Irritation blazed through her. Could no man speak to her without also wishing to part her thighs? The knowledge had never troubled her before. Nor had the prospect of flirting with

two men at the same time. Such pastimes were common entertainment for all involved and never taken seriously.

But Cameron did not flirt. And there was a gleam in Ross'
eyes that belied his light tone.

The prospect of an evening that involved Cameron and Ross
vying for her favor caused a wave of distaste to roll through her.
Except she knew Cameron would vie for no such thing. He
would probably turn and march away. The only wonder was why
he hadn't done so already.

The notion he would so easily abandon her heightened the
injustice bubbling in her breast. She inclined her head at Ross in
greeting and lowered her lashes, so neither man could glimpse
her true feelings.

"If your business with Lady Elise is concluded, MacNeil, we
will bid you farewell." Ross thumped Cameron on the shoulder.
Cameron folded his arms, his goblet hanging precariously
between two fingers and appeared unwilling to heed his superi-
or's unspoken demand.

Again.

Against her better judgment, Elise glanced at him from
beneath her lashes. She couldn't make him out. Why did he stay
when he had no intention of initiating a clandestine liaison? Just
because she wouldn't agree to such a liaison was beside the point.

Cameron didn't know that.

Her thoughts tumbled through her mind, tangled and sense-
less. Why was she so obsessed by what this particular Scot might
or might not want? And why did she want him to acknowledge
his lust for her when it could lead nowhere?

Goddess, her head hurt. The thought of enduring another
hour or more of Ross MacIntosh's practiced flatteries and
evading his inevitable invitation to continue the night in the
more intimate surrounds of her bedchamber made her feel ill.

"I fear I must leave you. The queen requires my presence." The
queen required no such thing, but it was the first excuse she

could think of. She held out her hand to Ross and with obvious reluctance, he took it and brushed a chaste kiss across her knuckles. "I bid you a good night."

She would not look at Cameron. And immediately did. His expression was curiously devoid of its normal glower, but he was still looking at her.

For a fleeting moment, she almost offered him her hand, too. But her nerve failed her. Instead, she swiftly turned on her heel, barely acknowledging Ross' extravagant words of regret at her departure, and left the feasting hall.

Only after she reached the bedchamber she'd so recently shared with Aila, did she remember her queen's edict. And her own personal reasons for wishing to speak with Cameron MacNeil in the first place.

Droston. Heat washed through her as his beloved face swam into her mind. How had she forgotten to steer the conversation in the right direction? She'd remembered him only fleetingly when Cameron mentioned her royal sisters and then remarked on the lack of a brother. Injustice at Droston's situation had momentarily cracked her façade.

That same injustice flooded through her once again. Droston, her half-brother, whose royal blood was a secret so tightly guarded even his mother's husband was unaware of it. The son her father refused to acknowledge, the boy her mother despised with every particle of her being.

None of her sisters knew. And if they did, why would they care? Droston had been her childhood playmate, her confident. Her savior.

The only reason her mother had finally told her the truth was because she had constantly called Droston's name while in the grip of delirium. Her mother had feared one day Elise would take Droston as a lover. Blood oaths had been sworn as soon as Elise's life was out of danger. She could tell no one the truth. Not even her half-brother.

She let out a silent breath. No, she could tell no one. But she wouldn't forsake him. Bride had brought Cameron MacNeil to her, and it didn't matter if the Scot troubled Elise in a way no other man ever had. He was the one who would help her. Her goddess had decreed it.

Elise would simply have to endure MacNeil's presence and find a way to encourage him to share whatever knowledge he possessed on the fate of the Pictish hostages.

She had no choice.

CAM WOKE the following morning with a fearsome headache and flung his arm across his eyes in a futile effort to stop the sun from blinding him. He couldn't remember returning to camp the previous night. He couldn't remember anything much after Elise had left the great hall, except that he'd ignored Ross' pointed glare and then proceeded to down five tankards of ale in quick succession.

But it didn't matter how much he'd drunk. All he could hear reverberating around his head was Elise telling him Ferelei mac Uurguist was her husband.

His stomach heaved. No amount of ale would ever drown that knowledge from him. The man who had ruined his sister was married to the woman he couldn't shift from his mind.

Did she love the bastard? He tried not to let his thoughts wander further, but it was impossible. All he could see between the crimson ribbons that ripped through his head was Elise, naked, her hair surrounding her like a golden river. And mac Uurguist touching her with his foul, decrepit body.

"Good morn, fierce Scot warrior."

The husky whisper, in accented Gaelic, shocked the image of Elise from his mind. His arm slid from his eyes and he squinted at the woman who leaned over him, her dark auburn hair tumbling over her naked shoulders.

His heart slammed against his ribs. He had no recollection of bedding a woman last night. Who was she? Where was he? Because now his senses were returning it was clear he wasn't in the camp.

Neither was he slumped in some flea-ridden tavern room. As the woman smiled and the tip of her tongue slid over her lips, the truth hit him with the might of a fist between his eyes.

God Almighty. He'd spent the night with a Pictish noblewoman.

She gave a soft laugh he imagined she thought seductive. Except it grated on his nerves. Who the devil was she? But even he, with his deplorable social graces, knew better than to ask her outright.

"Do not fear, Cameron MacNeil." She smirked down at him, but even though her accent reminded him of Elise's, her voice didn't cause his gut to clench or blood to heat. And the way she said his name served only to irritate him.

Why didn't it irritate him when Elise addressed him so?

The woman swayed over him, so that her hair drifted across his jaw. "Your secret is safe with me," she said. "But now I believe you owe me for what you promised last night."

His secret? What promise? A terrible thought assailed him. Had he, in a drunken stupor, told this woman of his thirst of vengeance against mac Uurguist?

He shoved himself up against the pillows, inadvertently pushing the woman back onto the bed. She kneeled beside him and regarded him with a faintly bemused frown. It was clear she was unaccustomed to men not falling at her feet.

"Secret?" His voice was raw. He felt like shit. And he still couldn't remember a thing that had occurred since leaving the great hall.

Her frown faded and she smiled at him again. "The ale affects a man in such a manner. So I have heard." She languidly brushed a length of hair over her shoulder, exposing her breast to his view. "But no matter. The morn is still young."

He stared into her face as his addled brain attempted to process her words. "We didn't fuck?"

Her smile faltered and a faint blush heated her cheeks. It was obvious she wasn't used to being spoken to so coarsely. And had she taken any of his fellow warriors to bed they would never have used such words in her presence.

But if she'd taken any of the other Scots to bed, this conversation would never have occurred in the first place.

Relief flooded him. He might not recall the last few hours but at least he'd betrayed neither his principles nor his private vendetta.

He pushed back the bed covering. He was fully clothed, apart from his boots. It appeared after reaching her room he'd collapsed, unconscious, on her bed. He hoped to God none of the others found out, but there was little he could do about it if the auburn-haired seductress chose to mock his lack of prowess in public.

"What are you doing?" She sounded astonished and he turned to look at her. She had dragged the sheet around her and was clasping it to her breast. Strangely, the sight of her discomfiture touched him in a way her provocative pose had not.

He rubbed his hand over his roughened jaw. How best to tell her he had to leave, without wounding her feelings?

But his mind was a blank when it came to such matters. He'd never been in this position before. He doubted any warrior of his acquaintance had been in this position before. What man in his right mind would leave a woman who looked like this one, when she was offering blessed relief?

He cleared his throat. "I need to—" The words lodged in his throat. He needed to what? Stick his head in a bucket of iced water in the hope it cleared his brain?

Find a way to scrub Elise from his mind so she was not an exasperating distraction every hour of the day and night?

It was no use. He could think of no pretty words with which to flatter this woman. "Go," he said, and before she could hurl angry words at his head, he picked up his boots and left her chamber.

As he closed the door behind him, he let out a relieved breath. And saw Elise standing not an arm's length away from him. Staring at him with her lips slightly parted, as though she could not believe her eyes.

CHAPTER 7

When it became apparent Elise had no intention of breaking the strained silence, Cam took a deep breath and attempted to wipe the glare from his face. Why did he always glare when he saw Elise? He couldn't seem to help himself.

"My lady." It sounded like an accusation. He gripped his boots tighter. Why hadn't he put them on before leaving the chamber? He felt strangely vulnerable without them on his feet.

As if to reinforce his thought, he watched Elise glance at his boots. Her lips compressed, as though she found the sight disagreeable. Then she stiffened her already rigid spine and looked back at him.

Why could he not have awakened in her bed this morning? It didn't matter how much he despised himself for the thought. He knew the truth.

If it had been Elise leaning over him, trailing her golden hair across his jaw, the last thing he would have done was leave.

But if it had been Elise, no amount of ale would have deadened his senses to the point where he'd been unable to make her his.

He shifted his boots so they hid his groin. He could only imagine the look of disgust on her face if she witnessed the extent of his arousal through the thickness of his plaid.

"Cameron MacNeil." There was a distinct chill in her voice as she inclined her head in a regal manner. "I did not expect to see you in this part of the palace."

Belatedly he realized she'd seen him leave the mysterious noblewoman's room. It was obvious what she thought had occurred.

He had the insane urge to tell her nothing had happened. He clamped his jaw shut before he could make a fool of himself. Why would Elise care if anything had happened or not? The only conclusion she'd draw was he was less than a man for being unable to pleasure a woman.

That was something he most certainly didn't want her assuming.

His head throbbed. Why was nothing simple when it came to Elise? Why did he care what she thought? It was glaringly obvious what she thought of him. Nothing he said or did would ever change her opinion.

"I was returning to camp."

"Of course." But she didn't sweep by him. She remained staring at him and he couldn't fathom the look on her face at all. It was a strange combination of disdain—which he expected— and despair, which he couldn't understand at all.

Probably because it was merely a figment of his ale-drenched senses. Why would Elise look at him with despair?

He cleared his throat. In his haste to leave the noblewoman's bedchamber he'd neglected to ask her which direction led to the nearest exit. "Could you direct me to the great hall?"

She didn't answer right away. He had the strongest impression she was battling the urge to tell him to go to hell—or whatever place of eternal suffering she believed in. But then she offered him a stilted smile that managed to wipe every other thought from his head.

"Certainly. I'd be happy to show you the way myself."

Despite her agreeable words, hostility radiated from her. But if it meant a few more minutes in her company then even her hostility was welcome.

He turned and fell into step beside her, as it appeared he had been going the wrong way. The bodyguard who shadowed Elise was unnerving, but at least she was protected. Where had he been the previous day, when the princess had been alone by the pagan stones?

He chanced a sideways glance at her. He racked his aching brains for a pretty compliment or turn of phrase. Something that would make her look his way with admiration at his wit.

But he'd never been known for his entertaining wit. Yet he was compelled in a way he never had before to have this woman look at him with favor, instead of disdain.

"Your gown is most becoming." He growled the words at her and they fell into the space between them, as graceful as rocks. She shot him a startled look and then her eyes narrowed as though she imagined he mocked her.

"Thank you." She didn't sound as if she meant it.

He exhaled a tortured breath and tried again. "It's nothing like the gowns the noblewomen of Dal Riada wear."

Back in the spring, when he'd first entered Pictland, he'd been taken aback by the quality of the Picts clothing. All his life he'd been taught they were little more than savages, and since the only time he had faced them was in battle, he had no reason to doubt it.

But the gowns of the nobility and those of royal blood were astonishing. They utilized every color of the rainbow and many more besides. Today Elise wore a gown of peacock blue, the shade enhancing her eyes, and her matching veil was a flimsy wisp that caressed her hair in a way that had never before occurred to him.

"Indeed." The touch of frost was back in her voice. Clearly, she'd taken his remark as a criticism. "I've never seen a Dal Riadan noblewoman so cannot offer my opinion on this matter."

Thank God he was prevented from answering by the fact they had reached the staircase. Elise preceded him, lifting her gown as she began to descend, and he caught a bewitching glimpse of shapely calf. He dragged his lecherous gaze away and followed her down the curved stairway, her bodyguard looming over him.

How he had navigated the stairs last night he couldn't imagine.

Elise waited until he reached her side. "The hall is yonder." She indicated the direction with a wave of her delicate hand. "I bid you farewell, Cameron MacNeil."

But instead of leaving she remained where she was and watched him pull on his boots. It was most disconcerting.

Finally, he was done. There was nothing to keep him from returning to camp. But the prospect of leaving Elise filled him with a strange hollowness.

Had he been blessed with a silken tongue, he could charm her into agreeing to meet with him later for an innocent stroll in the secluded copse.

Except when it came to this princess, his thoughts were far from innocent.

He gritted his jaw. This madness had to end. He stepped back from her, so he was no longer ensnared by her evocative scent and gave an awkward bow.

"Farewell." With that, he turned and marched away.

ELISE forcibly relaxed her tense muscles as Cameron MacNeil strolled toward the hall. It didn't matter that he had spent the night with Kila. What man would refuse what Kila offered? And she had certainly utilized all her charms to capture Cameron last night.

Except Elise did care. And she couldn't fathom why the thought of Cameron in bed with Kila bothered her so. When she'd seen him emerge from Kila's chamber, she had been dumbfounded. And had battled the irrational desire to smack his face.

As though he had somehow betrayed her.

How foolish she'd been to wear one of her finest gowns merely in the hope of seeing him. Well, she'd got her wish. She had seen him. He had even bizarrely complimented her although she couldn't imagine why he'd bothered. The glower on his face as he'd delivered the words gave the impression he meant the opposite.

And clearly, she had been quite wrong in her impression of him. He might still despise all Picts, but his principles weren't nearly as immovable as she'd thought. Perhaps the prospect of an indefinite stay in the Highlands had been enough for him to overcome his prejudice long enough to bed a Pictish noblewoman.

She took a deep breath. Every sense she possessed urged her to avoid the Scot. It wouldn't be easy, but scarcely impossible. And if not for Droston that was exactly what she would do.

But she couldn't. Because Cameron was the warrior who was destined to reveal Droston's fate to her.

It was bitterly unfair that the one man her goddess commanded she should use in such a manner was the one man who affected her so profoundly. But it wasn't her place to question Bride in such matters. For Droston, she would swallow her pride and seek out Cameron later.

And this time she wouldn't forget her sole purpose of doing so.

～

THE COPSE, situated beyond the village and some distance from the bronze smith's forge, offered a degree of peace and tranquility. But it took Elise longer than she liked before her blood cooled and mood calmed sufficiently for her to consider returning to the palace.

It was outrageous that one man, that a *foreigner*, could upset the balance of her life so thoroughly. She hardly even knew him. From this moment on, she would command her senses to treat him as any other warrior of her acquaintance.

With amused detachment.

She allowed her bodyguard to assist her up the grassy slope that led to the standing stones, even though she didn't need any help. She didn't need a bodyguard, but to her irritation, she couldn't quite forget Cameron's blunt comments of the previous day when he'd warned her of abductions.

Ludicrous. The closest Vikings were over a day's march from here, on the northernmost border of Ce's neighbor, Fidach. She was perfectly safe. She was—

Her thoughts collided as she saw Kila emerge from the nearby monastery.

For a moment she froze. Perhaps she could retreat to the copse before Kila caught sight of her. But before she could put her plan into action, the other woman turned, saw her, and lifted her hand in a wave.

Elise flexed her fingers and ignored the way her stomach pitched. It was merely because she had yet to break her fast. It had nothing to do with the knowledge that she was to be subjected to a graphic account of Kila's nighttime exploits.

Kila waited until Elise reached her side and then slipped her arm through Elise's.

"You are about early this morn." Elise was relieved her voice gave nothing away of her foolishly wounded feelings. She would listen and laugh at whatever the other woman confided about her new lover. Not by the slightest gesture would she allow Kila to guess how much the thought of Cameron bedding another woman made her feel ill.

So much for commanding her senses to behave.

"I couldn't sleep," Kila said. "I thought to confess my sins while they were still fresh in my mind."

Elise smiled. Her face hurt with the effort. "I could never confide my sins to any of the monks. I don't understand the concept at all."

Kila laughed. Elise shot her a sour look. Clearly her friend had been very thoroughly satisfied during the night.

"Unlike you, I enjoy scandalizing with my confessionals. I truly think the monks vie to be the one who unburdens the sins from my soul."

Elise tried not to scowl but wasn't sure she succeeded. She compromised by shaking her head so that her veil draped farther over her face, hiding her expression.

Like many of their people, Kila embraced the new religion without it affecting her devotion for the old. Elise's own cousin Aila had once been dedicated to the new God, but Elise had never wavered from the one true path of her goddess, Bride.

"It's a pity the Scots don't take advantage of our monastery. I've yet to see any of them confess to their transgressions." Surely now Kila would gush about her night. Elise wasn't sure why she was goading her friend to spill her secret, except that by doing so, Kila would never guess just how much the fact had shaken Elise.

It was of paramount importance nobody guessed that. For if even a whisper of it reached Cameron's ears, Elise would never be able to face him again.

"I fear our monks would perish if they were forced to endure hearing the Scots' confessions."

In spite of herself, Elise smiled at the notion. "Some of it would make fine entertainment, I'm sure."

"Yes. I'm quite sure MacGregor would singe the monks' hair should he confess his bedchamber exploits." Kila leaned closer and whispered in her ear. "Are you sure you did not sample his charms, my lady? Many of the ladies swoon over his technique. I'm sorely tempted to try him out tonight."

Elise frowned. Kila might enjoy illicit liaisons but she had never sampled two different men on consecutive nights. Had Cameron made it clear he didn't wish to share her bed again? Or was it Kila herself who had made that decision?

She desperately wanted to ask her friend but couldn't find the words. After all, Kila hadn't yet even admitted she'd spent the night with MacNeil.

"Don't expect me to wager on that outcome." She raised her eyebrows at Kila in a knowing manner. Hopefully, her comment would jog the other woman's memory. "Unlike Cameron MacNeil, Stuart MacGregor is only too eager to please every noblewoman in the palace."

Kila laughed, but there was an odd undercurrent, as though she forced the gaiety. "I'm inclined to believe MacNeil possesses ice in his veins. A more passionless man I have yet to encounter. All that succulent flesh—wasted." She made a sound of disgust, and Elise stumbled on the uneven ground. Familiar pain shot through her damaged leg, but she scarcely noticed.

Had nothing happened in Kila's bedchamber last night? How was that even possible? To be sure, Cameron didn't flirt and make hot promises with his eyes, but he was far from passionless. Every time he looked at her, she saw suppressed lust seething beneath his surly façade.

"He is nothing like his compatriots, that much is certain." For one thing, she couldn't get him out of her mind. She'd never had that problem with a man before, whether he had been Pict or Scot. It was most confusing. "If I didn't know better, I would imagine him to be a frigid Northumbrian."

Kila sniffed in mutual disgust of the barbaric Northumbrians, who frequently attempted to expand their boundaries by encroaching the borders of Pictland. The bloodied alliance between Pict and Scot had been forged not only to combine forces against the Vikings in the north, but also the Northumbrians in the south.

"It's a pity the Scots have been banished to a camp." Kila bit off her words and glanced at Elise, as though she suddenly recalled Elise's close blood kin with the queen. "Although I understand the reasons, of course. It's enough they've been allowed to attend the nighttime feasts again. Our queen could surely not be expected to accommodate them as she did before."

Elise dragged her errant thoughts back to the present. She had just been given the perfect opening to share the queen's edict with Kila. She drew her close and whispered in her ear.

"I have a confidential decree for you..."

THAT NIGHT, as the feast drew to an end, Elise attempted to subdue the nervous flutters that plagued her stomach. She hadn't seen Cameron all day but had hardly been able to take her eyes off him all night. She could only hope no one had noticed. She was certain he had not. Not once had she caught him glancing in her direction.

She had it all planned in her mind. Once the tables had been pushed back to the walls and the musicians began, she would draw him aside and be pleasant and amenable, no matter what he said or how he acted. And while a section of her mind couldn't imagine Cameron sharing any information with her, no matter what she did, if that was the case why would Bride have chosen him?

As the queen rose to leave the hall, she beckoned Elise to her side. "What progress have you made with MacIntosh?"

Elise had forgotten the queen had instructed her to all but seduce Ross MacIntosh.

"Bride led me to another, madam. I intend to question him tonight."

The queen's eyes widened. "Bride has come to you?" Her voice was barely above a whisper. "Why did you not inform me of this, Elise? What did the goddess tell you?"

Elise risked a surreptitious glance over the queen's shoulder, where the hall was being readied for the entertainment. Cameron was not in sight.

"My goddess only bade me to make the acquaintance of Cameron MacNeil. She gave me no other insights."

"Cameron MacNeil?" Her grandmother raised her eyebrows in obvious surprise. "He is the last Scot I imagined would be of any assistance to us."

The queen gripped Elise's hand. "If Bride has singled out this warrior, then there is no mistake. He is the one who will help us. If all else fails, you know your duty Elise."

CHAPTER 8

*E*lise strolled around the perimeter of the feasting hall and hoped she didn't look as flustered as she felt. Her nerves had been on edge enough at the thought of confronting Cameron again. But when the queen had reminded her of her duty should simple flirting not extract the information required, her half-formed plans had disintegrated.

Now all she could think about was taking Cameron to her bedchamber. She swallowed and licked her lips. It would never happen, of course. Even if the prospect of taking the Scot as her lover was strangely enticing, she knew in her heart she wasn't that brave.

For Ferelei to mock her was one thing. She had long ago hardened her senses against his verbal insults. But for another man to recoil at her unsightly scars—for Cameron to recoil—she wasn't sure her fragile veneer of pride could take it.

Before her marriage, she had naively imagined her damaged leg wouldn't matter to her husband or a lover. But Ferelei had shattered that hope on their wedding night. His shocked disgust at her flaw had been enough to discourage her from ever seeking a lover who might also be repelled by the sight.

Her subsequent introduction to the horrors of the marriage bed had only strengthened her resolve to avoid intimate contact with any man. And although, as the years had passed, she'd known not all men would treat her the way Ferelei did, she'd never been able to overcome the deep-rooted fear of seeing admiration turn into revulsion.

Far better to flirt and laugh and enjoy an uncomplicated dalliance that didn't involve her removing her gown. And besides, until Cameron MacNeil had entered Pictland she'd never wanted to take things any further with any of her admirers.

She caught sight of Kila holding court with three Scots warriors, but there was no sign of Cameron. From the corner of her eye, she saw Ross march purposefully across the hall toward her and she hastily slipped behind a couple of noblewomen.

Ross clearly intended to continue his pursuit of her. She didn't feel up to meaningless banter with him when she needed to find Cameron.

Where in the name of the gods was he?

Then she saw him, disappearing through the great doors. She frowned and followed him, ignoring the pain in her leg. The cursed thing had been giving her grief all day since her stumble that morning.

As she left the feasting hall, she caught sight of him marching outside. For a moment, she hesitated. Although the outside of the palace was well guarded, it was also a favorite place for ladies and the object of their admiration to enjoy the night air. Of course, the main reason was so they could find a secluded nook away from the guards' watchful eyes and the glow of the countless torches.

Elise had always been scrupulous in never accompanying a warrior outside after dusk had fallen. No matter that there were plenty of guards about. After an evening of suggestive banter, it was a tacit prelude to a bedchamber invitation.

But she wasn't accompanying a warrior outside. She was

trying to find Cameron so she could discover what useful information he possessed.

She stepped outside and realized her bodyguard hadn't accompanied her across the hall. But why would he? He would never imagine she intended to leave the palace. And if not for Cameron's unsubtle disapproval the previous day, such a thought wouldn't even have crossed her mind in the first place.

A touch of irritation fired her blood and she embraced it. It was better than the nerves that seethed in the pit of her belly. She would not have her movements dictated to by a Scot.

She surreptitiously massaged her thigh as she glanced around. Although torches blazed, the sun had not yet set, and shadows spread like dark pools, inviting danger. And then she saw him. Beyond the glow of the torches, it appeared he'd been making his way around the side of the palace.

But he wasn't walking anywhere now. His attention was riveted on her.

CAM HAD ESCAPED the confines of the palace as soon as he was able. The feast hadn't been unduly long or elaborate, but it had dragged interminably. The subdued conversation at the tables, in deference to the Pict queen's recent widowhood, scraped along his senses and the undercurrent of flirtatious intrigue caused his head to throb.

And throughout it all, he was acutely aware of Elise at the high table, with her royal relatives, as aloof and untouchable as a star in the sky.

He dragged in a deep breath of the fresh Highland air. Already couples were strolling from the palace, but a quick glance confirmed Elise was not among them. God, this was intolerable. It was as if she had bewitched him. He turned and marched away, along the side of the palace that, due to its impenetrable face, was unguarded.

A strange prickling sensation drifted across the back of his neck and he froze. In battle, such unnamed senses were essential for keeping one's head, but right now there was no reason to obey the overwhelming imperative to turn around.

Yet slowly he pivoted, and saw Elise emerge from the palace.

He stiffened, waiting. Surely Ross would follow her. His commanding officer had made no secret of his displeasure in the way Cameron had interfered in his affairs last night. Ross had told him in no uncertain terms that he intended to make Elise his, and Cameron could turn his frustrated lust elsewhere.

But no Scot warrior followed Elise. She paused and glanced around as though she was seeking something. Someone.

He couldn't believe he was the one she sought. And yet, as she pressed her hand against her thigh as though it pained her, her gaze caught his.

And held.

His gut tightened and blood stirred. She was too far away for him to see the blue of her eyes or inhale her elusive fragrance. There was no reason why his body should respond merely at the sight of her. Yet it did. He was powerless to resist.

For a long agonizing moment, she remained motionless. Did she expect him to go to her? Fall at her feet the way Ross and Stuart and who knew who else had?

He would never fall at her feet. He should turn and walk away. Elise was wedded to his bitterest enemy, the man he had vowed to kill. How could he even contemplate conversing with her, let alone anything else?

With a sense of inevitability, he watched her slowly walk toward him.

Had she truly followed him outside? Why would she do such a thing? He knew, from watching his fellow warriors that a twilight stroll with a Pictish noblewoman often led to her bedchamber.

Graphic images flashed across his mind. Elise, naked in his arms, her hair cocooning them in a haze of golden silk. His heart hammered and chest constricted, making it hard to breathe. Hard even to think. She was barely an arm's length from him, and now he could see the mesmeric blue of her eyes and her evocative scent drifted on the summer breeze, mocking his principles, and turning his resolve to dust.

"Are you alone, Cameron MacNeil?" Her voice was soft, her accent enchanting, and every word simmered with sin.

"Aye." He sounded gruff. But it was the best he could do. It seemed a rock was lodged in his chest. He was amazed he managed to say anything at all.

"No assignation with Lady Kila tonight?" She lowered her lashes, before looking up at him in a manner so provocative it scrambled what remained of his senses.

"I have no assignation with Lady Kila."

She smiled, as though his answer pleased her. "Then perhaps you would allow me to keep you company this eve."

He stared at her. Why was she going out of her way to be agreeable? Was it solely because he'd returned her heathen crystals to her? He found that unlikely. But why then had she sought his company tonight, when in the spring she'd done everything possible to avoid even looking at him?

"If you wish." He knew he sounded ungracious, even without witnessing the way Elise's smile wavered. She likely wished she had never bothered following him. Which brought him back to his original thought.

Why in the name of God had she?

"I wanted some air. But if you would rather be alone…" Her voice trailed away, and she glanced away from him, apparently fascinated by the wall of the palace.

He could not believe it possible, but he had the strangest

impression that Elise wasn't nearly as confident as he'd always imagined.

She was a practiced flirt. He'd seen her many times with many different warriors. But never had he seen her look the way she did now.

Uncertain. As though she expected to be rebuffed. Was his reputation really so bad?

He could feel a dark glare twisting his features yet again and made a monumental effort to keep the glower from his face. Elise was well aware of his reputation and that hadn't stopped her from approaching him. It was his own hostile nature that caused her to retreat.

He didn't want her to retreat. It didn't matter that she was bound to mac Uurguist. It was clear from her many liaisons she harbored little loyalty toward her husband. Why should he reject what she offered when what she offered was something that had tormented his sanity from the first moment he'd seen her?

"I welcome some company." He hoped he didn't sound as surly to Elise as he did to himself. Why could he not charm a woman the way his fellow warriors did? It had never bothered him before that all Picts thought him uncouth and disagreeable. It still didn't. It was only this woman he wished to charm and to think of him in less scathing terms.

Only this woman, despite her Pictish blood and heritage.

Elise smiled at him. It wasn't one that illuminated her face that she so freely bestowed upon her many admirers. It appeared hesitant, as though she didn't quite trust his words, but it was at least a smile.

"You must have traveled widely, Cameron. As befits a warrior."

He wasn't conversant in the arts of flirting, but he was certain it didn't involve discussing the merits of what being a warrior might entail. Or did it? He'd imagined it consisted entirely of pretty compliments and meaningless banter. He didn't understand meaningless banter, but he could surely speak of being a warrior, if that was Elise's preference.

"Aye." He knew that wasn't a sufficient response on its own and struggled to be more forthcoming. "Aside from Pictland and subduing the savage Northumbrians, I've been to the Isle of Iona twice."

"I've never ventured beyond the borders of Fib in the south and Ce-eviot is the farthest north I've ever been. The thought of crossing the sea quite terrifies me."

He didn't want to think of the Kingdom of Fib. The place her husband came from. "Why are you not in Circinn?" That was the kingdom of her birth, situated between Fib and Ce. If she wasn't overseeing the hillfort of her cursed husband, then why wasn't she under the protection of her royal parents?

"I came to visit my cousin Aila in the spring and... events overtook us. The queen is happy for me to stay here until I must leave."

He could feel a frown gathering on his brow. He knew what events she spoke of. The massacre in Dunadd. But instead of giving him a disdainful glance and stalking off, Elise appeared to accept that he, like all the other Scots warriors in Ce-eviot, had not been a part of that outrage.

A chill inched along his spine at his treacherous thought. It was one thing to find something amiss with the official version of that event. It was another to openly challenge it. Even if that challenge existed solely inside his mind.

"At least Ce-eviot is well protected." He growled the words, intending them as comfort. It was only as they left his mouth he realized how they could sound.

Aye, Ce-eviot was well protected—by Scots warriors. Because so many of their noble Picts were still imprisoned in Dunadd.

"Indeed." There was a strained note in Elise's voice, but she didn't appear unduly offended by his thoughtless remark. She looked away from the palace toward the distant mountains. The sun had sunk low in the western sky and Elise's profile was strangely ethereal in the pre-twilight glow. He couldn't drag his gaze from her. "Is your Dal Riada anything like the Highlands, Cameron? I cannot imagine a land without mountains."

"We have mountains. Why do you think we do not?"

She turned to him then and looked intrigued by his words. "I heard Dal Riada was a barren rock where nothing flourished. Of course, before the Scots invasion, that part of Pictland was beautiful beyond measure."

He laughed, the sound startling him, but not enough to quell his amusement. Elise also smiled as though she couldn't help herself. He took a step toward her. She did not retreat.

"Dal Riada is still beautiful beyond measure, Elise." Her name came easily to his tongue and she didn't look affronted by his liberty. "A different beauty to the Highlands, maybe, but she is the only home I've known." Dunmar had been a poor excuse for a home, with his tyrannical father and the tragedy of his sister. But there had been a time, long ago before his mother's death, when a fragmented memory of love and happiness illuminated his young life.

If only he could recall the details…

Roughly he pulled himself back to the present. Elise was gazing at him as though she found him fascinating. It had to be a trick of the light. He hadn't flattered her or even uttered a witty remark. Yet she looked at him as he'd imagined her looking at him.

As if she was unaware of everything but him.

"I should like to see Dal Riada." Her whisper was soft, husky, and his cock thickened as desire coiled through him like a serpent. Insane words hovered in his mind and tangled on his tongue.

Let me take you to Dal Riada.

But he would never ask her. She was not a village lass who'd caught his eye and was eager for adventure. Elise was a princess and even if she truly did want to go to Dal Riada, she wouldn't wish to go with him.

"Maybe someday you will."

"If the goddess wills it."

She said the words so simply it was hard to remember they were blasphemous. A hard knot tightened deep in his chest as the unformed certainty she was drawing disaster upon her gripped his senses.

There was no goddess. There were no gods but one. Her beliefs shouldn't disturb him the way they did. But he couldn't shift the soul deep fear that her carefree disregard wrapped chains of death around her.

Around them both.

A shudder crawled over his arms. He couldn't fathom where the thought came from. Elise might worship pagan idols. But she wasn't a witch.

Elise glanced over her shoulder. Although they were some distance from the others who had left the great hall, they enjoyed no real privacy. Was she giving him a subtle hint that she wanted to walk a little farther, where shadows hugged the ancient stone walls?

He turned, so he was once again facing the dark side of the palace. Elise fell into step beside him, and without looking at her, he began to stroll away from the guarded entrance. There were fewer torches blazing, and if they followed the palace wall along its southern length, they were unlikely to be disturbed.

At the corner of the palace, Elise came to a halt. He looked down at her. The top of her head barely reached his shoulder. She was so close it would take no effort to wrap his arm around her and pull her lush body against him.

He remained rooted to the spot, arms welded to his sides. In the half-light she looked like a vision from a dream, a fantasy made flesh. But she was no insubstantial illusion. And no matter how innocent she looked, he knew she was well versed in the pleasures of sex.

His mouth dried. There could be only one reason why she had silently agreed to walk with him. He still couldn't fathom why she had chosen him. Not when Ross MacIntosh had set his sights on her.

He reached out and took the gossamer wisp of her veil where it rested on her shoulder. She swallowed, and as he slowly tugged the length of veil across her breasts, he felt her tremble.

For a heartbeat he paused, her delicate veil trapped between his thumb and forefinger. "Are you cold?"

She shook her head, an oddly nervous gesture. But this was Lady Elise, the jewel of all Pictish noblewomen, and it was inconceivable that she was nervous. The fine fabric slid through his fingers and trailed over the swell of her breasts, fully exposing her throat and the curve of her shoulder.

Two long tresses tumbled over that shoulder. Before he could stop himself, he closed his fingers around one tempting lock. So silky soft. His gaze meshed with hers and if it wasn't such a ludicrous notion, he imagined he saw apprehension shift in those beautiful blue eyes.

But she didn't slap his hand away for his insolence. Or demand that he release her, this instant. She simply stood there, as if she had been turned to stone.

CHAPTER 9

Cam twined her hair through his fingers and watched it slide across the palm of his hand. The touch was feather light, a whisper of sensation across his callused flesh and yet he could feel each individual strand of silk brand him.

She made a small sound and he dragged his gaze up to her. Her eyes were dark with desire, her cheeks flushed. Her luscious breasts that threatened to overspill her tightly laced bodice, rose and fell with each uneven breath. An intoxicating trace of womanly scent ensnared his sanity. Barely daring to breath, he trailed his knuckles along the aristocratic line of her jaw.

Again, she trembled. If he didn't know better, he would imagine her an untouched maid, fearful for her virtue. But she was no virgin and he was no pillager. God give him strength. His heart thundered, echoing in his ears, and the blood seethed in his veins, a molten river of lust. He had taken enough women in the past to know every facet of passion. Yet here, with Elise, it felt like the first time.

The first time but with tantalizing foreknowledge of what was to come, and this time, he possessed the needs of a man, not a raw boy.

He lowered his head toward her. Her lips parted, a silent invitation, and his mouth captured hers.

Her lips were soft beneath his and his breath stilled as he savored the moment. She didn't move, either to push him away or draw him farther into her scented heat. A low groan filled his ears and vibrated through his head. The kiss was chaste. Nothing like he had imagined it would be with Elise. Yet his cock hardened as though she had sunk to her knees and taken him into her mouth.

The thought pounded in his mind, a heady counterpoint to the thundering of his heart. He cradled her face and traced her parted lips with the tip of his tongue. A tantalizing hint of spiced wine teased his senses and he couldn't hold back.

He claimed the short space that separated their bodies. Her breasts crushed against his chest and his erection burned through his plaid. Surely, she could feel him? Feel how much he wanted her?

His tongue penetrated her mouth. Her strangled gasp caressed his tongue. His fingers tightened around her face, holding her still as he plundered and explored. She tasted of heaven.

He would go to hell.

He did not care.

Her hands curled around his forearms. Her touch was oddly hesitant, not as assured as he expected. But the feel of her fingers against his skin caused lightning to spear through his loins.

He slid his hand into her hair, holding the back of her head. Her nails dug into him, needle sharp and unexpected, and he wrapped his other arm around her shoulders and held her close.

She molded to him so perfectly. A soft, scented haven in a dark world of chaos. He wanted her. Needed her now. But she was a princess and no matter what she had done before, he couldn't take her on the rough ground or up against a cold stone wall.

God, this was torture. A torturous pleasure he had never dreamed could exist. Would she invite him back to her bedchamber? Or should he demand that she do so?

Her body stiffened and she tried to pull back. He broke their kiss and panted into her face. Her breath was uneven and her eyes dark with passion but there was no mistake. She was trying to escape his embrace.

Fingers still tangled in her hair, he slid his other hand along her back, and then held her possessively against the swell of her arse. A shudder rippled through her and her eyes glazed, but she didn't fall against him. Didn't spear her fingers through his hair and drag him back.

Instead, she pushed back against his restraining arm, her palms flat against his chest. Her ragged gasps razed his senses, but something was off kilter.

Wrong.

He dragged in a pained breath and glared down at her. Her eyes widened and despite the frustrated lust pounding through his body, he recognized that look.

Fear.

It was the second time she'd looked at him in such a way. God Almighty, how could she fear him? Ancient distaste churned his gut and he loosened his hold on her, despite how every nerve he possessed balked at the notion.

"I must go." Her voice was breathless, but she didn't look away from him, as if searching for an escape route. She stared at him, and he had the strangest certainty that the lingering tendrils of fear that still clung to her were not directed at him.

It didn't make sense. None of this made sense. He gritted his teeth, fought to batten down the rabid lust that clamored through his blood and only then trusted himself to speak.

"Why?" It was a feral growl and Elise tensed. He had the surreal notion she was bracing herself for scathing insults. What was he thinking? No man would insult a princess. Certainly no man would insult Elise. He bared his teeth at her in a poor attempt at a smile. "Because I don't shower you with pretty words?"

She bit her lip. He caught a glimpse of her white, even teeth and the sight sent a shocking spear of need through his groin. But much as he wanted to despise her, he had the uncanny certainty that she hadn't deliberately led him on.

She had, after all, promised him nothing. It had all been in his mind. But it didn't ease the fire in his blood or the ache in his balls.

Or the grim knowledge that had he been Ross, this night would not have ended with harsh words or thwarted lust.

"Forgive me." Her voice was scarcely above a whisper. Her hands were still flattened against his chest, but she no longer pushed against him. He could almost believe she touched him because it gave her a degree of pleasure. But if that was the case, why did she wish to leave?

Had he been mistaken? Was this all a game to her?

He leaned toward her, until their breath mingled. He saw her lips tremble before she pressed them together, as though harnessing her courage. The thought that she needed to do any such thing while in his company raised both his ire and his frustration.

"I don't play games, Elise." It wasn't a threat. It was a statement of fact. "If you want me, tell me. If you don't, go back to the hall and pick a warrior who is more accommodating to your fastidious sensibilities."

She didn't slap his face for his insolence. For an incredulous moment, he thought he saw pain flash over her face, as though his words wounded her. Then she tilted her head in a regal manner he had come to recognize.

"Unhand me."

The insane thought thudded through his mind to sweep her into his arms and silence her protests with his mouth. A part of him was tempted. No matter that she pushed him aside now, moments ago she had lusted for him. But mainly his gut recoiled. Because if Elise truly did not want him and he took her by force, it made him no better than his father with his pitiful conquests.

No better than Elise's filthy pirate husband.

With damning reluctance, he released her. She didn't instantly turn on her heel and leave him. Instead, she remained where she was, and he couldn't fathom the expression on her face.

She looked as though she hadn't expected him to comply with her wishes.

He knew he should retreat but he couldn't move. She might not wish him to touch her, but she appeared to have no objection to his presence. This had to be a game to her. How could it be anything but? Did she play this game with all the warriors? What did she expect from him?

The questions hammered in his mind, but he had no words to voice them aloud.

And then she let out a ragged breath and shivered. He had to forcibly smother his instinctive urge to touch her again. To wrap his arms around her and ensure she was protected from the Highland's chilled breeze.

He folded his arms so he wouldn't be tempted to follow through on his thoughts. She had repelled him once. He wouldn't give her the opportunity to do so again.

"Cameron." Her voice was so low he scarcely heard her. She no longer had a look of regal disdain on her face. She looked...

He struggled to comprehend how she looked. But it was beyond him.

"Aye?" Why was he still standing here, as though he was her slave? Yet he knew he would never leave her until she was safely back inside the palace. No matter how many games she played.

"It is not that... I don't want you." She licked her lips and he stared at her, speechless. Not only because of her words. But because of the strangely haunted look on her face. He could almost believe she wasn't playing with him at all. "I understand if you must allow your fellow Scots to believe we shared a liaison. But..." Her voice trailed away, and she gripped her hands together before taking a quick breath. "But I've never chosen any warrior before."

Before he could hope to respond to that, she turned and stumbled. He reached for her arm to steady her, but she had already regained her balance. One hand pressed against her thigh, she returned the way they had come and with a silent curse, Cam followed her.

He had never quite understood women, but he didn't understand Elise at all. He drew level with her, but she refused to look his way. In only a few more moments, they would reach the great doors to the palace and any chance of conversation would, he knew, vanish.

"Elise." He took her hand and pulled her to a halt. She didn't look at him but didn't try to pull free. Except now, he didn't know what he wanted to say to her. Did she truly mean she hadn't invited any of his fellow warriors to her bedchamber? Or had he misunderstood?

"Please release me." Her words were soft and finally she looked at him. A sharp pain speared through his chest at the resignation he saw in her eyes. Did she think he would forcibly drag her into the hall, to proclaim to all present that he had conquered her?

Even if he had indulged in such barbarism, the guards would run him through with their swords before he had taken a dozen strides. Why then did she look as though she expected him to debase her in public?

Slowly he released his grip on her hand. He watched her take a ragged breath before she rearranged her disheveled veil. Without another word or glance in his direction, she turned and walked into the palace.

He stood there, blood seething, his thoughts a tangled whirl of confusion. Elise said she wanted him. But she wasn't prepared to go any further with him. In all his encounters with Scots women —both noble born and not—once mutual desire had been acknowledged between them, he had never been rebuked. He knew from his fellow warriors, if not from personal experience, that the Picts were no different.

But Elise was different. Discordant images stabbed through his brain. Why had Stuart MacGregor and the others claimed to have enjoyed the princess' charms if it wasn't true?

I understand if you must allow your fellow Scots to believe we shared a liaison. Her resigned words whispered through his mind. He'd barely registered her comment at the time. He'd been too staggered by everything else she had said.

Did she really think he would besmirch her name in such a manner? Outrage churned, burning through his chest and instinctively his fist closed around the hilt of his sword.

But it wasn't fury that Elise could think such a thing of him. It was because his fellow Scots had chosen to besmirch her name, rather than admit she had denied them.

He couldn't blame her for thinking he would do the same. She had no way of knowing he would cut out his tongue before he spoke of her, whether she had succumbed to his non-existent charms or not.

But beyond the anger, beyond the frustrated lust that still thundered in his veins, another thought pounded. A thought so revolting he could scarcely comprehend it, but a thought that gained traction with every infuriated beat of his heart.

Did Elise remain loyal to her husband because she loved him?

CHAPTER 10

*E*lise spent the following morning diligently working on her embroidery with several of the other noblewomen. She refused to think of Cameron MacNeil or the way she had so humiliatingly embarrassed herself in front of him.

And could think of nothing else.

Kila strolled into the chamber and took a place by her side. "Goddess, you look fit to faint," she remarked, giving Elise a frank look. Then she leaned in close and whispered in her ear. "Did you have an enjoyable night? I would hope so, to account for the fearsome shadows beneath your eyes." And then she smiled sweetly and picked up her needle.

It was no surprise to Elise she looked ill. She'd spent most of the night going over her encounter with Cameron in minute detail, and every time she did, her mortification multiplied.

What had possessed her to tell him that she wanted him? Except she knew the answer to that. It was because she couldn't bear for him to think she had been merely toying with him.

Not that it mattered. He was, after all, a man. He wouldn't care one way or another about her feelings, so why she'd had the inexplicable urge to soothe his, she couldn't imagine.

"Come, my lady," Kila said under her breath. "Don't keep me in suspense. Tell me everything. I promise not to breathe a word to anyone else."

Elise's needle pierced her finger and she flinched. But it was not the pain of the needle. It was the foolish pain that pierced her heart at the knowledge Cameron had already spread the rumor that they had spent the night together.

Why else would Kila be so insistent on wanting all the graphic details?

"There's nothing to tell." She kept her head bent over her work so Kila wouldn't see the truth in her eyes. "I believe I'm coming down with a chill."

Kila straightened. She clearly didn't want to risk catching a chill. "What a pity." Then she apparently couldn't help herself as she once again leaned close to Elise. "I simply must tell you, my lady. I can scarcely contain myself. *Two warriors.* Have you ever conceived of such delight? I confess I can barely sit still, my thoughts are so scandalous."

Elise shot her a frown, her own tumbling thoughts momentarily forgotten. "You had two warriors last night?"

Kila's smile left Elise in no doubt of the answer. "Every woman should experience such rapture at least once in her life," she whispered. "Can you imagine..."

Elise returned her attention to her embroidery, as Kila shared every rapturous moment in vivid detail. But her concentration wandered. Even with such delicious gossip to share, would Kila truly not have pressed Elise harder if she believed Elise had taken Cameron MacNeil as her lover?

Why couldn't she overcome her fear and take Cameron MacNeil as her lover? She could barely conduct a conversation with him without wanting to touch him. Last night she'd been determined to discover whatever knowledge he possessed of the hostages. She'd brought the conversation around to Dal Riada— and then all thought of pressing him for information had flown her mind.

He had kissed her. A ripple of remembered desire teased her damp sheath and she shifted on the stool. Nobody would believe it, but it was the first kiss she had ever had, not counting Ferelei.

But Ferelei did not kiss. He mauled. He took. The kiss she'd shared with Cameron had been nothing like she imagined. How could a warrior as surly and unapproachable as Cameron MacNeil kiss with such tenderness? With such gentle concern for her pleasure?

It was true he possessed no finesse when it came to conversation. But the touch of his large, callused hands on her face had all but undone her. He was a contradiction she could not fathom.

He touched her as reverently as the dream lover she harbored deep in her soul. But Cameron was a warrior. And her dream lover was not and could never be.

"Mistress." The voice of a servant who now stood before her interrupted her swirling thoughts. She blinked, and realized her embroidery lay discarded upon her lap. She looked up at the servant who dipped a curtsey. "The queen requires your presence."

THE QUEEN WAS in her private chamber, along with several of her ladies and Elise's grandmother. There was a subdued air of excitement, but oddly a few of the ladies avoided Elise's eyes.

She curtseyed and waited for the queen to indicate she might sit.

"It appears we were somewhat misled in the matter of your husband's arrival in Pictland." The queen smiled, but it was devoid of warmth.

"Madam?" Elise kept her voice calm, but inside panic began to churn. *Great Bride. Please do not let Ferelei have arrived in Ce so soon.*

She clasped her hands together on her lap so no one might see how they shook.

"Your husband has arrived with his band of warriors. Perhaps he will be gracious enough to allow you to continue staying with us for the remainder of the summer."

Perhaps he would. Perhaps he would even return to Fib and leave her alone for the summer. But Bride had not heard her desperate pleas for Ferelei to stay far from her. Why should she believe he had not come here to claim her and take her back to his sprawling stronghold?

She tensed her muscles as a servant opened the door that led to the queen's formal antechamber. Her husband strolled in, resplendent with the jewels he wore upon his plaid and on his fingers. He bowed extravagantly to the queen and with faultless eloquence conveyed his deepest condolences on the foul murder of her king.

Elise swallowed. *Remain calm.* But when his shrewd gaze caught hers, her stomach clenched with fear and revulsion.

On the morn of her wedding, her mother had whispered in her ear. *He is old, to be sure. But it's likely that within a year, he will be dead, and then you will inherit what is due to you from his vast estate.*

She'd thought her mother's words cold and somewhat cruel. Certainly, Ferelei was far older than she had dreamed her husband would be. But she wasn't ignorant. She knew how few warriors were both suitable and available for royal marriages.

Ferelei had always been kind to her. Flattered and complimented her. She had foolishly imagined she could wrap him around her little finger. That he would adore her and let no harm befall her.

How quickly that illusion had shattered.

How swiftly she had secretly echoed her mother's prediction for an early widowhood.

But Ferelei would not die. Perhaps in the end, he would outlive her as he had outlived his previous wives.

"My lady." Ferelei bowed before her. "You grow more beautiful every time I see you."

Elise offered him a thin smile. Beautiful was not the word he used when he looked at her scars. "You are too kind."

He took her hand. She forced herself not to snatch it back and wipe her palm on her gown. "I am the most fortunate of men." He brushed his dry lips across her knuckles, and she couldn't help the shudder that racked her body. If he noticed, he chose to ignore it. "My wife is the star that leads my ship home. I've brought you many exotic treasures, my sweet. I trust you will greatly enjoy them."

Elise inclined her head. She couldn't trust herself to answer. She only hoped he hadn't discovered yet another exotic aphrodisiac that promised to restore a man's vigor. No matter how many strange powders and concoctions he'd used over the years, none had worked. At least she could thank Bride for that small concession.

But it was only a small concession. Ferelei made up for his inability to claim his rights with a multitude of degrading humiliations.

She stifled the shudder that threatened to claim her again and remained frozen in place as the queen beckoned Ferelei toward her. The conversation flowed over her head, unheeded. Only one thought thudded through her mind and kept her from losing her fragile veneer of calm.

Escape.

THAT AFTERNOON, when her husband had left the palace to attend to the mercenaries who accompanied him, Elise once again eluded her bodyguard. Thunderclouds scudded across the gray sky and she shivered as she hurried from the shadow of the palace.

She sank to the ground in front of the sacred standing stone and with shaking fingers arranged her crystals. But even though she had cleansed and purified them after Cameron had handled them, his essence permeated every glittering facet.

She closed her eyes, and his unsmiling face flooded into her mind. How could she bear Ferelei's demands when the memory of Cameron's touch haunted every waking moment?

Great goddess, hear my prayer. Her fist closed over one of her crystals, its sharp edges grazing her palm. *I will do anything you command, if only you send Ferelei far from here.*

A strange vibration radiated across her palm and slowly she straightened her fingers.

Her heart slammed against her ribs. Her breath lodged in her throat. The crystal was no longer pure. Smears of crimson marred its translucent beauty. Elise gasped and dropped the crystal, her gaze riveted on her open palm.

At the blood that seeped from half a dozen tiny scratches across her hand.

CAM DREW BACK from his opponent, sweat blinding him, his broadsword heavy in his hand. For what seemed like hours, he and Ross had fought on this distant field, neither one willing to yield. But now they faced each other, and it was exhaustion that forced the impasse.

Ross had been spoiling for a fight all day. But until Cam had seen mac Uurguist arrive at Ce-eviot he'd been disinclined to feed Ross' aggrieved pride.

That had changed as he'd watched the murdering bastard enter the palace as though he owned it. And since he could hardly storm the stone walls and relieve mac Uurguist of his head, he'd accepted Ross' challenge instead.

But despite the ferocity of the sparring session, his mind had not been fully engaged. And he hadn't always been thinking of the bastard Pict.

It was Elise who occupied his thoughts. Elise, who belonged to mac Uurguist, and could even now be parting her thighs for her despicable husband.

The thought turned his stomach.

Ross came to his side and thumped him on his shoulder. "Women." He gave a short laugh. "It appears the princess is now beyond both of our reaches, Cam. You should have pushed forward with your advantage when you had the chance with her."

Cam grunted and shrugged Ross' hand from his shoulder. It appeared Elise's return to the hall last night, alone, had not gone unnoticed. He didn't know what Ross thought had happened between him and the princess and he didn't care.

If only he could forget that kiss. But it had haunted him throughout the night.

"Join me in the tavern," Ross said. "Who knows, one of the serving wenches might look past your glower and raise her skirts for you, if you're lucky."

Cam looked up at the darkening skies and welcomed the first cold drops of rain that splattered across his face. "I have no use for serving wenches."

The man he'd sworn to slaughter had saved him the trouble of hunting him down. He didn't believe in omens, but this could be nothing but a good sign.

Elise's face swam into his mind, distracting his purpose. Brutally he shoved the memory of her gentle touch and evocative scent aside. He couldn't let the unfathomable attraction between them alter his course.

He needed to plan how to get mac Uurguist away from his heathen mercenaries. And then, God help him, he would avenge his sweet sister's death.

In the end, Cam joined Ross and a couple of other warriors in the local tavern. It was likely mac Uurguist's mercenaries would be there and men often revealed what they shouldn't when under the influence of ale.

But it appeared that at last God was on Cam's side. Because mac Uurguist had also joined his mercenaries.

In keeping with Connor MacKenzie's instructions, none of the Scots were permitted to drink to oblivion while in Ce. The alliance between Scot and Pict was tenuous at best, and although the queen of Ce had extended hospitality toward them, they all knew the folly of losing their senses to drink.

Two nights ago, Cam had discovered that himself. He'd been fortunate to only end up in a noblewoman's bed, and not with his head embedded on a spike. If Ross knew how pissed Cam had been, he would certainly not have overlooked it, as he had overlooked the incident involving Elise.

It appeared mac Uurguist's mercenaries were under no such orders. Likely the old bastard believed himself safe here in the heart of Pictland.

His arrogance would be his downfall.

Night had descended early, with black clouds lowering over the land. Rain slashed against the tavern's roof and the few lanterns inside flickered from the gusts of wind that invaded every possible crack and gap in the structure. The cramped conditions intensified the stink of unwashed bodies, spilled ale, and the wet fur of wild-eyed dogs.

The compulsion to leave this rank outpost of hell clamored through every jagged nerve. But he remained on his rickety stool and watched his enemy from the corner of his eye.

"MacNeil." Ross' low voice, laden with warning, penetrated his blood-fueled thoughts of retribution. "There's no room in this alliance for long held feuds. You swore fealty to MacKenzie back in Dal Riada."

"Aye." But he'd sworn to avenge his sister long before he'd taken up arms for his king or joined Connor's ranks. He'd battened down his loathing for the Picts as a people and curtailed his natural inclination to smash the head of every male Pict he encountered. He'd done that because it was expected of him, and he had given his word.

But mac Uurguist was his.

CAM HAD BARELY TOUCHED his first tankard of ale when his fellow Scots, mellow but not drunk from their indulgences, heaved themselves to their feet. It would not do to be late to the feast and the prospect of securing a noblewoman for the night. Who knew how much longer the queen would extend such hospitality their way?

He saw mac Uurguist push his way through his mercenaries and disappear outside. Cam tensed and managed not to grasp the hilt of his sword as he left the tavern with the other warriors. The last thing he needed was for Ross to guess his true purpose.

The weather was foul, and it was fully dark although still

hours from sunset. Harsh wind and pelting rain attacked them and as they fought against the elements, Cam stealthily retraced his steps.

The others wouldn't notice his absence in this weather. And by the time he joined them in the great hall it would be too late for Ross to stay his hand.

He sank back against the cold stone of the tavern and made his way along the wall. Chinks of light escaped the ill-fitting shutters, giving him just enough illumination to discern his surroundings. There was a narrow alley between the side of the tavern and its neighbor, and at the far end, he saw the black outline of mac Uurguist taking a piss. Cam drew his sword and strode forward. Even the storm couldn't wash away the stink of decay that clung in the alley like a noxious cloud.

"Ferelei mac Uurguist. Draw your sword and prepare to meet your death."

The Pict swung around, just as lightning split the sky. Shock stabbed through Cam's chest at the sight of the other man's face.

He knew mac Uurguist was old. But he'd only seen him from afar earlier this day and the light had been gloomy inside the tavern. Up close, mac Uurguist looked eerily like a walking corpse.

Cam's guts clenched in revulsion and he resisted the urge to back away. Instead, he gripped his sword tighter, hands slippery from the rain.

"Who dares accost me?" Scorn dripped from every word and although it was too dark to see, Cam knew mac Uurguist swept his arrogant gaze over him. "A mere Scots pup. I could demand your head for this insult, boy."

"Draw your sword, coward." Rain slashed, and the mist made it hard to see clearly. Ominous thunder rolled across the heavens. He took another step forward. "I demand justice for the murder of my sister."

The Pict might not have cut her throat with his dagger as he had their father. But even that savage death would have been kinder than the one she had endured.

"I don't kill women."

"She wasn't a woman." A hard knot expanded deep in his chest and raw grief pumped through his veins. He tried desperately to cling onto his control. He was a warrior. He wouldn't fall victim to emotion that could get him killed. But the words could not be denied. "She was a child."

Silence greeted his words. Then mac Uurguist slumped, as though his spine had crumpled. In the gloom, he looked nothing like a warrior. He looked like an old, defeated man.

"I've done many things I'm not proud of. The bloodlust of battle does not make heroes of us all. Tell me who you are, boy, so I might know whose sword will deliver me to the gods."

Cam gritted his teeth and flexed his fingers around his hilt. These were not words he'd anticipated mac Uurguist saying. Yet he couldn't ignore the question. "My name is Cameron MacNeil from Dunmar. Now draw your sword."

Mac Uurguist raised one arm, his palm face up in a sign of surrender. His other arm remained by his side. Was it the shadows playing tricks, or did that arm look unnaturally twisted? Was it paralyzed? Had he used that arm in the tavern?

Cam couldn't recall.

"I no longer fight, Cameron MacNeil from Dunmar. If it's vengeance you seek, you will have to run me through while I stand before you unarmed."

Rage thudded in Cam's chest, making it hard to breathe. He would no sooner murder an unarmed man than he would cut his own throat. "Draw your sword, damn you."

"I'm not the man I once was. I'm old now and feeble." Mac Uurguist slowly lowered his arm. "Thanks to my beloved wife who has shown me the errors of my past. I care nothing for my own life, MacNeil. But I fear greatly for her peace of mind should she discover the violence of my death. She is gentle and does me the great honor of loving me, despite my foul faults."

Elise didn't love this bastard. She couldn't love him. Yet how fiercely she'd defended him when Cam had first learned who her husband was.

And she was loyal to mac Uurguist. She hadn't been with any other warrior and why would she stay true to a man such as this unless she loved him?

For a second his sword wavered before his grip tightened. This wasn't about Elise. This was about honor and avenging Isla.

But how could he ever look Elise in the eyes again if he killed the man she loved?

A man who bore no resemblance to the demon he'd harbored in his mind for nine long years. This was no warrior. Nor pirate. It was a man at the end of his life.

There would be no honor if he killed this creature. Only a sense of disgust that he, Cameron MacNeil, could sink so low as to murder a decrepit cripple.

He stepped back. His grip around his sword was so fierce his knuckles ached. Frustration burned through him at how retribution was within his grasp and he couldn't claim justice.

It would be so easy. One swift swing of his sword and the Pict's head would roll. Rain blinded him and the wind cut through him, but that was nothing to the violent storm ripping through his heart.

He cursed and swung on his heel. Lightning split the sky, illuminating the filth-strewn alley. In that second, he saw Ross at the end of the passageway. Saw him raise his arm in warning, heard his urgent shout.

Cam whirled around. The Pict, his arm no longer paralyzed, threw his dagger. The blade glinted and Cam ducked. Stinging pain razed along his cheek.

The thunder drowned out his ferocious roar as he attacked the lying bastard. Mac Uurguist, sword in hand, was far from frail. Metal clashed and Cam's boots slid on the foul muck coating the ground. He lunged forward and crashed into mac Uurguist who also lost his footing on the treacherous ground.

Cam collided into the wall and pushed himself upright and around in one furious movement. Panting he glared into the shadows to where mac Uurguist slumped against the wall of the tavern. Another trick? Cam would not be fooled so easily again.

"Christ, Cam." Ross was by his side. "Bastard was going to run you through from behind."

Cam shoved him aside. "Get up." He kicked the Pict's boot. No response. "Get up and fight like a goddamn man."

Mac Uurguist's head slowly slid toward his shoulder. His body remained motionless. Frustration pounded through Cam's blood and he battled the primitive need to thrust his sword through the Pict's black heart and to hell with honor.

"Wait." Ross shoved at Cam's chest and bent over the fallen man.

Cam tensed. "Beware, MacIntosh."

Ross swore and stood up. "He's dead."

Cam ground out a curse and bent over the man himself. The iron scent of freshly spilled blood filled his senses. The darkness that dripped from the wall behind mac Uurguist's head and mingled with the black puddles was more than mere shadows. It was the Pict's life seeping into the mud.

"No." Denial pounded with every thud of his heart. He should have killed mac Uurguist when he'd had the chance. Now the Pict had escaped justice and Cam had failed his sister. He stood over his fallen enemy and lifted his sword. It wasn't the same, but it would have to do.

"MacNeil." Before Cam could plunge his sword through the dead man's chest, Ross shoved him off balance. Cam rounded on his commanding officer, fury and frustration blinding every sense he possessed.

"I should have been the one to end his miserable life,

MacIntosh. What end is this, to die by accident? I'll carve out his shriveled heart and sever his head from—"

Ross shoved him again and he smashed up against the wall. Ross pinned him there, his hand around his throat. "You'll not touch him. Do you hear me? If the Picts discover his mutilated body there'll be an uprising. This way he's merely a drunk who lost his footing."

Cam bared his teeth as Ross released him. "That's not good enough."

Ross rounded on him. "That's the way it'll be. You'll speak to no one of this, MacNeil, on pain of execution. Do you hear me? The bastard fell and hit his head. That's the truth, and that's all the truth that will ever be revealed."

With that, Ross gripped his arm and forced him along the alley. Cam pulled himself free and marched toward the palace since it appeared he had no choice. He sheathed his sword and welcomed the stinging rain and buffeting wind that scoured the stench of the alley from his clothes. But he knew nothing would ever cleanse the darkness in his soul.

The darkness he had known would fade once mac Uurguist's blood was on his hands.

As the looming shadow of the palace came into view, Ross pulled him to a halt. "The only reason you're still breathing is because I saw you turn away, MacNeil. If you'd followed through and killed mac Uurguist in cold blood, I would've had your head for disobeying orders. Are we clear?"

"Aye." The bloodlust had faded, and instead a hollow sense of inevitability seeped into his veins. His vendetta was over but there was no victory.

Cam and Ross dried themselves as best as they could in front of the roaring fire in the outer hall. Several other warriors, both

Scot and Pict were also there, and none commented on his fresh wound or their late arrival.

None appeared to even notice their late arrival.

He didn't want to sit through another feast surrounded by Picts. He ached to return to Dal Riada. But it wasn't Dunadd, stronghold of his king, that he craved.

It was Dunmar. He needed to return home, to seek Isla's forgiveness for failing her.

As the royal party took their places at the high table, he steadfastly refused to look Elise's way. But it didn't matter whether he looked her way or not. He couldn't help but see her from the corner of his eye.

She didn't appear unduly concerned at her husband's absence.

The food turned to ashes in his mouth and he swallowed half a tankard of mead. He tried to kill the thought before it took form but could not.

Elise was free. Would she take a lover, now? Would she take *him*?

A Pict warrior bowed low to his queen and murmured in her ear. The queen's countenance didn't change, but she turned to Elise and a moment later, the entire royal party left the hall.

Speculation for the swift departure spread throughout the hall. Cam caught Ross' grim glare, but he hadn't needed the reminder.

He would tell no one what had happened outside the tavern.

ELISE FOLLOWED her aunt and grandmother to the queen's private chamber. She hadn't seen Ferelei since earlier that day and had been dreading his presence at the feast. But for an unknown reason he had risked the Queen of Ce's displeasure by not attending.

Elise didn't care what had delayed him. She only wished with all her heart the delay would be permanent. Would Bride grant her such a favor even though her goddess had allowed Ferelei safe passage through countless sea voyages?

She knew it was too much to hope for. But a tiny corner of her heart hoped, all the same.

"Elise, my love." The queen beckoned her forward and took her hand. "I have bad news of your husband. He's been taken into the gods' safekeeping."

The gods' safekeeping? She knew what that meant, of course. But they were speaking of Ferelei. "Madam?"

The queen squeezed her fingers. "He is dead, Elise. It appears he stumbled in the rain and hit his head. Nothing could be done."

The queen's words echoed in Elise's ears. *He is dead.* It couldn't be true. He was a pirate and a warrior. How could he have stumbled and hit his head?

Her grandmother approached and embraced her. "The goddess has set you free, Elise," she whispered in her ear.

She pulled back from her grandmother as the truth sank into her soul. She was free. Her heart thundered in her chest making it hard to breathe, and a whirlwind filled her head making the chamber spin about her.

Bride had heard her prayer. The enormity of her wish, and the manner in which her goddess had replied, crashed through her. She stumbled backwards as icy fear filled her veins, and she looked at her palm where the crystal had marred her skin.

Bride had released her from Ferelei. But nothing was truly free. She had pledged wildly and without due care to do anything, sacrifice anything, if only Bride would grant her this one favor.

What would her goddess demand in return?

Cam saw nothing more of Elise that night or the following morning. No Pict warriors marched through the Scots camp, demanding justice for the death of one of their own. From overheard conversation, it appeared mac Uurguist, while a wealthy and powerful noble, had commanded little personal respect in life.

He had been old. The facts had spoken for themselves.

When drunk, he'd slipped in the storm and cracked open his skull. An inglorious death for a warrior, even a retired warrior, but no one appeared inclined to investigate further.

It shouldn't have been this way. Cam had wanted public retribution, to grind the Pict's reputation into the mud. But had he done so, his own life would be forfeit.

"I have a bad feeling about the arrival of MacAlpin's men." For once, there was no laughter in Stuart MacGregor's voice as they and half a dozen others cleaned weapons and equipment in the camp.

Cam grunted in response and glanced at their commanding officer's tent. A score of Kenneth MacAlpin's warriors had arrived at Ce-eviot barely an hour ago. The leader, MacAllister, had not requested audience with the queen. He had demanded to speak with Ross.

The other new arrivals guarded the tent as though they expected to be attacked. Had something happened to Connor? It was unlikely any other Pict tribe would have attacked him. The eldest Princess Devorgilla of Ce was with him, and she was his wife.

Besides, MacAlpin's men would have left Dal Riada at the earliest over a week ago. Even if something had befallen Connor, how would they know of it?

IT WAS late afternoon before Ross called his men together.

"MacAlpin was not best pleased to discover Connor had brought his bride back to Ce-eviot." He swept his glance around each man. They had all known the mission back into Ce from Dal Riada had been undertaken without their king's knowledge, and all had been willing to risk his wrath. Cam knew each man was in conflict over the massacre of the Pictish nobles in Dunadd, and while they would always serve their king, their fealty was to Connor.

"Are we to return to Dunadd?" another warrior asked.

Ross held up his hand for silence. "They met up with Connor on the way here. The fact he was returning to Dal Riada with the princess goes in his favor as far as MacAlpin's concerned. But MacAllister wanted me to confirm what Connor had told him." His jaw tightened. "It appears our facts not only tallied but met with MacAllister's approval."

"What happens now?" Stuart asked.

Ross looked grim. "Six of us are to return with them, while ten of them will remain here. I will choose who stays and who is to leave and let you know my decision in the morning."

As the warriors dispersed, Ross beckoned Cam over. "You'll be leaving with them, MacNeil."

Cam had expected the order. But instead of relief that he'd soon be back in his own land, disquiet stirred his blood.

He wanted to leave Pictland. He wanted to return to Dunmar to try to appease the restless soul of Isla. But no matter how hard he tried, he couldn't fight the truth—he didn't want to leave Elise.

CAM RECOGNIZED the man standing a short distance from the pagan stones, arms folded across his massive chest. He was Elise's bodyguard.

A strange sensation churned his gut. He wanted to see her. But how could he look her in the eyes when he had been responsible for the death of her husband?

True, he hadn't killed mac Uurguist in the way the bastard had deserved to die. But if Cam hadn't been in the alley, the Pict would still be alive.

It was as well Ross had decided the full truth would remain buried. Cam didn't want Elise to ever discover the part he'd played in her husband's death.

God. When had things become so complicated?

He could feel the bodyguard's glare burning into his back as he made his way toward the stones. He knew where Elise would be even though he couldn't see her from this angle.

The same stone where he had almost fallen over her three days ago.

He saw the spill of scarlet gown across the grass and his chest tightened. She was sitting on the ground before the massive stone, as though she was praying.

Of course she was praying.

A shiver ripped over his flesh.

He couldn't interrupt her while she was communing with her

heathen gods. But neither could he stand here watching her without her knowledge. He hovered, uncertain, before the matter was taken from his hands as stones slid from beneath his boot.

Elise jerked upward and their gazes clashed. His stomach clenched. Had she been crying?

"You startled me." Her voice was soft. Husky. It reinforced his thought.

She had been crying. Because of his actions. It didn't matter how despicable mac Uurguist had been or how deserving of his fate. Elise still mourned him.

If ever a man needed a silken tongue, he needed one now. How could he comfort her when he was responsible for her grief? He was proficient neither at sweet talk nor lying.

"Forgive me." He sounded feral. Oddly, Elise didn't flinch beneath his tone. Her steady gaze encouraged him to continue. "I heard of your loss." He had damn well caused her loss. Should he have left mac Uurguist in peace? But what then of his sister's peace?

In one rain sodden moment, he had destroyed any chance of peace for both Isla and Elise.

She looked at the ground and he followed her gaze. It was no surprise to see her crystals forming the pagan symbol. He watched her gather them up and slide them into her pouch before she braced her weight on one hand and began to rise.

This time he offered her assistance, and with barely a moment's hesitation, she accepted his help. His hand dwarfed hers, and he couldn't bring himself to release her when she was standing before him.

She didn't appear offended. Unless it was his wretched imagination playing tricks, her fingers briefly curved around his before she gently disengaged.

A white shawl draped over her shoulders to keep the Highland chill at bay. It matched the color of her veil.

Scarlet and white. The Pictish colors of mourning.

"It falls to me to take Ferelei's body back to Fib. The queen believes I should remain here or return to my family in Circinn. But I believe I will do as my goddess commands."

He hadn't expected her to tell him of her plans. He had no idea how to respond to her disclosure. He didn't even understand what she meant by doing as her goddess commanded. But he had to say something. Because she was looking at him, and he didn't want her to think him disinterested in anything she might say.

"I also am leaving Ce shortly." Elise would need a full complement of guard if she traveled. But Fib was due south from Ce. Dal Riada was in the southwest. Would MacAllister consider a Pictish princess worthy of his warriors' protection for such a diversion?

Her eyes widened and lips parted in evident shock before she quickly recovered herself. He wasn't sure why her reaction made him uneasy, but it did.

"You are returning to Dal Riada?" He heard a trace of disbelief lingering in her voice, as though she needed further confirmation.

"Aye. MacAplin's sent reinforcements. Ce will not be left undefended."

He saw her grasp her crystal filled pouch but had the uncanny notion she had no idea that she had done so. Was she calling on her goddess again?

"I intended to travel with Ferelei's band of warriors. But if you are going in the same direction…" Her words trailed away but her meaning was clear. She wanted them to travel together.

ELISE HELD her breath as she waited for Cameron's reply. Vaguely she noted the fresh wound on his face. Thank Bride it didn't look poisonous. She'd spent half the afternoon begging for Bride's guidance, and despite how she'd sat upon a blanket, she was damp to the marrow of her bones from the wet ground.

But that was a minor concern. For Bride had once again answered her desperate prayers, and in the one way Elise had not imagined possible.

There was a price for everything. But Bride's price for releasing her from Ferelei was not leaving Cameron behind in Ce.

"Fib is not on the route to Dal Riada." There was a ferocious glare on Cameron's face, but she knew it wasn't directed at her or her question. It was because he spoke the truth but wished it otherwise.

How refreshing she found his directness. Another warrior would have played with words, offering her assurances he had no way of fulfilling.

But then, she had no intention of traveling to Fib. Bride had granted her freedom, and with that freedom, she would discover the fate of Droston. With no husband to answer to, she could command her own destiny. Once she was beyond the borders of Ce, the queen could no longer deny Elise's wishes.

She wanted to tell Cameron her plans. But the time was not yet right.

"No. But perhaps arrangements could be made that suit us all." The warriors who'd accompanied Ferelei on his sea voyage were not hers to command, but she would have no trouble with his mercenaries. So long as she paid them, they would follow her orders. And Ferelei hadn't been exaggerating when he'd told her he had brought many exotic treasures from his last adventures.

She would use those treasures to buy and bribe her way to Dal Riada. And once there she could pay whatever ransom the barbarous MacAlpin demanded for Droston's release.

"If I could influence MacAlpin's men in this matter I would. But..." Cameron hesitated and something dark haunted his eyes, something that made her want to reach out and take him in her arms. She pressed her fingers against her damp gown before she followed through on the thought. "I'm out of favor and doubt Ross MacIntosh would lend weight to my words."

Elise had lost count of how many warriors, both royal and noble born, had promised her the stars so she would look favorably upon them. But Cameron MacNeil, a foreigner from a savage land, stood before her and confessed he was powerless to change his commanding officer's mind.

An odd pain pierced her breast. His brutal honesty meant more to her than any number of pretty, insincere words.

"This is a matter for the queen. Neither you nor I have any influence on this outcome."

It was true the final word would come from her queen. But Elise was no longer prepared to accept whatever her aunt might decide. If the queen decreed Elise had to remain in Ce, then she would disclose that Bride was guiding her.

Even the queen wouldn't deny Bride.

Cameron stepped toward her. His dark hair whipped across his face in the breeze, but she could still see his intense frown. And the concern in his eyes caused her heart to ache.

She desperately wanted to feel his strong arms around her once again. To have his lips tenderly claim hers. He was a raw, uncivilized Scot, and yet he was the only man she craved to touch.

"Elise." His husky voice sank into her blood and her breath became uneven. His hand reached for her face and liquid desire heated her. Barely reined lust simmered in the air between them and tendrils of need enslaved her senses. But before his fingers made contact, he paused. "I don't trust the mercenaries."

She blinked and tried to gather her scattered wits. While she daydreamed of Cameron making sweet, undemanding love with her, he thought of Ferelei's warriors and her safety.

It wasn't what she expected or was used to when confronted by a man who desired her, but it was strangely fitting when that man was Cameron MacNeil.

"Neither do I." Goddess, had she really confessed that? But if he was surprised by her frankness, he didn't show it. "But they will guard me well for payment." Besides, once the queen had agreed to her request, she would ensure a small contingent of Ce warriors also accompanied Elise.

"They have no loyalty." The tips of his fingers traced the line of her jaw. His callused flesh enhanced the tenderness of his touch and tremors danced over her exposed skin. "They wouldn't think twice about killing you if that offered them greater financial reward."

She knew he was serious. Knew what he said was the absolute truth. Yet she couldn't help the breathless laugh that escaped. "You're such a comfort, Cameron MacNeil. I shall be sure to watch my back when among them."

His frown intensified, but his fingers remained gentle against her face. "It's no laughing matter, my lady. If the mercenaries are your only guard then may your queen forbid your request."

Had any other man said such a thing to her, she knew she would've been regally offended. But despite his blunt ways and lack of finesse, Cameron's concern was as enchanting as his accent.

He didn't expect her to stay in Ce because it pleased him. It was because he feared for her safety.

Tentatively she raised her hand to her face and threaded her fingers through his. He swallowed, as though her touch affected him as much as his affected her. Her pulses hammered and her chest constricted as his wild Scots scent filled her head. They were in full view of anyone who might pass by. Her bodyguard was within calling distance. Yet they might have been the only two people alive on this windy Highland day.

There was no doubt in her mind that, one way or another, she would travel with Cameron to Dal Riada. Bride was guiding them both to the same destination. But she couldn't tell him that. He didn't believe in her goddess and she had no wish to see that look of mingled disgust and horror on his face at the mention of Bride.

"Then we must pray to our gods my queen has no reason to deny my request."

"Aye." He might have agreed with her, but she saw the conflict in his eyes. The knowledge that she worshipped the ancient gods troubled him deeply, and she couldn't fathom why. None of the other Scots warriors had ever had a problem with it. But then, Cameron was unlike any other warrior she had ever encountered.

With reluctance, she pulled back from him. She had been out far longer than she'd intended, and the queen expected her back at the palace. There were rituals to perform and sacrifices to offer the gods to allow Ferelei safe passage beyond the veil.

But far more importantly, she needed to obtain her queen's permission to leave the Kingdom of Ce.

CHAPTER 13

Cameron marched toward Ross' tent, where he had been summoned. There had been no feast last night in the palace, in deference to the death of Lady Elise's husband, and he hadn't seen her since she'd left him at the pagan stones yesterday. But she'd invaded his dreams, except this time instead of leaving him hard and frustrated he'd awoken with a chilling sense of foreboding.

"MacNeil." Ross welcomed him with a curt jerk of his head. Cam glanced at MacAllister who stood by Ross' side. There was a calculating gleam in the other man's eyes that Cam didn't trust at all.

"So you're MacNeil." MacAllister ran his shrewd gaze over Cam. He gave a small, satisfied smile that made no sense. "The Queen of Ce tells me the recently widowed Lady Elise wishes to travel to Fib."

Was he supposed to answer that? It appeared self-explanatory, especially if the queen herself had told MacAllister.

And then the meaning of MacAllister's words hit him. Elise had spoken to her queen. And if the queen had told MacAllister of Elise's wishes that meant she was seriously considering Elise's request.

But why had MacAllister demanded to see him? Why was he being informed of this development?

"Does she?" He sounded surly even to his own ears. From the corner of his eye, he saw Ross clench his jaw, but MacAllister appeared uncaring of Cam's attitude.

"Aye." MacAllister took a step toward him. "Were you not aware of the princess' plans, MacNeil?"

Silence hung heavy in the tent, a tangible force. Cam slowly exhaled a long breath. MacAllister was testing him, trying to discover if Elise confided in him. He didn't know why. But he would never betray Elise by repeating those few precious conversations they had shared.

"Why would I be privy to the princess' plans?"

MacAllister regarded him through narrowed eyes for a few moments before he gave a nonchalant shrug and tossed a brief glance in Ross' direction.

"According to the queen, one of their heathen gods has foreseen that the princess will travel with us when we leave Ce." MacAllister's lips twitched as though he found this amusing. Cam attempted to control his scowl because MacAllister was the king's man and ranked higher than Connor MacKenzie. But despite his best intentions, he knew he failed. "What is more," the older man continued, "the queen appears to believe that her gods intend you should be the one to whom the princess' wellbeing should be entrusted."

He didn't know anything about that and was inclined to believe MacAllister had simply made it up to gauge Cam's reaction. He took grim pleasure in maintaining his scowl.

A flicker of impatience crossed MacAllister's face. Clearly, he had expected some kind of response to that disclosure. "Well?"

What the devil did MacAllister expect him to say? "You intend to escort the princess to Fib?" Cam asked.

"I'm weighing up my options."

Something was going on here. Something he couldn't quite grasp. It seethed beneath the surface, barely hidden, waiting for the right moment to strike.

But he couldn't imagine what.

"It would be a lengthy diversion." Why was he trying to put MacAllister off? Yesterday he'd wanted nothing more than to spend more time in Elise's company. This journey, if MacAllister agreed to it, would be the last chance he'd ever see her. So why was he raising obstacles, even if those obstacles were blatantly obvious?

"It would be an unacceptable diversion if our destination was Dal Riada." MacAllister offered him an insincere smile. "But our liege is currently in Fortriu, the kingdom that adjoins Fib."

Fortriu, Supreme Kingdom of the Picts. But now, after the massacre of the nine Pictish nobles in the spring, under the rule of Kenneth MacAlpin.

The sense of foreboding that had haunted him all morning thickened like a storm cloud in his chest. They would need to travel through Fortriu to enter Fib. But every sense he possessed warned him that if Elise entered the Supreme Kingdom, she would never leave.

He had to alert her to the danger.

"MacNeil." MacAllister stood in front of him, arms folded across his burly chest. There was no longer any hint of amusement in his expression. "I've decided we will escort the princess to Fib. I entrust her personal safety to you. And one more thing." An intangible sense of menace throbbed in the air between them. "You'll say nothing to the princess as to our true destination before we leave Ce, upon pain of death. Is that understood?"

IT WAS late afternoon before Elise managed to escape both the other ladies and her bodyguard and make her way to the standing stones. She needed to commune with Bride alone. But it didn't matter how many times she told herself that. The truth was quite different.

She wanted to see Cameron MacNeil. And she couldn't shake the certainty that she would see him if only she went to the sacred stones. Alone.

But he wasn't there. She walked around the great circle that surrounded the monastery, trailing her fingertips over the ancient monuments. The lingering remnants of the mighty storm two nights ago had vanished, leaving the air crisp and fresh.

As though the goddess had washed away the darkness and now offered a new beginning.

She sighed and leaned her back against one of the stones that faced the copse. How she secretly longed for a new beginning. A new life. But it was foolish to imagine she could have any such thing with Cameron.

He was a Scot. A commoner. And she was a Princess of Circinn.

But her cousin Aila had married a Scot. And Aila was the eldest Princess of Ce, not the fifth daughter as she was.

Ah, what was she thinking? She would have little say in the choice of her second husband. There simply weren't enough eligible royal or noble born Picts to choose from, especially since so many were still held hostage in Dal Riada.

The choice would be slender, but it was her duty to wed again. And no matter that the thought of the marital bed sent fearful shivers skating along her spine, at least the experience might one day lead to having a precious babe of her own.

But she would make the most of her year of widowhood. Not only would she secure Droston's freedom…

She would take Cameron as her lover.

The thought slid into her mind, unbidden, and heat flooded

her cheeks. Perhaps, in the darkest hour of the night, she imagined how it could be with Cameron. But in the harsh light of day, her courage always failed.

The ancient stone grazed her fingers where she pressed against it. Her heart thudded and nipples peaked against her bodice. Bride had chosen Cameron, and Elise had thought it was because he was the one who would take her to Dal Riada and help her find Droston.

But she no longer needed Cameron for that. The queen had now agreed to allow Elise to leave Ce. She had enough treasure to find out what she needed without coercing Cameron.

There could be only one reason why Bride continually allowed their paths to cross.

As if to reinforce her revelation, a figure appeared on the slope that led down to the copse. Tall, broad shouldered. Achingly familiar. Her mouth dried and she was grateful for the solid rock that kept her upright.

Surely there could be no doubt left in her mind.

He paused at the top of the ridge and looked down at her. The breeze whipped his plaid around his legs, and even from this distance, she could see how the material molded his muscular thighs. He didn't appear inclined to come to her, so she pushed herself from the comforting presence of the standing stone and slowly made her way toward him.

"Cameron MacNeil." Her voice was breathless as she greeted him. "Are you on your way back to your camp?" She hoped not. And surely he couldn't be if Bride had led them both here.

"Aye." His answer was uncompromising, and her fragile courage wavered. But she should have known Cameron would be blind to her subtle invitation. If she wanted to walk with him, she should have simply said so. He wasn't, after all, adept at the accepted nuances of light banter. "But I'm in no hurry if you are in need of protection during your walk."

She stared at him, secretly shocked. Clearly, he'd noted the absence of her bodyguard and disapproved. But instead of telling her so, he had offered her his company instead.

"I should like that." She smiled at him and he stared at her as though mesmerized. It was unnerving and her smile faltered. She had never been the one to initiate a clandestine liaison and despite her extensive experience in the art of flirtation, she had no idea how best to approach the matter.

Kila and the other noblewomen would be scandalized if they knew the true extent of her inexperience in the bedchamber. What Ferelei had subjected her to didn't count. She'd never been a participant, only a vessel for his depraved pleasure. A chill raked over her flesh and she forcibly shoved the memories aside.

She wouldn't allow Ferelei in death, any measure of power over her. He had passed through the veil and she hoped the gods judged him fairly.

The thought of his suffering the gods' judgment gave her some small satisfaction.

She turned and began to walk down the slope, ignoring the ache in her leg from the damp grass yesterday. Cameron fell into step beside her. He didn't offer his hand to assist as another warrior might have done, but simply having him so close to her was enough to send her pulses racing.

Goddess, she would likely pass out from bliss if they did any more than kiss.

The thought amused her, and she bit her lip to stop herself from smiling.

"Are you well?" He sounded hesitant, as if unsure whether his question would be unwelcome.

"Very well." She chanced giving him a sideways glance. His usual frown was in place. What would it take to wipe that look from his face for all time? How dearly she would love to be the one to accomplish such a feat. "It seems our gods listened to our prayers. I am to leave Ce in two days."

Instead of vanishing, his scowl noticeably deepened. She

hadn't expected that reaction. Did he no longer wish to travel with her? But why wouldn't he?

"It might be wise if you remained in Ce, where you're safe."

They had already had this conversation. "Ah, but now I will also be protected by a contingent of fearless Scots warriors." She smiled up at him, willing him to smile back. But it appeared today such a thing was beyond him. Yet she couldn't stop herself from trying. "Indeed, I believe my queen would not have granted permission had you not been accompanying us." Surely that would rouse him from his dark thoughts?

"Why?"

She blinked, uncertain as to his meaning. She hadn't expected him to challenge her comment. Then again, Cameron never did anything she expected. Clearly, her expression mirrored her thoughts as he drew in a great breath and came to a halt.

"Why does your queen place such trust in me?"

And now he wanted specifics. She knew he wouldn't be impressed that Bride had chosen him. But that was the very reason why her queen had finally relented.

Perhaps she could tell him the partial truth, instead.

"Because I told her I trusted you."

He stiffened and if it weren't such a ludicrous notion, she could have sworn bleak despair gripped his features for a fleeting moment. It was as if her confession had somehow wounded him.

But she hadn't offended him. If anything, she had complimented him. Truly, Cameron MacNeil was the most intriguing man she'd ever met.

"I'll do everything within my power to protect you, my lady." His formal address combined with the underlying hint of raw passion was a powerful combination. She swallowed, suddenly aware that here, by the stream, they were utterly alone.

The stream. Instinctively she drew back. Her heart hammered and palms grew sweaty. The storm had swollen the normally tranquil waters, and now it reminded her more of a treacherous deluge.

It reminded her of the river where she had almost lost her life.

"Elise." Cameron took her hands and the concern in his voice dragged her back to the present. She took a deep breath and forced herself not to think about that terrifying time. And with Cameron's intense gaze on her, it wasn't hard to let those memories slide away. "What is the matter?"

His strong hands held her steady. She was about to laugh off her panic attack as nothing when something stopped her.

Perhaps this was Bride's way of telling her to warn Cameron of her injuries. So that he wouldn't recoil if he saw them.

But she never spoke of her accident. Those who knew of it never mentioned it, and those who did not remained in ignorance. And, except for the ladies who attended to her needs, nobody since it had happened knew of the damage she had sustained.

Nobody but Ferelei mac Uurguist. But Cameron was nothing like Ferelei.

She owed it to him to warn him. So he wouldn't be repulsed by her disfigurement.

So she would not have to bear witness to his shocked disgust.

"Forgive me." Without meaning to, her fingers tightened around his. Somehow it gave her the courage to continue. "When I was a child I almost drowned. I've had a fear of fast-flowing rivers ever since." And today the stream was a fast-flowing river, with hidden dangers swirling beneath the frothing surface.

She took a fortifying breath. Now she should tell him. But the words locked in her throat. Suppose her confession caused him to retreat without even seeing the damage?

Cameron was frowning. But since he invariably frowned, she didn't think that had any bearing on what she'd just told him.

She licked her lips. Surely Bride wouldn't have chosen

Cameron MacNeil if he could be so easily repulsed. And then he spoke.

"Is that when you injured your leg?"

The tortured words fled her mind. She stared at him, staggered by his words. How did he know? Who had told him?

But it was impossible anyone could have told him.

"What?" Her voice was barely above a whisper.

"You favor your right leg at times."

She did? But she was always so careful not to draw attention to her leg when in company. She trawled through her mind but couldn't remember any time when she had done such a thing in front of Cameron.

Yet the fact remained. He had noticed.

She wasn't certain whether his powers of deduction impressed or shocked her.

"Yes. I..." she hesitated. It was one thing to decide she wouldn't allow Ferelei's contempt rule her life. But it was another to face her fear of rejection so blatantly. Countless men had told her she was beautiful. Perfection. She had always smiled prettily and accepted their outrageous compliments. And all the while she had thought *how quickly you would run if you saw the damage beneath my gown.*

Compliments meant nothing to her. But Cameron's opinion...

Great Bride. Cameron's opinion meant so very much.

Her goddess had given her this opportunity to forewarn him. Now it was up to Elise.

"I fell from a crag into the river below. My leg shattered on impact." There. The words were between them. She searched his face for any sign of disgust but all she saw was dawning comprehension on how close she had been to passing through the veil.

Or was she merely deluding herself?

"You could have died." There was a trace of awe in his voice, as though the fact she hadn't was something of a miracle. To be sure, her grandmother always maintained it was only the intervention of Bride that had saved her life, but marriage to Ferelei had diminished the miraculous by focusing on what had been damaged.

The hard knot in the center of her chest eased. "I didn't emerge unscathed. My leg is…" She swallowed and Cameron squeezed her fingers. She hadn't imagined it. It gave her the courage she needed to continue. "My leg is quite disfigured."

"I cannot believe you still possess your leg."

The nervous fluttering in the pit of her belly faded as the absurd desire to giggle assailed her. How like Cameron to say something like that. "It was a close thing. The Healers were divided as to which path to take. But I am significantly… scarred."

It was the first time she had said the word aloud. Before her marriage, she had tried to pretend her scars didn't exist. And after her marriage, Ferelei had flung that word, and worse, at her so frequently she hated the very sound of it.

"Aye," Cameron said, as though the revelation was of little significance. "I am badly scarred also, Elise."

This time she couldn't contain her laugh. "But you're a fierce warrior, Cameron. Of course you have scars. What warrior does not?"

"They shape the course of my life."

"Indeed, they do." Goddess, was Cameron concerned she might find his scars abhorrent? She'd never believed a warrior could ever think such a thing. "You could scarcely be the man you are today without them."

"Aye." That was all he said, but he looked at her as though he could see deep into her soul. For a long moment, she luxuriated in the dark intensity of his eyes. But as the silence lengthened, an odd sensation curled through her breast.

Heat washed through her and once again, she could feel a blush suffuse her face. Surely, she was wrong. Surely Cameron had not just turned her own words back at her?

CHAPTER 14

By unspoken agreement, they walked upstream toward the untamed woodland ahead. Cameron continued holding her hand and she had no desire to pull free.

His hand enveloped hers. No man had ever held her in such a manner. It was intimate. Comforting. Yet there was a thrilling undercurrent of danger that wove through her blood and caused her skin to prickle with heightened awareness.

Cameron might think they were enjoying a simple stroll. But she knew exactly where they were heading. The knowledge that she was about to embark in an illicit liaison caused molten desire to pool low in her womb and curl with delicious heat between her thighs.

"How did you fall from a crag?" His question was blunt, and she knew what he really meant. How could a princess fall from a crag? And of course he was right. No young princess of Pictland would be allowed to play such dangerous games. But then, she and Droston had always loved daring each other to their limits.

"I was playing on the wet rocks and slipped." She shivered as the memory of falling through air and nothingness rushed through her once again. "It was a harsh lesson to learn but as you can see, I still evade my bodyguard and ladies on regular occasions."

He stopped dead and turned to face her. "You were alone?" His voice was harsh. "How did you survive until you were discovered?"

His evident concern was a balm to the ragged memories that haunted her. She couldn't help the small smile that curved her lips, even though she knew he must think her mad for it.

"I wasn't alone. My dear friend Droston was with me. He pulled me from the rapids and carried me back to the palace. He is scarcely a year older than me." Droston had been only twelve, but his bravery and single-minded purpose to save her had barely been acknowledged by her mother. And her mother, Elise had soon realized, ruled her father in such matters.

CAM WATCHED the smile fade from Elise's face as a shadow clouded her eyes. A sharp pain stabbed through his chest and he clenched his jaw against the unfamiliar sensation.

He ignored it. Because it was clear to him that Droston was so much more to Elise than merely her friend.

Were they lovers? Elise had told him she'd never taken a warrior to her bed and he believed her. But she had been speaking of Scots warriors. Not Picts. And the man who had saved her life as a child would not be merely a passing liaison.

Elise had shown no special favor to any Pict warrior that he could recall. But the suspicion Droston had been her lover strengthened and with it came another.

Now Elise was free of mac Uurguist, would she wed the other man?

"Will he be waiting for you in Circinn?" They had to travel close to the border of Circinn to reach Fortriu—and Fib.

A frown creased her brow, as though she found his question

completely unexpected. "No. He—I believe he is held hostage in Dal Riada."

The pain in her voice was obvious. Cam tried to ignore the spike of relief at the knowledge Droston wouldn't be joining Elise in the journey from Circinn.

He didn't know why. It wasn't as though the existence of Droston changed anything between Cam and Elise. And yet he couldn't shift the feeling that somehow—it did.

"You care for him." He sounded surly. Could not help himself. Because the thought of Elise caring for another man churned his guts.

"I love him as though he—" Elise bit off her words, blushed in that entrancing manner she had, and then took a deep breath. "As though he were my brother. It grieves me that I don't even know whether he is alive or dead."

Why didn't she simply tell him the truth? It was obvious she felt more for Droston than brotherly affection. She was more concerned for his fate than she appeared by the death of mac Uurguist.

Perhaps he'd been mistaken when he'd thought Elise cared for her husband. God, he hoped so. The bastard Pict hadn't deserved a fleeting glimmer of regret from a woman such as Elise.

He didn't want to think of Droston. But the haunted look in Elise's eyes tore through him. "To my knowledge no Pict warrior without a claim to Fortriu died."

The shadows miraculously cleared from Elise's eyes and the smile she bestowed his way was like no other he had ever seen from her. It should have fired his blood. Instead only a dull sense of despair filled his chest.

"Thank you." She took a deep breath and her relief was so great it became a tangible thing, hovering between them like a heathen specter. "I prayed he was alive but to know for certain has lifted a great weight from my heart. We were all but insepa-rable as children. I have four older sisters, as you know, but

Droston is so much closer to me in age. We couldn't care for each other more if we were related by blood."

She gave him an oddly earnest look, as though willing him to believe her. Of course he believed her. Why would she lie? Her affection for the cursed Pict illuminated her like a star in the heavens.

"If he's held in Dal Riada there's no need to fear for his safety. The hostages are afforded all privileges their rank deserves."

"Of course." Her tone was oddly formal, and he cursed his brusque manner for shattering her happiness. As much as the existence of Droston irked him, he had meant to comfort her. But all he had done was reinforce the fact Droston was little more than a political prisoner. "My father is also held hostage. But I doubt any ransom would secure *his* release."

It was true some of the minor hostages could be released upon negotiation. It was equally true the most valuable ones would continue to be held until all of Pictland acknowledged MacAlpin's claim to Fortriu.

He tightened his grip on Elise's hand as they continued to walk through the woodland. Not that she'd tried to pull free, even after his inept attempt to ease her concern. He stole a sideways glance at her.

She was looking ahead, but he noticed how she scanned the ground and how carefully she stepped over tangled roots and shallow dips in her path. In her scarlet gown and white veil with a plain gold circlet upon her head, she looked every inch a princess.

Untouchable.

Yet she had no objection to holding his hand.

He edged closer to her, so their entwined fingers pressed against his thigh. He had never walked hand in hand with a woman—or a girl—before. A sad reflection on his past. But after mac Uurguist had destroyed Isla, Cam had lost what little social graces he'd ever possessed. Girls were not enamored of his terse manners and while his friends broke countless young hearts as they practiced their seduction techniques, he had plotted dark retribution.

Elise led them farther into the woods. He had no idea where they were going and didn't care. The sunlight filtered through the dense canopy of leaves overhead, giving a mystical diffused illumination. She looked like a mythical fae from a child's tale, an ethereal wood nymph from pagan times and for once, the thought didn't fill him with a nameless fear.

Elise might worship pagan gods. But she wasn't evil. She wasn't a witch. While there was breath in his body no man would harm her for her beliefs.

She glanced at him and offered a smile of such sweetness that his chest ached. Her elusive scent drifted in the air, spinning through his blood and stirring his ever-present lust. He battled the primitive need to pull her into his arms, to feel her body meld with his.

He would do none of it. No matter that she had taken him deep into the woods where the only sound came from birdsong and the breeze rustling through the leaves.

She brought him here because, God help him, she trusted him.

"We have arrived, Cameron MacNeil."

He realized he had been staring at her profile as they walked and had no idea where it was they had arrived. He dragged his gaze from her to look up ahead.

An ancient stone roundhouse nestled among the trees. Its roof had long gone, and ivy twined around the structure. Far from looking out of place, the roundhouse gave the impression that the woodland had embraced its presence and was as much a part of the landscape as the trees themselves.

They might have arrived. But he still had no idea where they were.

"This place is inhabited?" His disbelief was evident in his tone. A chilling thought struck. Had Elise brought him to visit an ancient one who communed with her illusory gods? But why would she do that?

Elise tugged on his hand. "Why do you look so fierce? It's only a deserted roundhouse. Not a secret outpost of Vikings."

He looked at her. She was smiling up at him, but her earlier easy demeanor had vanished, and there was an undercurrent of tension radiating from her.

A memory stirred. In the spring, Stuart MacGregor had told of a deserted roundhouse deep in the woodland where he'd enjoyed the favors of two Pictish noblewomen. Cam's mouth dried and cock thickened as he recalled Stuart's indiscreet boasts.

Just because Elise had brought him here did not mean she intended to seduce him.

He cleared his throat and tried to gather his scattered senses. But all he could think of was lifting Elise's skirts. Tasting her succulent heat.

Making her his.

"I thought perhaps," Elise hesitated and looked back the way they had come. "But it does not matter. If you would rather continue our walk that would be most—"

"Elise." Her name burned through his chest and he cradled her face with his hand. Her skin was warm and smooth as silk. She looked back at him, wariness clouding her beautiful blue eyes and he cursed himself for making her believe, for even a second, that he didn't want her. "If we enter the roundhouse, I fear I might never let you leave."

The guarded expression on her face vanished. She leaned very slightly into his palm and he caressed her cheek with the pad of his thumb. Such a fleeting touch. Yet it scorched through his blood, constricting his chest, and gripping his vitals.

He had never wanted a woman as much as he wanted Elise.

"I may never wish to leave." Her soft whisper threaded through his pounding head. He raised their entwined hands between their bodies and pressed his lips against her knuckles.

Somewhere in the lust-soaked depths of his mind, a sliver of caution stirred. A primal warning that echoed through his soul. If he entered the primitive Pictish ruin with Elise, the course of his life would be irrevocably changed.

But his life had already been turned inside out from the moment he'd first seen Elise. All his nighttime fantasies of having her in his arms collided in his mind. If MacAlpin himself appeared and forbade him to enter the roundhouse, he doubted he could obey.

"Are you sure this is what you want?" His voice was uneven. She had led him here and she looked at him with desire. But a thread of disbelief tugged on his senses.

She was a princess. All his compatriots lusted for her. Yet she had chosen him.

He could not truly fathom it.

For answer, she bent her head and pressed her lips against his knuckles. A mirror image of his own action. Her lips were soft, and her breath drifted across his fingers. It was a chaste kiss, but exquisite promise swirled beneath the surface.

"I have never wanted anything more," she whispered and led him through the open door.

CHAPTER 15

 $\mathcal{E}$ lise stepped over the threshold into the roundhouse. An ancient stone table set back from the door was the only furniture. The light was muted as the open roof had been claimed by creeping vines and overhanging trees, and she couldn't help the relief that washed through her.

She didn't want Cameron to see her in the full force of daylight.

He kicked the door shut. Before he could pull her into his arms, she spied a timber rod propped against the wall.

"We can secure the door." She indicated the rod and the weathered bolt holders that, at some distant point in the past, had been attached to the door and wall.

Only the slight raising of his eyebrows showed his surprise before he hoisted the rod and dropped it into place.

"You've been here before." There was no censure in his tone, yet Elise had the strangest certainty that Cameron had believed she had not.

If she had taken lovers in the past, and Cameron was any other warrior, then what he believed in this matter was irrelevant. Did a warrior remain celibate when away from his wife?

Elise knew few were faithful. It was not even expected unless a love match was involved. And how often did those with royal or noble blood wed for love?

But she hadn't taken any lover. And Cameron wasn't any other warrior. She didn't care for the elaborate games played out between lovers, despite having spent so many years indulging in the frivolous pastime of flirting.

She curled her hand around his bicep. Even through his sleeve, she could feel the heat of his flesh and the rigid strength of his muscles. The knowledge that they were utterly alone thudded in her mind and caused her breath to catch in her breast.

"I've not been here before with anyone. But some of the ladies love to gossip. It appears this roundhouse has been used as a lovers retreat for many generations."

His fingers trailed along her cheek. It was such a gentle gesture. Almost reverential. As though he wasn't certain whether his touch was truly welcome.

"I didn't imagine having you in a ruin." His husky whisper, combined with his irresistible accent, was as potent as the feel of his fingers on her face. Spellbound she gazed at his harsh, unsmiling face that no longer caused her to shiver with unease. Because she could see beneath that surly exterior. She hadn't been mistaken when she'd thought he presented a façade to the world.

"How did you imagine it?" She slid her hand up his bicep and over his powerful shoulder. Even though they were both fully clothed, her fingertips tingled from the contact, and a thousand fluttering wings collided within her chest.

"In a bed. For your comfort."

Unlike another man, she knew Cameron didn't say such a thing merely because he knew it would please her. He said it because it was true.

"The moss is springy and quite comfortable, so I have been told."

"I wouldn't take you on the wet ground." Lust spilled through every word but there was an undercurrent of masculine outrage. As though the thought she expected him to do such a thing offended his sense of honor.

For a second, she was entranced. And then the meaning of his words penetrated.

What a fool she was. She had forgotten about the storm. The moss beneath her feet was likely still sodden. She should have brought a blanket with her.

"Elise." There was a hint of laughter in his tone now as though he didn't share her dismay, and she stared at him, bemused. Cameron wasn't given to amusement and what in the name of Bride was there to find amusing in this situation? He traced his forefinger along her bottom lip. Goddess, she had never imagined her lips were so exquisitely sensitive. And who could have imagined how beautiful Cameron looked when he didn't scowl?

"Elise?" He repeated, as his voice dropped to a decadent rumble, but the frown was back on his face. She blinked, clearing her vision, but frown or not Cameron still struck her as beautiful as an immortal god.

"Yes?" Her breathy whisper was all she could manage. She wound a length of his hair around her finger. It was surprisingly soft, like threads of silk. She had never before done such a thing. How wonderful it was not to cringe at the thought of touching a man.

"I will not take you on the ground." He wound his arm around her waist and tugged her tight against his hard body. "But I have every intention of having you before we leave here."

The length of his rigid cock pressed against her stomach. Tremors rippled through her. She felt deliciously swollen between her thighs and pressed her legs together. The friction was not nearly enough to satisfy.

She rose onto her toes, pressing her aching breasts against his chest. His eyes were so dark they appeared black, and his unwavering focus was as potent as any pretty words.

Their lips touched. It was everything she remembered from the other night and so much more than the dreams she'd had since. His kiss was tender, and he coaxed her lips to part. The tip of his tongue teased and explored but did not thrust inside. She sighed and shifted in his embrace and wrapped her arms around his neck.

Holding her securely with one powerful arm, his other hand drifted up her back and over her shoulder. She felt him tug her gold circlet from her head and heard it land upon the mossy ground. Her veil slid onto her shoulders, and Cameron speared his fingers into her hair and held the back of her head.

Her eyes closed as she savored the feel of his hands on her body. Yet all he did was hold her still while his fingers slowly massaged her head. It was oddly intense and intensely arousing. She'd never imagined a man would do such a thing to her, or that it could feel so good.

His kiss deepened. His tongue slid into her mouth and liquid darts of a strange pleasurable pain tumbled between her thighs. She dug her fingers into his hair, wanting him closer. If only they didn't have the barrier of clothes between them.

He tore his mouth from hers and she gasped, trying to catch her breath. He looked at her as though she was the only woman in the world. In this moment, she felt like the only woman in the world, and Cameron was that world.

"I cannot believe you're here with me." There was a hint of awe in his voice and she gave a breathless laugh before she could stop herself. His fierce expression softened as though her response, far from spoiling the mood, merely added to it. "You could take your pick of my compatriots. Why me?"

She cradled his jaw. His faint stubble grazed her palms. Cameron MacNeil was a tough, taciturn warrior. Yet she had glimpsed his soul, and he was the unlikely man who had haunted her secret dreams.

"I took my pick of warriors, Cameron. Not one of them stirs my passion as you do."

He brushed a lock of hair from her cheek, his fingers lingering on her warm skin. "I don't know how to say sweet words, Elise. They are foreign to me."

"A man can say anything and mean nothing. All that counts are his actions."

A look of anguish flashed across his face, as though she had plunged a sword through his heart. "I would never wish to hurt you."

"I know," she whispered. "You won't." Yet deep in her heart, she knew he would, even though it wouldn't be his fault. When the time came for them to part, she would grieve for what might have been until the last breath left her body.

But she would never regret this time with him.

She watched him as he loosened the laces of her bodice. The look of utter concentration on his face sent need spiking through her. He tugged open the material and pulled her gown over her shoulders revealing her breasts to his gaze, and she hitched in a jagged breath.

Her breasts felt heavy, aching for his touch. He trailed a finger over her exposed flesh and heated shivers coursed over her nakedness. Then he cupped her breasts, squeezing them together to create a deep cleavage. Every erratic breath pressed her sensitized globes into the palms of his hands. It was beyond anything she had imagined.

He lowered his head and pressed his lips to her. She threaded shaky fingers through his luxuriant black hair and gasped as his mouth captured her erect nipple.

Mesmerized she stared at him as he sucked on her sensitive peak. Pleasure streaked from her captive nipple straight to her swollen clitoris. The sound of her heartbeat pounded in her ears and she dug her fingers through his hair, pinning him more securely to her throbbing nipple.

His tongue swirled and his teeth very gently nipped. She gave a strangled groan and shifted helplessly as he abandoned her untouched breast and molded the shape of her waist and hip.

He grasped her gown and began to tug the material up her leg. In a tiny sane sliver of her mind, relief spilled that he was exposing her left leg and not her injured right. But almost instantly, the thought fragmented when his hand curved around her naked thigh.

Her nipple slid from his wet mouth as he straightened. Impeded by her disheveled gown she could no longer cling onto him and instead gripped his shirt where it sculpted the taut planes of his stomach.

His hand slid around to the apex of her thighs. His knuckles brushed against her curls in a touch as light as a feather, but liquid flames ignited deep in her core.

She swayed and her grip on his shirt tightened. A hint of a smile tilted his lips, as though her reaction pleased him. Shock flickered through her as she found herself smiling back at him.

In the past, sex had never been something to smile about it. Warmth flooded through her blood and heightened the need surging through her veins. "Should I be smiling?"

"I like to see you smile." Raw lust wove through each word and primitive desire tugged low in her belly.

"I like…" she swallowed, mouth dry, as he nudged her throbbing clitoris. "That." She gasped the word and clutched desperately onto his shirt to keep from collapsing onto the ground.

For answer, he cupped her sex and drew one finger along her wet seam. He didn't penetrate but teased her unmercifully until she writhed with wanton need.

"Are you ready for me, Elise?" His words were uneven, and

she couldn't drag her gaze from his. She could not find the wit to answer him, either.

Clearly her ragged breath and burning face were answer enough. Slowly he dipped a finger inside her cleft and then another. She groaned out loud and then bit her lip in mortification.

"Don't." His command was rough. She stared at him, bemused, while he rotated his fingers inside her, building the intense pressure between her thighs. Goddess, it was too much... "Don't be silent. I want to hear you."

"Cameron." Her voice sounded strange to her ears, breathless and sultry. "I fear I may fall if..." If she didn't lie down. But she couldn't lie down because the ground was wet, and Cameron wouldn't allow her to lie on the rain-soaked moss.

He wrapped his arm around her waist and pulled her with him as he backed up to the stone table. Still teasing her swollen clitoris with the tip of one finger, he sat on the edge of the table, released her waist, and hiked up his heavy plaid.

His muscled thighs were glorious, all she had dreamed. Her gaze shifted upward to his mighty cock and she forgot how to breathe.

She had only ever seen her husband's before, and there was no comparison. Cameron radiated vigor and youth, everything she had ever hoped for as a young maid.

"If you continue to look at me like that, I will likely spill my seed before even possessing you." His tortured growl thickened the desire pooling low in her belly and she dragged her eyes up to meet his penetrating gaze.

"That would be a grievous disappointment." She edged forward, straddling his thighs. The musky scent of arousal drifted in the air. He slid his fingers from her and the chill air against her wetness caused her to quiver. She braced most of her weight on her good leg and licked her lips. "Are you ready for me, Cameron?"

He laughed, the sound echoing around the roundhouse, and a startled look flashed over his face. Entranced by how young and carefree he'd looked in that fleeting moment she smiled back at him, as a strange ache gripped her heart.

"Aye." His voice was rough. "I've been ready for you for a long time, Elise."

He palmed her bottom, rubbing his hand over her rounded flesh. His thighs spread her wide and tremors raced over her naked breasts as he tugged her even closer. Her gown now concealed his erection, but somehow that heightened her breathless anticipation.

Tentatively she lowered herself and his thick cock penetrated her wet cleft. She gasped and froze, savoring the sensation of having Cameron MacNeil enter her body for the very first time.

"Christ, don't stop." His agonized command and the way his hand gripped her bottom caused fiery tremors to spiral through her sheath. She sank a little farther down his shaft, and his groan was the sweetest music she'd ever heard.

Feverishly he pulled at her gown so he could bury his hand beneath her skirts. He wrapped his hand around his cock and his thumb massaged her swollen nub.

She panted desperately and sank down his shaft a little more. Goddess, he was big. He filled her in a way she had scarcely dreamed possible. Yet there was no pain, only a sensation of such raw possession, her senses spun.

His hand slid from his erection as she took more of his length inside. But his thumb continued to torment her, building such exquisite pressure it seemed the earth rocked beneath her feet.

"Come for me, beautiful princess," Cameron said and fastened his mouth around her nipple. The shock of his words and the feel of his lips tugging on her erect flesh ricocheted from nipple to clitoris like lightning.

Cameron flexed his hips, thrusting his length inside her. She gasped and clutched onto his shirt for balance and sanity. Liquid heat built and she convulsed around him.

Her nipple slipped from his mouth and he looked up at her, eyes black with passion. Her body quivered and heart pounded as he rammed into her again and again. Forcing her to abandon her will and her reason as pure sensation consumed her.

Her vision blurred and the world receded. There was only Cameron and this moment in time. She could scarcely breathe. She sagged over him, their foreheads touching, and only his arm, now wrapped around her waist, prevented her from collapsing.

He dragged his hand from beneath her skirts and rubbed his thumb over her nipple. His gaze never left hers. "Elise, my princess." The words were jagged with a primitive edge of possession. He kissed her, a savage plunder that caused another wave of pleasure to ripple through her core.

Before she realized his intention, he lifted her from his rigid cock. She fell against him, his arm still securely around her waist, and watched him grip his shaft.

The heady scent of sex and arousal perfumed the air. She watched, mesmerized, as Cameron pumped his seed onto the mossy ground. His strangled groan of completion pierced her enchantment and she looked at his face.

His eyes were closed, his teeth gritted. He looked in the throes of agony. She leaned closer, although how that was possible she would never know, and slipped her arm across his chest and clung onto his shoulder.

As his tortured gasps receded, she trailed kisses from the corner of his mouth and along the line of his strong jaw. After an eternity, when her heartbeat had slowed and Cameron's rigid muscles had relaxed, he turned to her.

She smiled and brushed a chaste kiss across his lips. "The next time I will take precautions to prevent conception. There will be no need for you to withdraw so hastily."

He trailed a finger along her face and across her lips. It was a gentle gesture that caused her tender flesh to once again quiver with need.

"I look forward to that." His husky voice wrapped around her heart. "But nothing will ever compare to our first time, my princess."

Cam left the roundhouse first, leaving Elise inside, while he scanned the area. He knew the Pictish noblewomen indulged in countless affairs and nobody appeared to care.

But Elise was a princess, and he cared deeply that her reputation remained unsullied. She had never taken another warrior, despite his compatriots' veiled insinuations, and he had no intention of anyone discovering that she had shared herself with him.

The woodland appeared deserted. The sky was obscured by the canopy of leaves, but he guessed it was late in the afternoon. He turned and opened the door and Elise stood there, looking demure and desirable, her veil back in place. But a mischievous smile lit her face and it was hard to remember they had to leave when all he wanted to do was shut the door on the world and take her once again.

"Is it safe?" Her whisper filled with laughter as she stepped outside. Her hair, only partially concealed by her flimsy veil, tumbled in glorious disarray and there was an inviting blush on her cheeks. She looked as though she had been thoroughly pleasured. He hoped he was the only one who noticed.

"Aye." He wanted to take her hand, but an odd reluctance held him back. He glanced over his shoulder but there was nothing but trees and bushes and grass. Yet he couldn't shift the unformed sense of unease.

"Ah, you are a man of such few words, Cameron MacNeil." Elise clearly harbored no reservations as she slid her arm through his and hugged him close. "How delightfully refreshing you are."

He offered her an uncertain frown. She sounded as though she meant every word, but how could that be so? A woman enjoyed flirtatious banter. Elise excelled in the art. It was one of the reasons his fellow warriors found her so charming.

Yet still she had chosen him. It would remain a mystery to him until the moment he died.

But he had no intention of allowing his perplexity in this matter prevent him from enjoying her as often as possible. "Tomorrow is the last day we spend in Ce-eviot. We can go to the roundhouse again in the afternoon."

"Indeed, we could." She looked up at him as she clung onto his arm and a hollow pain pierced his chest. When they reached Fortriu would MacAlpin allow her to continue onto Fib? He wanted to warn her. But if he did, MacAllister would have his head. And if he died who then could protect Elise from his king's machinations?

Elise laughed and squeezed his arm. "Why do you look so fierce, brave Scot? To be sure, we could meet here again tomorrow. But I have a better idea." She raised her eyebrows in an enchanting manner. It was all he could do not to simply stop walking and stare at her instead. "Tonight, you must come to my bedchamber."

He stumbled on a root but even that indignity wasn't enough to prevent his cock thickening at the thought of visiting Elise in her bedchamber. But of course it was merely a fantasy.

"What of your bodyguard? I'm certain he wouldn't allow a Scot warrior to enter your chamber unaccompanied."

Elise waved her free hand in a regal gesture. "It can be arranged. And besides, it is not even as though I'm bound to another anymore."

Were her vows to mac Uurguist the only reason she'd never taken a lover before him? He contemplated the possibility for a fleeting moment before discarding the notion.

Elise would have told him that the other night if it were true. But something else snagged at his conscience. He wanted to ignore it, but he was compelled to speak.

"But you're in mourning. I would not wish your people to look on you with disapproval for any reason." In Dal Riada, a widow was expected to remain chaste and above reproach until a new marriage was arranged for her. Of course, many enjoyed an illicit lover but if publicly denounced, the woman's reputation was ruined.

Elise sighed and gave him a strangely furtive glance. "I wouldn't blatantly make love with you in the middle of the feasting hall," she said, and he narrowly avoided tripping over another cursed root. She said the most outrageous things at times. He wasn't certain whether he should enjoy her remarks as much as he did. "But it's no great secret that Ferelei and I did not care for each other. I would never disrespect his memory, but I won't allow his passing to spoil what we've found together. In any case," she hesitated and then gave him a strangely sad smile. "We have only weeks together at the very most. In a year, I will be wed again. Should I be denied the pleasure of your company while I remain free, Cameron?"

Relief speared through him that Elise hadn't cared for that bastard Pict. It was a salve to his conscience knowing he hadn't been responsible for depriving her of a beloved husband. But with the relief came a bittersweet resignation.

Elise was right. Their liaison would be short lived in the extreme. That knowledge had never bothered him in the past with other women. But the thought of losing Elise to another man didn't sit right with him at all.

"How shall I reach your bedchamber?' He'd scale the palace wall to find her if he had to. But he was sure Elise had a different plan in mind.

"I'll send word to you," she said, with all the assurance of one who had never had her word denied before. He felt his frown dissolve as he soaked in the radiance of her smile. She was a princess. Of course she was used to having her way. And he certainly had no desire to deny her anything that was within his power to give.

WHEN HE RETURNED TO CAMP, after ensuring Elise had safely entered the palace, Ross approached. "MacAllister wants to leave Ce tomorrow." His voice was low. "I don't trust any of them, Cam. Watch your back."

"Aye." Cam had already reached that conclusion. Why had MacAllister changed his mind about leaving? Elise believed she still had two days left in Ce. Whatever the reasoning behind the decision, Cam didn't trust the king's man. "I'll protect the princess with my life, Ross. You know that."

Ross folded his arms and squinted into the distance. "I have no doubt you will. You're a loyal bastard. In your boots I can't say I wouldn't have done the same to mac Uurguist."

Cam grunted. There was nothing to say in response to that. But he knew what Ross was really saying. That, although he would have executed Cam for disobeying Connor's orders, he understood Cam's reasoning behind it.

"I've told the men you had nothing to do with his death. But there's speculation, Cam. No getting away from that. The important thing is, nothing can be tied to you that might lead to repercussions on the Scot-Pict alliance."

Aye, because nothing was more important than the cursed Scot-Pict alliance. And yet there was little bitterness in his thought. Unlike a few short months ago, he now wanted this alliance to succeed.

Because Elise was a Pict.

Ross turned toward him. There was a calculating gleam in his eye. "Tell me. You and the princess. Have you sampled her charms?"

Cam's scowl deepened. "I've learned one thing about the princess. She shares her charms with no warriors. I've a mind to smash Stuart's skull for slandering her name in the spring."

"Aye, that doesn't surprise me. Stuart's mouth is larger than his brain." Ross grinned. "But you, Cameron MacNeil, have been singled out by both the princess and the queen. That has to give you an advantage. What I fail to understand is why their heathen gods chose you. Miserable bastard that you are."

Since Cam didn't believe in their heathen gods, he could only conclude it was Elise herself who had singled him out. But he was hardly going to tell Ross that.

"THAT HE SHOULD DARE present *me* with an ultimatum." The queen stood tall and rigid in the center of her chamber, her rage barely contained. Elise glanced at her grandmother, but the older woman's face was impassive. "That filthy common Scot. The very air around him reeks of blood and betrayal. I don't believe I will entrust your safety to any of them after all, Elise."

"Madam." Elise stepped toward her aunt and tried to ignore the flare of panic that tightened her chest. The queen couldn't change her mind now. She wasn't ready to say goodbye to Cameron so soon. "MacAllister is doubtless an uncouth savage who deserves nothing but our contempt. But Cameron MacNeil is not the king's man. He is Connor MacKenzie's man."

The queen's lips thinned. "And you are a royal princess with links to all seven kingdoms of Pictland. You are not to be ordered to leave my domain a day earlier than we decided simply because it suits a foreign dog."

"You are right." Elise inclined her head so her aunt wouldn't see the dismay in her eyes. It was one thing to let the queen know both Elise and Bride looked upon Cameron MacNeil with favor. But she wasn't certain she wanted her aunt to guess she had taken the Scot as her lover. "But there is little to arrange. Ferelei's body is prepared and the treasures he brought with him from his last travels are still packed in the wagons. In truth, I would prefer to leave earlier, if it does not offend you."

"Why should it offend me that you cannot wait to leave my side?" Her aunt's voice was chilly.

Elise took a deep breath. She hadn't intended raising the queen's hopes, but knew she had no choice if she wanted her blessing.

"I believe during this journey I'll discover the fate of our hostages." Because once she was in Dal Riada, surely she would not only be able to secure Droston's freedom but also discover how her father and cousin Talargan fared.

"Why didn't you tell me this before?"

"I can't be certain of the outcome. I didn't wish to promise something I might not be able to fulfill." She felt her face heating and stared at the floor. She knew she was implying Bride would intervene and share her knowledge with Elise. But she couldn't tell her aunt the truth—that she intended traveling to Dal Riada herself.

She couldn't risk the queen flatly denying her permission.

The queen was silent for a moment. "This revelation is connected to the Scot, MacNeil." It wasn't a question.

"I believe so." But unlike a few days ago, when Bride had first thrust Cameron into her path, Elise no longer intended to use him as a means of information. There was no need, not now she had her freedom, both personal and financial.

"Then we shall have a farewell feast in your honor and invite the newly arrived Scots. They had best make the most of it. There shall be no more feasts for them in Ce-eviot until my daughter and son return home."

The queen turned and swept from the chamber, her ladies following in her wake. Elise went to follow, but her grandmother took her hand and pulled her to a halt.

"I know you plan more than you have told us, Elise." Her voice was low so no one could overhear. Elise's stomach knotted with trepidation. Had her grandmother guessed the truth? "The goddess hides your true purpose from me. I can only imagine whatever you intend is with her blessing."

Elise released a relieved breath. If her grandmother had asked her outright, she knew she could never have lied to her. Thank Bride it hadn't come to that.

"I serve the goddess in all things, Grandmamma. It's her path I follow."

Instead of looking reassured, a troubled frown creased her grandmother's brow. "Beware, my love," she said. "Our ways are changing whether we want them to or not. Wherever your path leads you, do not allow Bride's memory to die."

A shiver inched over Elise's arms at the glazed look in her grandmother's eyes. What did she mean? Of course she would never allow Bride's memory to die. No matter how many new gods might emerge, the ancient ones would always prevail.

THE FEAST WAS A SUBDUED AFFAIR, but Elise had little interest in the restricted platters on offer. She could scarcely keep her gaze from Cameron despite how she tried to be circumspect as her status demanded.

Truly, no other warrior, Pict nor Scot, could compare. Even from this distance, she could see the magnificent way his biceps bulged beneath the sleeves of his shirt, the breathtaking width of his chest and the way his black hair glinted in the lamp light.

She shifted on her seat, but it did nothing to ease her sensual discomfort. She tried to regulate her uneven breath and calm her racing pulses. But it was impossible. Even when she concentrated on her plate, all she saw in her mind's eye was the way Cameron had looked at her earlier that day in the roundhouse.

It was a relief when the feast finally ended, and the tables were pushed back to the walls. Elise knew there would be gossip and speculation when she didn't immediately follow the queen from the feasting hall before the entertainment began. But she didn't care. In her heart, she wasn't newly widowed. She had been released from an oppressive dungeon fashioned from darkness and fear.

She accepted condolences on her recent loss from several of Connor's warriors. Not one of them attempted to engage her in flirtatious conversation. It appeared her widowhood had erected an invisible barrier around her, and stilted phrases and awkward pauses replaced the previous easy-going manners of the Scots. It also appeared few of them could meet her eyes.

How odd the Scots were in the face of death. Did they treat all widows in such a manner? No wonder Cameron had been concerned for her. Thank all the gods her people were not so inhibited in such matters.

And then a thought slid into her mind. Kila had also been recently widowed, and yet no Scots warrior to her knowledge had been made uncomfortable by her status. Why the difference between them? Was it because Ferelei had not died in battle?

The crowd parted and from across the feasting hall she saw Cameron looking her way, as though he had known exactly where she was. Warmth bloomed deep in her heart and she tried not to let her delight show on her face. What did she care how any other Scot treated her? There was only one warrior whose actions mattered to her.

They met midway as though by chance and not design. He bowed, an economical gesture completely devoid of the extravagance of his countrymen, yet Elise found it perfectly elegant.

"Cameron MacNeil." She offered him her hand and after a second's hesitation, he took it and brushed his lips across her knuckles. He held onto her hand longer than protocol dictated before slowly releasing her fingers.

"My lady." Only two words but they caused her sheath to quiver with delightful anticipation.

"Walk with me." She gave him a sideways glance as he fell into step beside her and led him through the great doors into the massive entranceway. Warriors, guards, and servants mingled, all busy with their duties or leisure making, and none gave her and Cameron more than a cursory glance.

With seeming nonchalance she strolled around the perimeter until she passed by the concealed staircase. Then she paused and daintily rearranged the folds of her veil. "There is a secret stair behind me, located between the inner and outer walls of the palace. I will send my bodyguard to wait for you at the top of the stair in one hour."

CHAPTER 17

They returned to the great hall and after a few moments, Elise left him without a backward glance, as though they were merely acquaintances. She disappeared through the door that led to the royal chambers, her bodyguard shadowing her. Many surreptitious glances followed her.

Cameron exhaled a long breath. So far, her reputation remained intact. He knew it wasn't something that especially concerned Elise, and he doubted any of his fellow warriors would think less of her if they knew she had taken him as her lover.

But that was beside the point. Elise was a princess. She should not be spoken about in such a way, and the fact that she had been in the spring was a poisoned thorn in his side. He caught sight of Stuart MacGregor flirting outrageously with the noblewoman Cameron had found himself in bed with the other morning, and his scowl deepened.

He would take great pleasure in bloodying MacGregor's nose for such lies. But MacGregor wasn't the only one. Did he intend extracting retribution for every warrior who had claimed to share Elise's favors in the past?

It was a tempting proposition. But one he reluctantly acknowledged would remain unsatisfied.

Instead, he prowled around the hall and watched Connor's men and the newly arrived king's men vie for the Pictish noble-women's approval. Scandal and sexual intrigue thickened the air, and the haunting strains of the harps added to his building frustration.

But he could not go to Elise yet. It was too soon.

He swung about and grabbed a tankard of ale. And saw MacAllister watching him with barely concealed speculation. Cameron raised his tankard in a mocking gesture before swallowing half the contents.

There was something about the older man that made his flesh crawl. It wasn't the fact he deliberately wanted Elise kept in the dark about their destination or the way he'd threatened Cam. It was connected, certainly, but it went much deeper. A fundamental conviction that MacAllister had a hidden agenda.

Of course he did. He was MacAlpin's man. Cameron's grip on the tankard tightened. His thoughts regarding his king bordered on treason lately, but he couldn't seem to stop himself. The suspicions were polluting his mind.

He had to discover the truth of what happened to the nine Pictish nobles last spring in Dunadd.

FINALLY, it was time. It was a simple matter to leave the hall without attracting attention, and he found the concealed staircase without a problem. An iron grill gate at the foot of the stairs was unlocked and ajar and after a stealthy glance around, he entered the enclosed staircase.

It was dark as he climbed the ancient stone steps. It hadn't occurred to him to bring a torch. But eventually he saw a glimmer of light ahead.

He emerged through another iron gate where Elise's body-guard, torch held aloft, regarded him in stony silence. Cam glowered back. He wasn't used to resorting to subterfuge when it came to sexual affairs. But his ill temper wasn't because of the secrecy. He, after all, was the one who had insisted upon it. It was the disapproval etched on the Pict's face. The expression told Cam as clearly as if the words had been spoken aloud that he wasn't good enough for the princess. Not even as a transient liaison.

The bodyguard led him along the passage then knocked on a timber door. A servant opened it and Cam stepped into the antechamber, slinging a glance at the bodyguard who folded his arms and radiated menace.

He hoped the man was accompanying Elise on her journey. She needed loyal men around her. And although he trusted Connor's men with his life, only five were leaving with him tomorrow. The rest were MacAllister's men and mac Uurguist's mercenaries.

He followed the servant across the antechamber and waited while she went into, he presumed, Elise's bedchamber. He took a moment to look around. The antechamber was luxurious in the extreme, with thick rugs covering the floor and tapestries on the walls. For some reason it brought to mind his own hillfort, Dunmar, and the sorry state he'd left it in the last time he'd been there.

Even aside from Dunmar's sordid history, the grim interior held nothing that would please a princess like Elise.

He glowered at the ornate fireplace. Why was he thinking of Elise and his hillfort? The chance of her ever setting foot inside Dunmar was non-existent. His father might have been a noble and his mother related to cursed foreign royalty, but no royal Scots blood flowed in his own veins. Elise would never be anything more to him than a fleeting liaison.

"Cameron MacNeil." There was a trace of laughter in Elise's

voice and he swung around. She stood in the open doorway to her bedchamber and his heart slammed against his ribs at the sight of her. She was wearing a sleeveless white under-gown and her hair tumbled over her shoulders, unhindered by any veil.

She was a vision.

"Come." Her whisper was seductive, and she stepped back as he entered her chamber. Even with only the flicking light from the fire, he could see it was as lavishly decorated as the antechamber. "You look entirely disagreeable to be in my company." Elise smiled up at him. Obviously, his scowl didn't worry her at all and why was he scowling in any case?

This was a brief affair. It could never be anything else. To wish for something more would bring nothing but disappointment.

More than disappointment. He shoved the thought aside. He wouldn't waste the time he and Elise had together wishing for the impossible.

He kicked the door shut with his heel. Shadows spilled from distant corners. Why had her servants not lit her torches?

"I don't find your company disagreeable." He took a lock of her hair and it slid through his fingers, like golden sunbeams. He gave a twisted grin at the thought. When had he ever been so poetic?

"I'm happy to know it." She reached up and trailed her finger across his lips. "I like to see you smile. It illuminates the chamber."

He laughed and wrapped his arms around her, tugging her close. "You say the most outrageous things, my lady. I have never before been told my presence illuminates a chamber."

"Then the ladies of Dal Riada must be insensitive to your charms."

She linked her fingers together around the back of his neck. Her luscious body melded against his, warm and soft and full of promise. It was too dark to see the color of her eyes, but he saw them anyway. They were the blue of a summer sky, when no clouds marred the horizon.

"I have no charms." He searched her face, memorizing every feature for the years ahead when she would no longer be in his arms. "But I've often been called insensitive."

She sighed, her breath a seductive caress along the line of his jaw. "Perhaps I'm the only one who sees beneath your scowl, Cameron." Her fingers twined in his hair and her nails teased the back of his neck. "Perhaps I'm the only one you want to see beneath your surly façade."

He hadn't thought of that before. But now he considered her words. And realized she spoke the truth.

He did want Elise to see beyond the man who had spent more than a third of his life pledged to avenge his sister's death. For nine years, bitterness had corroded his soul and concealing his devastating memories and vow of revenge had become second nature.

But deep in his shuttered heart, it wasn't who he was. Except the boy he had once been had never had the chance to be anything else. Had never known he could want anything else.

Until he had met Elise.

"You're the only one who's ever wanted to." He hadn't meant to say that aloud and could feel his familiar scowl masking his feelings once again. His protective barrier against the outside world where ugliness ruled, and evil claimed the lives of innocents.

Elise cradled his face. Her hands were soft, her touch gentle, and his taut muscles slowly relaxed. She didn't say a word, simply gazed up at him as though she could somehow ease his burden through silence alone.

Moments passed. The only sound in the chamber was from the crackle of the fire. The tightness in his chest eased and he exhaled a long breath. Elise hadn't laughed at him. Had he really expected her to? But it had been so long since he'd said anything that came close to exposing the black turmoil that imprisoned his heart, he'd forgotten a tender touch could soothe an aching soul.

For a second an eerie sense of familiarity whispered through his mind. But he had never shared such a moment with a woman. His previous encounters had been earthy and enjoyable, but not once had he discarded his battle-honed veneer long enough for his bed partner to glimpse what seethed beneath.

He wasn't sure why he had now. Except that with Elise, he wanted so much more than he ever had before.

"My brave Scot warrior." Her hands drifted over his shoulders and she began to loosen the ties on his shirt. "You need no mask when we're alone."

It was true. He didn't. Except for one.

She could never know the part he had played in mac Uurguist's death.

With reluctance, he released her so he could lay aside his sword, strip off his plaid and pull his shirt over his head. Elise stared at him, and it must have been the flickering light from the fire that distorted her expression because she looked... enthralled.

No woman had ever looked at him in such a manner before. His blood heated and cock thickened, but he refrained from pulling her into his arms. He wanted to enjoy that look on her face a little longer.

"Are you admiring my scars, my lady?" God, where had that come from? He never felt the need to speak during such sexual encounters. He certainly never felt the need to gently mock the reminders of his battles. But even as the thoughts thudded through his mind, he couldn't stop his grin.

Elise's look of almost reverential awe as she gazed on his body aroused him in a way he had never imagined possible.

"Do you have scars?" Her voice was breathless. "I did not notice."

He laughed. Unbelievably, he flexed his biceps, in a pose designed to entice the favor of a lady.

"What do you notice, princess?" Was he flirting? Could it be this easy? Yet he couldn't imagine speaking this way to anyone but Elise.

"I notice…" She hesitated, and finally her gaze once again caught his. "I notice you are the most beautiful man I've ever encountered."

A strange pain twisted through his chest. He'd been called many things in his life. But no woman had ever called him beautiful.

"A man is not beautiful." His voice was gruff, and his arms dropped to his sides. "But you're beautiful, Elise. I have never seen another to compare."

She brushed the tips of her fingers over his chest, a look of wonderment on her face. He wasn't certain whether it was her touch or her expression that caused his balls to throb with need. He clenched his fists so he wouldn't be tempted to rip the gown from her and take her where she stood. But he was tempted, regardless.

"I want you, Cameron MacNeil." Her breathless confession stretched his control beyond his limits. He wrapped one arm around her and pulled her roughly against his body. She laughed, a breathy whisper against his jaw, her palms flattened against his nipples. "Come to the bed."

He ignored her command and with his free hand grasped her under-gown and tugged the soft material upwards. He wanted to see her naked before him, bathed in nothing but the glowing light of the fire. The vision burned into his brain and it took an agonizing moment for him to realize the pressure against his chest was Elise trying to break free of his embrace.

"What's wrong?" He loosened his grip around her waist but continued to drag her gown up her leg. Until she clasped his wrist in a silent but eloquent gesture.

"Nothing is wrong." Without releasing his wrist, she attempted to pull him toward her bed. "Cameron, come to bed." There was the faintest undercurrent of desperation in her tone and buried beneath the thundering beat of lust suspicion stirred.

He let go of her gown and cradled her face. Her hand slid along his forearm to nestle in the crook of his elbow. Her eyes were dark pools of temptation and he almost forgot what had to be said.

"I don't want your gown between us this time, Elise. I need to see you."

She swallowed and the tip of her tongue moistened her lips. He knew she didn't do it deliberately and yet he still found her action intensely provocative.

"You will. I'll take my gown off in bed. Beneath the furs."

His suspicion solidified. "I don't care about your leg. You know that, don't you?"

She flinched as though he'd struck her. Instinctively his fingers tightened around her face. Why would she react in such a way?

"Of course." But her gaze dropped from his. Disbelief seared through his chest. Did she truly believe he lied? "But... I would rather not risk your... I would rather you remember me like this. That's all."

The flames from the fire threw shadows across the chamber. Darkness claimed the corners and inched across the floor. It seemed to him that Elise was truly bathed in a halo of light.

But there was a darkness beneath her smile that he had never really seen before. He could agree to her wishes and take her beneath the furs. But if he did, something rare and precious within her soul would wither.

He had no idea where the thought came from or why he should imagine such a fanciful thing. But it wouldn't shift.

And neither would he.

He rested his forehead against hers. "Three nights ago, you

followed me, unaccompanied, outside the palace. Today you took me to a deserted roundhouse. And now I'm in your chamber, alone with you. Why would you do all this, my princess, unless you trusted me not to harm you?"

She wound her arms around him, her hands gliding over his taut skin. Her touch was light, almost tentative, but his flesh burned beneath her questing fingers and his cock ached for release.

"I do trust you." Her whisper was husky and sank into his blood like the finest wine. "I know you would never harm me."

He closed his eyes, savoring her words. Just a few short months ago, he considered her and all her people his bitterest enemy. But that was before he'd met her.

Before all his bloodied prejudices had been ripped from his embittered soul.

Once again, the silence wrapped around them. All he could hear was the sound of his heartbeat in his ears. All he could feel was Elise in his arms.

Need pounded. Frustration warred. He reined in his lust, subdued his passion. He didn't know—didn't want to know—what mac Uurguist had done to Elise to make her so uneasy. But he knew one thing.

She had to make the decision herself.

CHAPTER 18

Cameron could see indecision flicker over Elise's face. Slowly she slid her arms from around his neck and his heart slammed against his ribs. Had he pushed her too far?

Without taking her gaze from him, she loosened the ties of her bodice. With tantalizing restraint, she pulled her gown over her shoulders and then her breasts. For a moment, she clung onto the material as though it was a shield before she took a deep breath and released her grip.

His mouth dried and his breath lodged in his chest. With her golden hair cascading over her shoulders and the firelight bathing her in an ethereal glow she looked like a goddess from pagan times.

His goddess. A secret he would confess to no one.

He ached to cup her full breasts, to rub his thumbs over her erect nipples. But he resisted and his mesmerized gaze drank in the shapely curve of her waist and hips before focusing between her thighs.

Before he could stop himself, he dropped to his knees and pressed his lips against her sweet slit. Her curls dusted his lips and she tasted of heaven.

"Cameron." The uncertainty in her voice and the way she dug her fingers through his hair penetrated the lust pounding through his body. He dragged his face from her succulent flesh and looked up at her. *Goddess.* The word slid into his sex-drugged mind and it sounded so right. "What are you doing?"

Her breathless question made no sense. He offered her a savage smile and grasped her thighs. In the same second that she stiffened, he felt scarred ridges burn his palm.

Instantly he relaxed his grip. He'd forgotten about her injured leg. Without dropping his gaze from her, he slid his hand over her thigh. Something kicked against his heart. Even without looking, he could imagine the damage she had sustained. "Am I hurting you?"

She swallowed. "No." She didn't sound certain.

He wrapped his hand around the back of her knee. "Do you trust me?" He wasn't sure whether he asked the question more for her or himself. He knew she trusted him not to harm her. But did she trust him not to shatter this precious moment?

Her grip on his hair tightened, as though she was bracing herself. Then she gave the smallest nod. "Yes."

He drew back. He could feel tension radiating from her. Slowly he raked his gaze down her body. The primitive urge to forget everything and possess her once again hammered through his mind.

With rigid determination, he dragged his ravenous gaze from her tempting sex and focused on her leg.

Shock speared through him and gripped his heart in a merciless vise. The light was muted, but he could see how her flesh and muscles had been mangled by her accident. God Almighty. He'd watched men die on the battlefield with injuries less severe than these.

Tenderly he traced a finger along one jagged scar. The flesh was raised, and he could see how the wound had been closed by stitching the edges together.

Whoever had saved her life had been guided by the hand of God.

Or the gods from ancient times.

A shiver rippled over him. Not merely at the errant thought but at the possibility behind it. There was no doubt in his mind Elise should have died that day when she'd fallen into the river. He would thank any god responsible for the miracle of her survival.

"Cameron." Her voice was soft, but he could hear the grief behind it. "Please…"

He kissed her disfigured skin, his fingertips trailing along the back of her thigh. He heard her catch her breath and tremble beneath his touch, and he wrapped his other arm around her, flattening his hand against the small of her back to hold her steady.

He inched down her leg, pressing his lips against every particle of twisted, damaged skin. One hand caressed her thigh and his other molded the curve of her backside. He reached her ankle and retraced his path, but this time he slid his fingers between her thighs and teased her wet folds.

As he reached her hip, the heady scent of her arousal invaded his senses and thickened his blood. He cradled her waist and tugged her forward. She gasped and clutched at his hair as he bent his head to taste her once again.

His tongue circled her swollen nub and she moaned softly before her fingers dug into him, a silent command he was only too willing to obey.

He sucked on her clitoris and her gasp of shock arrowed straight to his heavy balls. He groaned inside her slick cleft and relished the taste of her juices in his mouth.

All he could hear was her ragged breath and it was the sweetest sound he'd ever heard.

She pulled on his hair. Her request was plain. He teased her silken slit with the tip of his tongue until she writhed with need before rising to his feet. Elise's eyes were glazed, her lips were parted, and he couldn't hold back any longer.

He plunged his fingers through her glorious hair, gripping her head. His mouth captured hers. She was so soft. So willing. His tongue thrust into her wet heat and he heard her muffled gasp. Her tongue met his, an intimate kiss, and need thundered through his blood like a ravenous beast.

With a smothered curse, he tore free and lifted her into his arms. She wound her arms around his shoulders and her erratic breath matched his own. He strode to the bed and laid her on the furs. Her hair spilled across the pillows like sunlight and he gave a twisted grin as he ripped off his boots. Why did he always think such fanciful things when he looked at this woman?

He straddled her thighs and planted his fists into the furs beside her shoulders. "You have bewitched me." His voice was raw with lust and for answer, she smiled up at him as though she knew quite well she had bewitched him and saw nothing wrong with it.

"And you, Cameron MacNeil, have stolen my senses." She brushed his hair back and then wound the strands around her fingers and gently tugged. "I never thought to find a man such as you."

Her artless words made him laugh. She could always make him laugh. He'd forgotten how good it could be, to laugh at irreverence.

"You deserve a prince." He was a Scot and with that heritage could never be a prince. "No. A king." He slid one knee between her thighs and spread her legs. He wasn't a prince and would never be a king, but for Elise he wished, futilely, he could be both.

She wound her leg around his backside. He hastily shifted position so she might wind both legs around him and let out a relieved breath when she did.

"I have no use for a prince or king." Her heels dug into him, enticing him closer. He resisted for a few moments so he could continue to admire her, and then lowered himself onto her lush body.

Her erect nipples pressed into his chest and he swayed over her, just so he could feel her full breasts rub against him. She scraped her nails along his back, and he arched into her, his cock branding her belly.

She rocked her hips in clear frustration. "You tease me unmercifully."

"I enjoy teasing you, my princess." He shifted, so the head of his erection nestled against her swollen bud. She groaned and arched her throat. He couldn't resist such a blatant invitation. His mouth fastened on her unblemished flesh and he sucked her sweet skin, relishing the way she writhed beneath him. Panting he released her, and satisfaction speared through him at his mark of possession.

His. Forever his.

Her fingers tangled in his hair and she pulled his head down. Their mouths met, hungry and demanding. She thrust her tongue inside, feverishly exploring, and he could wait no longer.

He penetrated her slick folds and a guttural groan razed his throat. She was so hot. So tight around his cock. Her choked gasps as she tried to catch her breath stoked his lust and his body shook as the pressure built.

But he remained unmoving, savoring the way her sheath expanded around him. Memorizing the way she looked at him as though he was her world.

Trying to prolong this moment so it would live inside his heart for all time.

But like all moments of perfection, it was fragile and transient. Elise wrapped her legs around his back and speared her fingers through his hair. Her musky scent invaded every breath and fired his blood. Her silken core rippled around his shaft, and he shoved into her, up to the hilt, and her moan vibrated through every straining muscle.

Bracing his weight on one hand, he cupped her breast, squeezing her succulent flesh and dragging his thumb across her hard nipple. He bent his head and licked her peak, then trailed possessive kisses over her ripe mound.

"Cam." Her voice was choked, and although he knew she didn't realize she'd used the shortened form of his name, he relished the sound.

He rocked into her and pressed his thumb against her clitoris. She bucked frantically and her nails tore into his head. He tried to go slow, but her uninhibited cries of pleasure and the way she writhed and clutched at him were too much.

With a guttural growl, he hammered into her, pinning her into the furs with every savage thrust. His balls tightened, drew up and he gritted his teeth. *Not yet.* But the scent of sex and passion thickened the air. Filled his lungs. Elise hitched in a strangled breath and her tight crease flexed around his thrusting shaft.

He held on as long as he could. But he was at the edge. He started to withdraw, and Elise's legs tightened around him.

"No."

"Elise." He could scarcely think let alone speak. But she had to understand, surely she knew…

"The goddess protects me." Her ragged words made no sense. "Come inside me, Cam. I want to feel you come inside me."

And his last remnants of discipline shattered.

Hands flattened on the furs he rammed into her. Her core quivered, squeezing his cock, and the frenzied beat of his heart filled his ears. He stared into her passion-flushed face. His princess, the woman who had filled his nighttime fantasies for endless weeks, the woman he had never believed could be his. For even a fleeting moment.

As her second orgasm consumed her, he followed her over the

edge. His hot seed filled her as he pumped inside her. Her slick sheath milked his cock, demanding everything he possessed.

With a final thrust, he collapsed onto her willing body. He could barely breathe. His heart thundered so fiercely that his ribs ached. Elise's legs slid onto the furs and her arms wound around him, holding him tight.

He kissed her throat. Her skin was damp, and her tangled hair caressed his face. He could feel the erratic beat of her heart against his chest and her uneven breath feathered his shoulder.

A strange sense of peace engulfed him. A soft, warm wave that flowed through him, cleansing the darkness in his soul.

He closed his eyes. It was an illusion. He knew that. But for now, he would embrace it. This was as close to heaven as he was ever likely to be.

Minutes slid by. Timeless moments. He breathed in Elise's womanly scent and gently threaded her hair between his fingers. Their breathing calmed and heartbeats slowed. And Elise stealthily shifted beneath him.

Instantly he was on alert. "Are you all right?" He propped himself onto his elbow and stared down at her. He cursed his negligence. He was no lightweight and Elise had an injured leg to consider. "Did I hurt you?"

She laughed softly and cradled his face, as though he was the one who should be comforted. "Of course not. And I don't want you to move but alas I can't breathe properly with you crushing my chest."

He could feel a frown gathering. "I didn't mean to crush you." He eased out of her slick sheath and rolled onto his side. "You should have told me earlier."

Elise sighed and rolled onto her side, so they were facing each other. "Why would I do that? I didn't wish to break our connection until the last possible moment." She smiled as though the thought amused her and once again cradled his jaw. "You take my breath away, Cam, and I am very happy for it."

Despite cursing himself for his thoughtlessness, he couldn't help a reluctant grin. "No woman has ever said such things to me before."

She pouted her luscious lips in mock disapproval. "I should hope not. You are mine, Cameron MacNeil, and I savor every second we're granted together."

He wrapped his arms around her and hauled her on top of him. She nestled into him as though they had been made for each other. "Aye, that goes both ways, princess. You are mine and don't you forget it."

She laughed and wriggled, teasing his cock. His shaft thickened and he groaned as she slowly sank down his length. She was his for tonight. His for another few nights. He would look no further into the future where nothing was certain.

He cupped her breasts, feeling their weight fill his palms, and squeezed her ripe nipples. She arched her back, thrusting her breasts forward and flattened one hand on his chest.

Her eyes never left his as she started to ride him. He sculpted the curve of her body down to her waist and then grasped her hips.

Her breath shortened and she fell forward, both hands braced against his chest. Her breasts bounced with every thrust and his mesmerized gaze flicked between them and the look of ecstasy on Elise's face.

She rode him harder. Her hair tumbled over her shoulders giving her a wild appearance. Her mouth opened as she sucked in air and her slick heat tightened around him.

Primal need hammered through his groin. Gripped his balls. As Elise gasped his name, he pounded into her, grasping her hips so she took every last inch of him.

He took her hard, giving her everything that he was. It shouldn't be possible, but his seed flooded her, filling her, and still he could not let this moment end.

Until she finally slumped onto him, her head on his shoulder.

He wrapped his arms around her. Exhaustion and satisfaction radiated from her, an intoxicating mix that spun a fragile cocoon around them both.

It was a false sense of serenity. But he would enjoy it while he could.

They had been traveling for three days. With the two wagons filled with pirate treasure that Elise had brought with her, as well as the wagon containing the body of mac Uurguist, the pace was painfully slow. Cam was only surprised that MacAllister hadn't complained.

As he and his four compatriots rode back to the main train from their scouting trip, he could imagine the other man's reaction to what Cam was about to tell him. The men he'd ridden on ahead with, to check the lay of the land, had seen nothing wrong with their intended path.

But they weren't responsible for the princess' safety. And he was.

"Well?" MacAllister spared him a fleeting glance as Cam rode up beside him.

"We need to change direction due west. The river will be easier to cross nearer its source."

This time MacAllister favored him with a longer look. "We can't ford it directly ahead?"

Without Elise, it wouldn't be an issue. With any other woman, royal or not, it wouldn't be an issue.

But he had witnessed the look on her face when she'd seen how the storm had caused the stream to rise. Compared to that, the river ahead raged.

"Not with the princess." Cam stared at MacAllister, daring him to contradict him. He knew ultimately the final word would be MacAllister's. There was little Cam could do if the other man ignored his warning. He also knew that every time he crossed swords with MacAllister he risked putting his future in jeopardy.

MacAllister, after all, was the king's right-hand man.

But Cam had never been good at politics.

MacAllister was silent for several minutes. Finally, he appeared to come to a decision. "How long will this diversion delay us?"

"At a guess, two days."

"Very well." MacAllister shot him a smile Cam didn't care for at all. "Anything to ensure the princess' comfort, MacNeil."

Cam watched him ride off to give the change in orders but instead of relief that MacAllister had taken heed of his words, unease seethed through his gut. MacAllister was, in Cam's opinion, taking far too much interest in Elise's wellbeing. He asked after her health every morning, as though he expected Cam to have intimate knowledge of her habits.

But he hadn't spent the night with her since they had left Ce. Eyes were everywhere and he trusted none of them. Not even Connor's own men when it came to the reputation of Elise.

He galloped down the flank of the train until he reached Elise. She had brought four ladies with her, a small contingent of Pict warriors and her bodyguard.

"Cameron MacNeil. How delightful to see you once again." She smiled at him, as though they were flirting at a great feast and not traversing the countryside beneath a cloudy sky. She leaned toward him and her voice dropped to a sultry whisper. "I had hoped to see you last night in my tent. You are altogether too circumspect."

"I will not compromise your honor." But God, how his body burned for her at night. It didn't help knowing that he could see her tent from outside his own.

"Then perhaps I should disguise myself and visit you at night instead."

Sometimes he couldn't tell whether she was jesting or not. "There are too few men here I trust." What had possessed him to tell her that? Except it was the truth. And he wanted to tell her the truth whenever he could, because there was so much he had to conceal from her.

The mocking smile slid from her face and she sighed. "I'm sorry for that, Cam." She had continued to call him by his shortened name since the night they'd shared. Neither of them had remarked on it, but a strange warm glow curled through his chest every time she said it. "I know only too well how it feels to be surrounded by those you can't confide in." A pensive look crossed her face as she stared into the distance.

Was she referring to her marriage?

"Do you not trust your ladies?"

Her eyes widened. "But of course. Except... that's not what I meant. Some things can never be discussed, no matter how dearly one might wish it."

Her blue eyes were so beautiful, so trusting. She continued to gaze at him, almost as though she was trying to convey a hidden meaning.

He cleared his throat and tore his besotted gaze from her. There was no hidden meaning in her words. Elise said what she meant, and she wanted him in her bed. But he couldn't see how it was possible. Her ladies shared her tent at night, and he shared his with three other warriors.

But her artless comment ate into his heart. She would never know how dearly he wished to confide in her as to their true destination. He could only hope that before they went their separate ways, she would forgive him for the deception and understand why he had done it.

"We're traveling upriver to find a shallower fording point. It could add two days to our journey."

"That will take us closer to Dal Riada." Her tone was casual and yet there was a strange undertone of excitement. He must have imagined it. There was no reason why Elise should sound excited at the thought of being two days nearer Dal Riada.

"The distance is nominal." But it did take them farther away from the Kingdom of Circinn. He knew the queen of Ce had sent a messenger to the queen of Circinn informing her of the death of mac Uurguist. But he found it strange that, despite how their travels took them close to the borders of Circinn, Elise had not once expressed the desire to visit her kin.

Was it because she suspected MacAllister wouldn't grant her request? But Cam was no longer certain what MacAllister might agree to when it came to Elise.

He could no longer contain himself. "Do you not wish to visit your family, Elise?"

She lowered her lashes, then appeared to reconsider and looked him fully in the face. "My mother would never allow me to leave Circinn once I entered the palace. She would have Ferelei's body returned to his stronghold in Fib and I would remain under her dominion until a new husband was found for me. I choose another path, Cam."

"You would rather live in Fib, away from your blood kin?" He had no idea what rights Elise might have to her dead husband's estate. Would Pict law allow his children to inherit his goods? Why did she not simply keep the treasure the bastard had brought back from his final travels and set up her own household?

A Scots noblewoman might not be permitted to do such a thing. But Elise was a Princess of Pictland, and the Picts' ways were not the Scots'.

"There's something I've been meaning to discuss with you." She bit her lip, as if she wasn't entirely sure what his reaction might be. "I would dearly love to see my cousin Aila. Instead of continuing onto Fib, which I know takes you many days out of your way, I want to return with you to Dal Riada."

He stared at her, speechless. Before his frozen thoughts could find some order, she reached across and briefly squeezed his hand. "I have it all planned." Her voice was breathless. "The mercenaries will accompany Ferelei's body back to Fib and ensure he is accorded every honor he deserves. I can afford to pay them well for this service. Would you speak to MacAllister about my wishes? I cannot see how he will object as I'm saving him a great diversion."

He gritted his teeth against the suicidal urge to tell her the truth. It would get neither of them anywhere. All he could do was promise to relay her request to MacAllister.

"Aye." It was a bitter growl and he couldn't look her in the eyes as he made her a promise that was little better than a blatant lie. When Elise reached over and laid her hand on top of his once again, shame burned through him at the trust she so freely bestowed on him.

"Don't look so fierce." There was a note of laughter in her whisper. "It means we have more time together. Unless you're tired of me already and wish nothing but to see the back of me?"

He shot her a glare. She cocked her head to one side and gave him a mocking smile. Obviously, she was once again jesting. But he saw nothing amusing in the situation. Not least because he couldn't even begin to fathom the day when he ever tired of Elise and wished never to see her again.

The day when he and Elise parted forever would come. Only too soon. He shoved the knowledge into the darkest recess of his mind.

"I'll speak to him when we make camp."

$\sim$

Elise sat on a stool as one of her ladies meticulously combed through her hair. They had made camp some time ago, eaten and retired to their tent while the warriors went about their business.

Was Cam speaking to MacAllister about her request? She couldn't see where there would be a problem. But she had learned it was never wise to assume anything.

Idly she trailed her fingers over her belly. Had Bride blessed her during the few times she and Cam had been together? She'd let Cam believe she was protected and for that she grieved. But she knew what he was like. So noble and honor bound, he would never risk leaving her with child.

But she wanted his child. A child she could lavish with all the love in her heart. She didn't care for scandal. No one would dare slander her in any case. For all anyone would know a baby she conceived during this magical time could be Ferelei's.

Only she would know the truth for sure. And in time so would her child. Because her child deserved to know its father was the finest man she had ever met.

She sighed softly. It was too soon to tell. But aside from that, Cam was being most obstinate. She had imagined they would spend every night of this journey in each other's arms. It wasn't because he didn't want her. She knew that.

His insistence on protecting her good name was endearing. But also dreadfully frustrating. He might think she was jesting about taking on a disguise to seduce him, but she was perilously close to carrying through with her threat.

It wasn't only because she wanted to take advantage of her fertile moon time. She wanted his arms around her. Wanted to breathe in his wonderful, wild scent that made her think of freedom and remember every girlish dream she'd ever had.

They had only spent one night together, but she wanted that again. Wanted to see him smile at her with no shadows darkening his eyes. To hear him laugh and feel his heartbeat beneath her palm. To lay her head on his shoulder and hold him close while they spoke of everything and nothing.

She wanted to store a thousand memories of him. Memories that would have to last her a lifetime without him.

"Madam." One of her ladies approached. "The Scot, Cameron MacNeil, requests audience with you."

She blinked, and her bittersweet dreams faded. "Cameron MacNeil is here?"

"Yes. He waits in the outer entrance."

The tent she shared with her ladies was divided into two sections. This section, where they slept, and an outer section separated by a flimsy wall of material where her bodyguard slept.

She took a deep breath to calm the fluttering of her pulses. But of course they didn't calm. She didn't really want them to.

"Then send him in. I will speak with him alone."

Elise stood as Cam marched inside, and her ladies discreetly retreated to the outer section of the tent.

His hair was windswept, and his familiar scowl darkened his features. Did he never smile when away from her? The thought that he endured an existence without laughter tugged at her heart. She stepped toward him and held out her hand.

He took her hand. But instead of bowing and brushing a chaste kiss across her knuckles as another warrior might have done, he roughly pulled her into his arms.

She gave a breathless laugh as she looked up into his grim face. "And it's good to see you too, Cameron MacNeil."

His forbidding expression didn't alter. Concern fluttered through her breast and she cradled his jaw, his stubble grazing her palm. "Is something amiss?"

It was absurd to feel indignation that another Scot might have slighted Cam. But he wasn't one of MacAllister's men, and she agreed with her aunt and grandmother. MacAllister was a creature of MacAlpin's and couldn't be trusted. It wouldn't surprise her at all if the king's man attempted to undermine Cam. Or worse.

She couldn't bring herself to dwell on the worst. And surely she was overreacting. MacAllister might not approve of Cam—she knew that much from the little she had seen of them together—but he wouldn't murder him. They were, after all, both Scots.

But the thought lingered, nevertheless.

For answer, he raked his fingers through her hair, forcing her head back. Her shawl slid from her shoulders to pool, forgotten, at her feet. She caught her breath at the fierce look in his eyes, at the determination she could feel emanating from him.

"Will we be disturbed?" His voice was low, rough with need. It sent a shiver of anticipation along her naked arms.

"Not unless I scream for assistance." It was true her ladies would likely hear everything, but they would never interrupt unless she called for them. She dug her fingers into his shoulders to keep her balance. "But I cannot promise not to scream in ecstasy."

His lips tugged in what looked like the beginnings of a reluctant smile. "I promised myself I wouldn't come to you. But I fear I can't stay away."

"I don't want you to stay away," she whispered. How had she ever imagined he had looked on her with contempt? He kept his passion so tightly leashed it was a wild beast roaring beneath the surface, desperate for escape.

Was she the only woman who affected him so profoundly? How dearly she would love that. To affect a man such as Cameron MacNeil so deeply was something to cherish.

His mouth claimed hers. A savage kiss of possession that sent hot sparks of desire from her breast to her core. She clung onto his shoulders as he wound her hair around his fist and thrust his tongue inside her.

There was no gentleness, no finesse as he wrapped his arm around her waist and pinned her to his body. Before she realized his intention, he lifted her from the ground and backed her toward the makeshift bed.

She gasped and he broke their kiss, panting into her face. She laughed, a breathless sound, delighting in the notion that he could pick her up in one arm as though she weighed no more than a feather.

"You find me amusing?" His low growl caused wet heat to bloom between her thighs. She wanted to pull off her under gown, rip off his plaid and feel his hard warrior body against hers.

But she was his captive. The thought sent hot arrows of need through her.

"I find you endlessly amusing." He would never know how often she thought of him when they were not together. Or how the memory of him warmed her heart, as though his mere existence was enough to erase the years of torment she'd endured at the hands of Ferelei.

A tortured expression crossed his face. How strange he was, to find it so hard to accept a compliment. She tried to kiss him but his grip on her hair was brutal and allowed her no quarter.

His gaze raked over her. His eyes were so dark they appeared black in the glow from the lanterns. Anyone could be mistaken in thinking he was a foreign savage from a barbarous land, but she knew better.

Beneath that harsh exterior, he was truly the kindest man she had ever met.

Not that she would ever tell him. She would never tell anyone. No man wished to be thought of as kind. It wasn't a trait a warrior would boast of.

But it was all she had dreamed of finding in a man for too many years.

He lowered her to her feet and loosened his grip in her hair as he tugged her down to the bed. Roughly he pulled her gown up and kneed her thighs apart.

"Goddess, Cam. No one will disturb us, I promise you." Not that she didn't enjoy his haste. It was thrilling to know he could scarcely contain his lust. But she didn't want him thinking speed was necessary.

"I need you, Elise." He poised over her with such an agonized look on his face her heart melted. She speared her fingers through his hair and hooked her ankles over his hips.

"You have me." Her whisper meant so much more than he would ever know. He would take a vital part of her with him when this liaison ended. She could only pray to Bride that her goddess would allow a part of Cam to stay forever with her, too.

"My beautiful princess." He stared at her for a moment as though he couldn't quite believe she was in his arms. It should have delighted her, but a strange sense of unease haunted her mind. He was so intense, as though he was imprinting her image on his soul. Yet there was despair in his voice, so deeply buried she wondered if he even knew it existed. But why would looking at her bring him despair? What did he truly mean by his words?

He braced his weight on his forearms and cradled her face as though she was something precious and fragile. His eyes enslaved her, and her disquiet fled.

Of course there was no hidden meaning in his words. Why did she look for shadows when there were none?

His breath was ragged as he tore one hand from her face and hiked up his plaid. The head of his cock nudged her wet folds, a teasing caress. She lifted her hips, desperate to feel him inside her, and with a smothered groan he complied.

His thick shaft stretched her, filling her so completely. Her eyes fluttered shut so she could savor every tiny sensation. He didn't move, and neither did she. It was a timeless moment. A fragment of eternity she would treasure forever.

"Look at me." His harsh command tore through her mind and she opened her eyes. He gazed at her, a look of fearsome agony on his face. But his dark eyes transfixed her with their burning passion.

Once again, he cupped her face as his fingers tangled in her hair. His focus was absolute. It was breathtakingly arousing.

Slowly he withdrew, and she felt every inch of his length drag against her sensitized sheath. She dug her heels into him, a silent demand. He didn't immediately obey, and she shifted beneath him, but his control was formidable.

"Do you wish me to beg?" She smoothed her palms over his roughened jaw, backward and forward, loving the abrasive scrape against her flesh. Lightning sharp tingles raced through her blood and collided low in her womb. How much longer would he keep her hovering on the precipice? "Goddess, Cam. I want you."

He gritted his jaw and pushed into her, stealing every coherent thought she possessed. Her eyes closed and her mouth opened. Her breath rasped and her heart pounded, and a frantic beat filled her head.

His fingers bit into her and his thrusts became frenzied. He pounded her into the furs, his jagged breath feathering her face. She dragged her eyelids open and he was still looking at her. His intensity was as potent as the feel of his hard body inside her.

She quivered around his cock. He gave a muffled groan and drove deeper. She gasped, couldn't breathe, and clung onto his hair as he rode her.

With a final savage thrust, he spilled his seed. She could feel him pumping inside her, filling her womb, filling her soul. Her legs gripped him, holding him tight. And still he came, his fierce concentration never wavering.

Her tight channel convulsed around him, demanding everything he had. His mouth crashed down on hers, swallowing her mindless gasps of pleasure. He possessed her strangled cries as her orgasm claimed her, his teeth grazing her lips.

Even as her breathing eased and her legs slid from his back, he didn't collapse onto her. She smiled up at him, exhausted and sated. He didn't smile back but continued to gaze at her with the same fierce concentration and finally she could ignore the sliver of doubt no longer.

"Cam." Her voice was low, and she battled the urge to merely pull him onto the furs beside her and wrap herself around him. Something was wrong, and if it affected Cam then, no matter how illogical in reality, it also affected her. "Tell me what has happened."

Cam stared down at Elise. Her hair tumbled in tangled disarray over the furs, her face was flushed, and lips swollen from his rough kisses. He burned the image into his mind because once he told her MacAllister had no intention of traveling to Dal Riada, Elise would have questions. And since he was no longer constrained by MacAllister's order to keep the truth from her, she'd discover how he'd lied to her about their destination.

A woman as honorable as Elise would have no use for him after that. He despised the desperate desire that had driven him to her tent this night. But he'd been unable to stay away. If tonight was the last time she would look on him with favor he'd wanted to take full advantage of it.

Aye, he was a despicable bastard. But even knowing that hadn't been enough to make him stay away.

With grim self-control, he withdrew from her slick heat. Hollowness filled his chest as he shoved himself upright and away from her. He raked a hand through his hair and couldn't look at her. But even without looking at her, he knew she stared at him with a bemused frown. Knew also that if he did turn toward her, he might not be able to stop himself from taking her one last time.

"I spoke to MacAllister." From the corner of his eyes, he saw Elise sit up and push her hair off her face. She leaned toward him and he cursed the fact he hadn't stood up and put more distance between them.

"Yes?" Her breathy response dusted his jaw as she curled her hand around his biceps. Her musky aroma of woman and sex invaded his senses and made it hard to think.

He dragged in a heady breath. "Our destination is Fortriu." He braced himself for her withdrawal. But she remained where she was.

"Fortriu? Why does he journey to our Supreme Kingdom?"

Cam resisted the urge to scrub his hand over his face. He was guilty enough without making himself look more so. "MacAlpin has taken up residence in the palace of Forteviot."

Again, he waited for her to snatch her hand from him, but she remained where she was. He couldn't help but glance at her, and then of course he couldn't look away.

Her eyes were narrowed, and no hint of laughter lightened her expression. He braced himself for her condemnation.

"Of course." There was a distinct chill in her voice that caused a shudder to inch along his arms. But she still held onto him. Perhaps she was unaware of her action. He certainly wasn't going to draw attention to it. "That was his prize. Naturally, he would claim it as swiftly as possible."

Cam said nothing. Her accusation was true however the deaths of the Pictish nobles had come about. He had no defense to offer.

She sighed and to his confusion caressed his arm. "Cam. I don't blame *you* for your king's actions. We know his despicable betrayal was undertaken without the knowledge of any of Connor MacKenzie's men."

She knew that? How did she know that? Another shudder

crawled over his arms but this time it had nothing to do with the fact that soon Elise would scorn him. It took him more than a few seconds to realize he hadn't attempted to refute her implied accusation that MacAlpin had murdered to gain the prize of Fortriu.

But since a reply appeared necessary, he grunted and glowered at his boots.

"When did MacAllister know of this change in plans?" Elise sounded thoughtful and Cam tensed for her next inevitable question. "But no matter," she said, and he gave her a sideways look. She appeared oblivious to the possibility that he had known of their true destination all along. "I can request an audience with MacAlpin as easily in Forteviot as I could in Dal Riada."

He forgot about his guilt as disbelief hit him. "You wanted an audience with MacAlpin in Dal Riada?" But she had told him she wanted to see her cousin, Aila. The knowledge that she hadn't told him the entire truth stung, despite the fact he knew there was no reason why she should confide all her plans to him.

It wasn't as if he'd been entirely honest with her, either. That stung, too.

"Yes." A faint blush heated her cheeks. "There is a matter I wish to discuss with him concerning the fate of certain hostages."

He remembered a conversation they'd had when Elise had remarked on the unlikelihood of any ransom securing her father's release. Did she mean to request her father's freedom to MacAlpin's face in the hope he might show mercy?

The thought of Elise begging for any favor from his king turned his stomach. It wasn't riches MacAlpin wanted for his most valuable hostages. It was the loyalty of the Pictish clans.

"MacAlpin doesn't talk politics with women."

It wasn't a tactful thing to say, but it was the truth. Elise stiffened in clear affront by his side. "I am quite certain your king will receive me, a Princess of Circinn."

Aye, he was damn sure MacAlpin would receive the princess.

With open arms. Unease stirred deep in his gut, the same unease he suffered every time he thought of MacAllister's undisclosed plans, but this time it was worse.

He turned to Elise. She still looked irritated by his remark, although he had the notion it wasn't him she was annoyed with for saying it, but his king for deserving it.

He couldn't stop himself from warning her. "Promise me you'll be careful around him."

A small smile caused her hauteur to flee. She threaded her fingers through his and gave a gentle squeeze. "I promise."

IT TOOK another two weeks before they entered the Kingdom of Fortriu. The palace of Forteviot was formidable. Protected by its elevated position and the numerous outlying hillforts, it commanded an unequalled view of the surrounding countryside. Its defenses appeared impenetrable.

No wonder MacAlpin had been so eager to claim his mother's legacy. To take Fortriu by sheer force alone would have led to a bloodied Scots massacre. Whoever ruled the Supreme Kingdom held an unparalleled strategic advantage.

MacAllister had sent a messenger on ahead a week ago to let them know of their royal visitor, and as they approached the palace, a small contingent emerged to greet Elise. Cam gritted his teeth and gripped his horse's reins until his knuckles ached as he watched her disappear into the palace.

He couldn't shift the fear he had led her into an elaborate trap.

IT WAS LATER that day when he was summoned to the king's inner sanctum. MacAlpin was surrounded by his intimate circle of advisers, including MacAllister. Cam dropped to one knee and bowed before his king, but his thoughts were far from those of a loyal subject.

He could only hope MacAlpin couldn't read his mind.

"Cameron MacNeil." There was a note of amusement in MacAlpin's voice, and he jerked his head indicating Cam should rise to his feet. "We always knew one day you would do your father proud."

Cam kept his mouth shut and tried not to glower. As a child, he had feared his father, and as a youth, he'd despised him. Was MacAlpin suggesting he believed Cam was turning into his father?

He'd rather slit his own throat first.

MacAlpin didn't appear to notice Cam's simmering anger. He strolled toward him and slapped him on the shoulder in a show of camaraderie. Cam had never been in the king's favor before. He didn't like the fact that he was now.

"Your father and I were inseparable in our youth." MacAlpin smiled in a benign manner that sent Cam's senses onto full alert. He knew all about the friendship his father and the king had shared years ago. He didn't know why MacAlpin felt the need to dig up that ancient history now. "It was I who encouraged him to pursue your beautiful mother who had stolen his heart."

Thunder roared through Cam's head and tangled rage lodged hard in his chest. Many times when drunk his father had recalled the sordid tale, as though he expected his son to applaud his actions.

All Cam had ever wanted to do was wrap his hands around his sire's throat and squeeze the life from him. The same urge consumed him now as he looked at his king.

God help him.

"It is fitting, is it not, that you follow so closely in my old friend Neil's footsteps?" MacAlpin stood in front of him. It was almost as though he dared Cam to raise his hand in defense of his long dead mother. "He brought a foreign princess back to Dal

Riada and you have brought a princess to our new Kingdom of Fortriu."

"My liege." The words all but choked him. "The princess travels of her own free will." Which was more than his mother had. Abducted and raped and then forced into marriage. His stomach churned at what she had suffered at the hands of his father.

"Excellent." MacAlpin folded his arms. "You've done well, MacNeil. And don't think we are unappreciative of your actions in avenging the deaths of your father and sister. We will not forget it."

Cam's fetid memories froze as the king's words penetrated. How did MacAlpin know he had anything to do with mac Uurguist's death? The only other who knew was Ross, and Ross would never have confided in MacAllister.

"My liege, I swore I would not let vengeance interfere with my duty." He could feel sweat trickle along his spine at the lie. But he couldn't confess the truth. The repercussions could fall not only on himself but Ross for covering for him and Connor for being his superior officer.

"Of course not." There was an unpleasant twist to the king's lips. "We cannot afford any more unfortunate incidences involving prominent Picts. Nevertheless, justice has finally been served." MacAlpin paused, a calculated move, Cam knew, to put him on edge. "How fitting that Ferelei mac Uurguist's timely demise freed his delectable wife. One might think it a gift direct from God."

Cam had several answers to that remark, but none fit for his king's ears. So he remained silent and fought to keep his face impassive.

The silence became oppressive. Was it his imagination or were all the king's men eyeing him as though he was an exotic insect?

MacAlpin gave a dry laugh. "Your reticence does you credit.

Much as I admired your father, restraint was not one of his virtues." He glanced at MacAllister and the two men shared a knowing smile. Cam battled the self-destructive urge to run the pair of them through with his sword. "You must have inherited the trait from your royal mother. Perhaps it's time her blood finally served us."

If MacAlpin mentioned his mother one more time, God help him. Cam fisted his hands and forced his thoughts away from drawing his sword. If he did such a thing in the king's inner sanctum, it would be the last action he ever performed.

But in all the years he'd known MacAlpin, the king had barely acknowledged his mother's existence. Much less her royal blood. As far as Cam was concerned, his mother's blood meant nothing. Her people were despicable, and he claimed no kinship ties with them.

"This Princess of Circinn," MacAlpin said, "cannot be allowed to slip through our fingers."

Cam's futile sense of injustice about his mother's tragic fate vanished. Every sense sharpened, like the moments before a battle commenced. He could feel the subtle shift in the atmosphere, a palpable tension radiating not only from the king but all his advisers.

The claws of the trap he had feared were real. They were here, in this chamber. And it was not only Elise the king had in his sights.

"The princess is not our captive." His snarled retort was out before he could consider any possible consequences. Several of the advisers stiffened and glanced at their king, but both MacAlpin and MacAllister appeared uncaring of his breach in protocol.

"No. But she is a widowed princess of Pictland. And unwed princesses of Pictland of marriageable age are rare, especially ones who possess such personal wealth. But rarer still are Scots born princes."

It seemed a great rock lodged in his chest, constricting his breathing. Insane images raced through his mind.

In the darkest, silent moments of the night, he had sometimes imagined a future with Elise. A real future where she was his wife and happy to be so.

But they had just been wild dreams because Elise was a princess and he was a commoner.

A commoner with foreign royal blood in his veins.

And MacAlpin was prepared to exploit that to his advantage to get what he wanted.

Another Princess of Pictland married to a Scot.

For an agonizing moment, the vision taunted him. Elise could be his. But it was only for one fleeting moment. He would never trap her as his father had trapped his mother. If Elise didn't want him as her husband, he wouldn't force her. He wanted her love, not her loathing.

He looked his king in the eyes. "I am not a prince of Dal Riada."

"But you are our loyal subject." MacAlpin offered him a cold smile. "And your bloodline is undisputed, even if it has been neglected until now. Tell me, MacNeil. Does the thought of bedding this princess repel you so utterly? We've heard reports that she is a rare flower indeed. Wasted on a wizened bastard like mac Uurguist. And even if her appearance doesn't thicken your cock, think of the dowry she brings with her."

Cam had taken a step toward MacAlpin before he even realized. The king merely cocked his head, as though waiting for Cam's reply.

He reined in his churning fury. Only the fact MacAlpin was his king allowed him to speak of Elise in such a derogatory manner. But by God, Cam would not forget the insult, nor would he forgive it.

"The princess does not repel me, my liege." He shoved the

words between his teeth and forcibly stopped himself from gripping the hilt of his sword.

"MacAllister tells me the princess appears to enjoy your company, despite your surly countenance." The king appeared to find this mildly amusing, if the look he slung MacAllister was any indication. "Therefore, it would be a simple matter to compromise her and form an alliance between us and the Kingdom of Circinn."

Compromise her. Form an alliance. The words thundered in his mind. All MacAlpin cared about was strengthening his bloodied alliance. He didn't give a shit if he besmirched Elise's reputation on the way.

"I will not compromise the princess."

Nothing stirred for a heartbeat. Then, at a sign from MacAllister, the rest of the advisers left the chamber.

"You've already compromised the princess." MacAllister's voice was low but there was no disguising the menace behind his words. Cam gritted his teeth and cursed his lack of willpower. During the journey, he'd stolen several nighttime visits with Elise, so certain no one had witnessed his stealthy maneuvers. "I followed you to the roundhouse in the woods the day before we left the Kingdom of Ce."

CHAPTER 21

Cam recalled the feeling of being watched as he'd left the roundhouse that day. But he hadn't followed up on it.

No wonder MacAllister had been so solicitous of Elise's well-being. He had likely been formulating this trap for her from that moment.

"The only way to preserve the princess' honor is for you to take her as your bride." There was no hint of amusement in MacAlpin's voice now. "We don't think you'll care for the alternative, MacNeil."

What alternative? "I will not coerce her."

The king scrutinized him through narrowed eyes, and then shrugged as though the matter no longer concerned him. He turned, strolled around the great desk, and sat down on the carved chair.

"Very well." He waved a regal hand. "We have many warriors who are not hindered by your scruples. Before the night is out one of them will only too eagerly compromise the princess and leave her no option but to accept their suit."

Something akin to horror gripped Cam's heart at the thought of Elise being so cruelly betrayed. "No." He slammed his hands down on the desk and leaned across, momentarily forgetting this man was his king and held his life in his hands. "I won't stand by and let Elise be used in this manner. She doesn't deserve it."

"What do you suggest?" The king's voice was hard. Cam straightened. There was only one thing he could do. It was the thing he most wanted in the world, but this was the last way he had wanted to achieve it.

"Even if I ask the princess and she accepts, there's no guarantee her mother, the queen of Circinn, will agree to it. For all my royal blood." The last words dripped with bitterness.

"Your royal blood," MacAlpin said, "is the sweetener that will remove any resistance the queen of Circinn might have raised. We certainly don't need to wait on her permission for the marriage. As to whether the princess will accept you, MacNeil—you had better ensure she has no reason not to."

ELISE and her ladies followed their escort to the feasting hall. When they had arrived some hours ago, they'd been taken to a chamber that Elise was sure had once belonged to the queens of Fortriu. Refreshments had been brought and they had been treated like honored guests.

But something was wrong. She couldn't quite fathom what, but had the uncanny certainty that the guard outside their door was there not to protect them from possible attack, but to prevent them from possible escape.

And now, finally, she was to meet Kenneth MacAlpin, upstart king of Dal Riada and murderer of the nine Pictish nobles who had also laid claim to the Kingdom of Fortriu.

Her cousin Aila had met him and told Elise of his cold-blooded arrogance and lack of mercy. A shiver skated over her arms and her stomach churned at the prospect of facing him. But it was the only way she knew of trying to secure Droston's release.

They were led to an antechamber adjacent to the feasting hall. There were about a dozen men who all bowed as she entered. She scarcely glanced their way. Because at the far end of the chamber was Cam.

Relief flooded through her at the sight of his familiar face. He even wore his usual scowl and somehow that comforted her more than a welcoming smile would have. Cam, after all, was not the kind of man to offer welcoming smiles.

"Elise, Princess Clodrah of Circinn." MacAllister stepped forward. "Kenneth MacAlpin, King of Dal Riada and Fortriu."

Elise stiffened. How dare he call himself king of the Picts' Supreme Kingdom to her face? Had he no shame?

"I welcome you to the palace of Forteviot." The man standing beside Cam gave her an elegant bow and took her reluctantly proffered hand. He kissed her knuckles, but his eyes never left hers. She hoped he couldn't read her thoughts. Droston would have no chance of freedom if so.

She inclined her head. Nothing would induce her to extend the courtesy of a curtsey as she would to any true-born king.

"Please accept our heartfelt condolences on the recent loss of your husband, my lady." Insincerity dripped from MacAlpin's words like deadly acid. Did he truly think she would believe anything he said?

Then she remembered why she had engineered this meeting in the first place. Her personal feelings had no place here.

"I've arranged for Ferelei mac Uurguist's body to be taken to Fib with all haste," MacAlpin continued, as though he had the right to interfere with her arrangements. But since he was merely doing what she wished to do herself she could scarcely complain.

"You are too kind." Her voice was chilly, but she couldn't help it. With luck, MacAlpin would put her attitude down to her mourning. The most important thing was she elicited a promise from MacAlpin to receive her the following day, when she could make a formal request for Droston's release.

But before she could draw a calming breath, MacAlpin indicated Cam. "You know, of course, Cameron MacNeil of Dunmar, Prince of Northumbria."

All thoughts of Droston and the need to speak with MacAlpin fled. She stared at Cam, shock ricocheting through her body. He was a prince? Of Northumbria? Why had he never told her of his royal heritage?

She desperately wanted to ask him. But instead, she remained cool and aloof and merely once again inclined her head. As if the revelation that Cam was a prince meant nothing to her.

MacAlpin wanted to shock her. He wanted to feed on her reaction like a demon fed on fear and decay. She didn't know why she was so certain, only that she was right. And if MacAlpin wanted that from her, she most certainly would not oblige him.

"Come, let us join the feast." Far from appearing irked by her refusal to rise to his bait, MacAlpin appeared faintly amused. She ignored him and focused on Cam who came to her and offered her his arm.

"Would you do me the honor of allowing me to escort you?" He growled the question. Anyone would think he asked her under duress. She smothered the smile that wanted to surface and accepted his offer.

She resisted the urge to stroke her fingertips over the back of his wrist. His muscled forearm fascinated her, and she had to forcibly drag her mesmerized gaze away as they followed MacAlpin into the feasting hall.

Great goddess. Bride had not simply thrust the finest Scots warrior in creation in Elise's path. She had ensured that warrior possessed royal blood.

Why would Bride go to such trouble unless she wished far more for Elise than a simple affair?

Her stomach fluttered as she took her place at the high table,

Cam by her side. She stole a sideways glance at him. His face was stony.

As MacAlpin gave a sickening speech about how honored he was to have her as his guest, her thoughts wandered into possibilities that until now she had never allowed herself to hope for.

Could Cameron MacNeil be her second husband? Would he want to be? Until this moment, the prospect that she would one day have to remarry had been something she'd tried not to think about. But if that man was Cam, she not only wanted to think about it…

She wanted to do everything within her power to ensure it came about. The sooner the better.

But first, she had to discover if this was something Cam wanted. But how could he not? Bride had sent him to her. It didn't matter whether he believed in her goddess or not. It didn't change the facts.

MacAlpin finally sat down, to a storm of applause. Elise realized it was not only Scots warriors in the hall. There were many Picts, and they looked relieved that one of their princesses was a treasured guest in the palace.

As servants brought in steaming platters and conversation filled the hall, she leaned toward Cam.

"I am astonished you forgot to tell me you are a prince of Northumbria, my lord." It was the first time she'd addressed him as my lord. It had never even occurred to her, but she decided she enjoyed the words on her tongue when they referred to Cam. The dark glare he shot her, however, indicated he didn't feel the same.

"I have never considered myself a prince of that cursed place."

Her smile wavered. "It must be hard to trace your heritage through two peoples who have been enemies for so long." She paused but Cam didn't appear inclined to respond. "For many generations it was like this in Pictland. Clans intermarried but their descendants still fought for land and honor."

"The Northumbrians have no honor." He stabbed a slab of beef with his knife. "Save for my mother."

Elise watched him tear the meat with his teeth. It was obvious he had no desire to continue this conversation. She took a sip of wine, but it was no good. She was consumed with the need to know everything about his tangled lineages.

"Your mother must have loved your father very much to give up her people and live in a foreign land." Even as she said the words, there was a strange throb of discontent in her mind. Something was out of balance, but she shook the feeling aside. Because the idea of voluntarily giving up everything she had been used to in order to follow her lover to a foreign land was wonderfully romantic.

It also seemed a favorable portent. Cam's mother must have been a princess too.

Cam dropped his meat onto his platter and turned to her. There was such a look of fierce anguish in his eyes that she instinctively recoiled.

Goddess. She had been wrong. So wrong. Why hadn't she listened to the voice of caution in her mind?

"My mother was a younger princess in one of the borderland royal houses. My father had seen her during a raid and pledged to make her his. One day when she escaped her bodyguards, he abducted her and took her to Dunmar."

There was no need to wonder whether the Northumbrian princess had secretly wished for such an abduction. The look on Cam's face told her everything.

She licked her lips and swallowed, but her mouth was dry. Now she understood why Cam had been so blunt when she'd escaped her own ladies and bodyguard, that time he had come upon her by the sacred stones.

To be sure, the Vikings were a more pressing threat in the north of Pictland. But it was his mother's fate he had been thinking of.

"Cam," she whispered, her heart aching, but it appeared he hadn't finished.

"My father thought his fortune was made. He thought her family would prove useful. He had a foreign princess as his bride, what could be finer than that?" Bitterness hammered through every word. Elise slid her fingers through his and held him tight. He didn't appear to notice. "He demanded a dowry fit for a princess in exchange for visitation rights." Cam's lip curled in disgust. "Her family disowned her. She'd been ruined and as such, was of no further use to them. They didn't even try to get her back. They cut her completely, as though she had died."

A hard knot lodged in Elise's breast. With every word he uttered she could feel the hopeless love he had borne his mother. And while Cam hadn't said, Elise knew in her heart that his mother was dead. The loss radiated from him. A frustrated, forlorn loss that could only manifest from a young child.

Goddess. How old had he been when his mother had died?

"I'm sure having you gave her great joy." Her voice was husky. She hoped Cam couldn't see the tears prickling the back of her eyes. How dearly she wanted to take this tough warrior into her arms and soothe his pain.

How dearly she would love to take him into her arms every night, for the rest of their lives.

"I couldn't protect her." He stared down at their entwined fingers. "I was barely five when she died giving birth to Isla. But I can remember her smile, even now. Although God knows she had little enough to smile about."

Elise stared at Cam's averted face. His jaw was clenched, and she knew it wasn't only his mother who was now haunting his mind.

His sister Isla had died in his arms when she was eleven years old.

If only they were alone. If only this feast wasn't destined to drag on for endless hours. Even by holding hands, they were doubtless drawing unwanted attention, but what did the idle speculation of strangers matter?

She caressed his fingers with her thumb. "I am so grieved for your losses, Cam."

He looked at her, his dark eyes filled with pain. "I wanted to hate Isla as only a child can. But the first time I looked at her she stole my heart." He gave a low, mirthless laugh. "Yet when she needed me most, I wasn't even there."

Elise pulled his reluctant hand to her lips and brushed a kiss across his knuckles. She didn't know how Isla had died, but guessed it was from some cruel disease. "You were there when she needed you most. You told me yourself. She was in your arms."

A spasm of such intense agony flashed across his face that she again ignored protocol and pressed her lips against his knuckles. He hitched in a ragged breath and she held hers, as the sudden certainty assailed her that he was about to share something of utmost importance.

But then he gritted his teeth and forced their hands back to the table. Tension thudded in the small space between them, but Elise already knew the moment had shattered.

He was not yet ready to confess the unwarranted guilt that tortured his soul.

But that day would come. She would ensure it. Because otherwise the memories would consume him forever.

LATER THAT NIGHT Elise sat on a stool in her chamber as one of her ladies combed through her hair. The feast had been magnificent and the entertainment lavish. She had barely tasted a mouthful and the epic songs of the bards had slid over her head, unnoticed.

All she could think about was the man by her side. The man

who had spilled the darkness in his soul, and yet she knew he harbored so much more.

Another of her ladies entered from the antechamber. "Madam, Cameron MacNeil requests audience with you."

Elise attempted to contain her delight, but knew she failed when her ladies glanced at each other and smiled. "Please, bid him enter." She fingered her hair and rearranged her shawl and then simply stared at him as he marched into the bedchamber. She scarcely noticed her ladies retire to the antechamber. All she could see was Cam.

"I didn't know if you would visit me tonight." He had given no indication that he would. She had feared his sense of propriety would prevent him but thank goddess he was here. Now, at last, she could hold him in her arms the way she'd wanted to all evening long.

"My chamber is next door." His heavy glower suggested this fortuitous arrangement didn't meet with his approval. She wanted to tell him it was only proper he had a chamber of his own, but she bit her tongue. He didn't care for his royal blood and now that she knew how his Northumbrian relatives had treated his mother, she understood why.

She stood and went to him and held his hands. It seemed the only time buried anger and heartache didn't etch his features was when they made love. She was happy for it, but how she longed to possess the power to heal his hidden wounds, so they no longer continually haunted him.

"And why is this such a terrible thing?" She tilted her head to one side and smiled at him.

He let out a tortured breath. "Give me the word and we'll leave Fortriu this night. I swear on the memory of my mother and sister I'll see you safely to the Kingdom of Circinn."

Her smile faltered. They were not the words she'd expected from him, but when did Cam ever do the expected? He spoke from his heart and swore on the memory of his beloved mother and sister. It was obvious he was still concerned for her safety. So concerned, he was willing to risk the wrath of his king.

She pressed his fisted hands against her breast. "Do not fear for me. MacAlpin will not harm me." She didn't know why she was so sure of that. MacAlpin was, after all, an unscrupulous barbarian without honor. But the feeling wouldn't shift. She could only hope Cam believed her.

He wrenched his hands free and cradled her face in a hard, possessive gesture. His gaze roved over her, his eyes dark with bridled lust. Desire quivered between her thighs and she gripped the front of his shirt.

"Be sure this is what you want, Elise." His voice was harsh. "For if you stay with me tonight, I will never let you go."

CHAPTER 22

*C*am's words echoed in her mind. *I will never let you go.* She wanted to tell him she felt the same way about him, but surely he knew.

His mouth captured hers. A demanding kiss that stole her senses. His tongue invaded and tangled with hers. It was a kiss like none other they had shared. Wild and savage yet beneath his passion she caught the faintest hint of desperation.

She pushed herself against him, still clutching his shirt, and tore her mouth free. She panted up into his face, intoxicated by the dark passion in his eyes and the primitive aura of possession that pulsed from him.

But dark desolation still seethed beneath the surface. Perhaps he didn't know how she felt, after all.

"I'll never leave you, Cameron MacNeil." Her voice was breathless. She would tell him anything, everything, if it would ease that aching void she sensed within him. "You are everything I want in this life. Do you hear?" She tugged on his shirt for emphasis. "You are truly the man of my dreams."

He stared at her as though she had just plunged a dagger through his heart. "Everything, Elise?" He speared his fingers through her hair and gripped her head. "Enough to consent to be my wife?"

Her heart kicked against her ribs and she forgot how to breathe. Without any warning and no finesse, Cam had just asked her to wed him.

There were no pretty words and outrageous compliments. He didn't even smile. Anyone would think he had just imparted devastating news.

But she could see beneath his façade. She always had, even when she had denied it to herself. She gave a small laugh and tugged on his shirt once again.

Cameron MacNeil had asked her to be his wife. She had been right. This was the moment Bride had led them both toward. It didn't matter that protocol had not been observed. She didn't care that neither her mother nor father had approved the match.

She'd done her duty by the Kingdom of Circinn when she had taken Ferelei, and her parents had accepted his lavish gifts in exchange. This time she would take a man of her own choosing. A man who had managed to break through the brittle shell she'd erected around her heart and opened her eyes to the true meaning of passion.

"I gladly consent to be your wife, Cameron MacNeil of Dunmar." Her mother's undoubted fury to the news Elise had wed another man would, she knew, be greatly appeased by the knowledge that man possessed royal blood. But Cam despised that blood and Elise would not insult his mother's memory by alluding to it ever again.

The fierce glare on Cam's face faded. He looked staggered by her acceptance and she laughed again as she wound her arms around him, delighting in the feel of his hard muscles beneath her hands.

How different this proposal was from her first, where her acceptance had been a mere formality. This night would remain in her heart forever. The night when Cameron MacNeil had pledged his life to her.

Unbidden a thought slid into her mind. Would he, in time, pledge his love to her?

How wonderful that would be. How rare and precious. But surely not an impossible wish. Not when Bride herself had ordained this match.

"Do you have nothing to say to your betrothed, my love?" The endearment came so easily, before she had even considered it. But the words were true. He was her love.

One day she would be his.

"Aye." His voice was rough. "I swear I will do all in my power to make you happy, Elise. To ensure you never regret this decision."

She smiled, but a distant thread of unease weaved through her. To be sure, Cam said the strangest things. It was one of the reasons he so fascinated her. But his last words haunted her, nevertheless.

"Is this something you want, Cam?" She was almost afraid to ask the question, although she couldn't imagine why she feared the answer. Why would he have proposed to her if he didn't want her?

His hands skimmed down her throat. He hooked his thumbs into her shawl and slid it from her shoulders. Without breaking eye contact he loosened the ties of her bodice and she leaned back to give him easier access.

Finally, he spoke. "You'll never know how much I want this, my princess. God knows I've wanted this since the first moment I saw you after entering Ce."

Her unease vanished and she tugged on his belt. "You did nothing but glare at me. I swear I thought you wished to murder me in my bed."

With a smothered curse, he ripped her gown over her arms,

and it slithered to her feet. She dropped his belt to the floor, and he removed his plaid with inelegant haste.

"It was never murder on my mind when I looked at you." For the first time that night, he offered her a grin, and her heart seemed to expand at the mesmerizing sight. "I tried to fight it. You were my despised enemy, but it made no difference."

She sighed. "You have such a sweet tongue when trying to flatter a lady."

He frowned, but it wasn't a fierce frown. More a frown of confusion. "I don't flatter. I don't know how. You know that. I thought you didn't care." He pulled his shirt over his head and Elise licked her lips at the glorious expanse of honed flesh he displayed.

"I don't care." She pressed her lips against his heart and his hands splayed across her back, holding her close. She closed her eyes and breathed in deep, the scent of his body all the aphrodisiac she needed. "I don't need pretty words. But I'm not your enemy. I never have been."

"I know." His words were muffled as he buried his face in her hair. "It was never you, Elise. Never you."

She wound her arms around him and hugged him tight. His body was hard and unyielding, the body of a warrior. With him she was safe. Nothing else mattered. His manner was rough and for that, she was grateful.

He would never tell her charming lies simply to get his own way.

She trailed kisses over his impressive chest, lingering on the battle scars that scored his body. How wonderful it was to take her time to explore every ridge and plane, to run her fingernails over his taut backside and feel him tense with need.

His nighttime visits to her tent had been scarce and fleeting, and he had never stayed until morning. Tonight, she would show him how much he meant to her and leave him in no doubt that to make her happy all he had to do was be himself.

She kneeled before him, her hands cupping his firm backside, and gazed at his cock. His erection thrust upward, thick and proud, and her mouth watered at the bewitching sight.

"Elise." His voice was tortured, and his fingers tangled in her hair. "No."

"I've wanted to do this for weeks." She tore her fascinated gaze from his shaft and looked up at him. He was staring down at her, an expression of desperate lust and disbelief etched on his features. A surge of thrilling power chased through her blood at the knowledge of how much he desired her. "I want all of you, Cameron MacNeil."

"You have me." He growled the words at her, as she had whispered them to him the first night he'd come to her tent. "You've always had me, princess."

She leaned forward, never breaking eye contact, and his rod burned her cheek as she pressed against him. He swallowed and his grip on her hair tightened.

Slowly she moved her head until her open mouth nuzzled his rock-hard flesh. The tip of her tongue licked and tasted, and a strangled groan vibrated along Cam's body. She smiled, her teeth grazing him, and she curled one hand around his hot length.

She wanted him inside her, stretching her delicate flesh with his rigid cock and filling her womb with his seed. But they had all night. Goddess, they had the rest of their lives to conceive a longed-for babe. She no longer needed to mourn the fact that Bride had not blessed her this moon time.

Bride had known there was no need for such haste.

She licked him from his root up to his glistening slit. His salty taste entranced her. She swirled the tip of her tongue around his swollen head, and his stifled groans of pleasure spiraled through her core.

She fastened her lips around him. His fingers bit into her head, forcing her downward, and he slid farther into her. For a second she tensed and her nails dug into him, before her muscles relaxed and she could breathe once again.

"I never thought to witness such a sight." Cam's agonized words caused her to look up at him. He was staring down at her, a wild light in his eyes, and tension throbbed around the chamber as though a fearsome storm brewed. "My aloof Pictish princess naked and on her knees before me." He groaned and wound her hair around his fists, pinning her in place. It was savage and shocking, and she loved it. "Your sweet lips wrapped around my cock. Suck me harder, Elise. God, that's good. So fucking good."

Her eyes fluttered shut as she savored the exotic thrill of his shaft inside her mouth. She sucked him hard, as he had ordered, and the echo of his tortured words continued to seduce her.

Her cheeks hollowed with effort and she abandoned his backside to cup his heavy balls. His grip on her hair became brutal and the sound of his ragged breathing filled her head.

He claimed her mouth, pinning her head in place so she could not move. But she didn't want to move. Every thrust filled her mouth and sent tremors of deprived delight spinning through her quivering core.

"Can't hold on." His voice was raw, and his hard fingers pulled her from his cock. She let out a mewl of protest and fastened her lips around him once again. He gave a choked laugh and tugged her tight to his body.

His thrusts became frantic. If he hadn't held her, she would have fallen onto the floor from his savagery. Juices trickled from her sheath and her clitoris trembled for release. He gave a strangled roar and stilled, his muscles rigid with effort. And then his seed pumped into her, filling her mouth and she swallowed desperately, wanting to take everything he had.

But it was too much. She gagged and instantly he pulled free and sank to his knees. Holding her close she felt him finish between them, the sweet warmth bathing her belly.

"Christ." His voice was uneven, and he speared shaking fingers through her hair, pushing it from her hot face. His lips crashed down on hers, kissing her as though it had been years since they had last kissed.

He slid one hand between their sweat-slicked bodies and found her sensitive pearl. His finger circled, teasing her and she gasped her pleasure while he continued to ravish her mouth.

The pressure built, a wild storm of pure sensation. She arched against him and the friction became unbearable. His hand slid from her head, along her back and grasped her bottom in a possessive gesture.

It was too much. Frenzied waves of pleasure consumed her. She was boneless, floating on a sea of bliss. Only Cam was her anchor, working magic with his mouth and his fingers as she slowly drifted back to reality.

An eternity later, she raised her heavy head from his shoulder and looked at his face. He grinned down at her, and the sight caused her heart to tug within her breast.

With Bride's help, she swore she would find a way to make Cam smile like this outside the realms of lovemaking.

"We will wed as soon as possible." He gathered her into his arms, stood, and strode to the bed. "I don't want to risk anything delaying us."

Did he mean the objection of her mother? She smiled up at him in sated contentment. If Cam wished them to wed this night, she would be only too happy to oblige.

"Nothing will delay us." She trailed languid fingers along his roughened jaw. "You have my word."

CHAPTER 23

They had been traveling for almost two weeks when the hillfort of Dunmar came into view. Cam looked at his wife, riding beside him, and as always when he looked at her, a surge of mingled pride, disbelief and fierce protectiveness consumed him.

They had wed five weeks ago, the day after she had accepted him. It had been hasty by any standards, but MacAlpin had been only too happy to ensure the occasion was infused with as much regal ceremony as possible.

Afterwards MacAlpin had drawn him aside. "You've done well, Cam. Such great service to your country deserves a mighty boon. Name it and if it's within our power you shall have it."

For once diplomacy had curbed Cam's tongue and he'd refrained from telling the older man he hadn't taken Elise as his bride for either his king or his country. He'd done it not only to protect his princess but because she was the only woman he could imagine wanting for his wife.

And as for a boon. He wanted nothing from MacAlpin. But mellow with the knowledge that his wife awaited him, he'd simply thanked his king and returned to her.

And now he was taking her home. A familiar knot of dread gripped his gut as they approached Dunmar. Three weeks ago, he'd sent on a messenger, so his servants had time to clean the hillfort and make it as welcoming as possible for his bride.

But it was still the place where Isla had died. Where, in the darkest hours of the night, he feared her restless spirit haunted the dreary halls.

MacAlpin had invited him to remain at Forteviot for the winter, doubtless because he knew of the lack that awaited Elise at Dunmar. But much as Cam didn't want to return to the home of his forefathers, he wanted to remain under the same roof as MacAlpin even less.

Elise requested an audience with his king every day. He was running out of excuses as to why MacAlpin refused to see her. But the truth was Cam didn't want her to see him. He had a fear that if she did, she would somehow learn the sordid truth that had led to their marriage.

In his heart, he knew he was being irrational. MacAlpin wanted this alliance to succeed. He would surely not jeopardize it by poisoning Elise's mind against Cam.

But the fear remained. And with it the determination to put as much distance as possible between Elise and all those who knew of his involvement with mac Uurguist's death and that conversation in MacAlpin's inner sanctum.

Even so, the king had assigned a dozen warriors to him and with the men who had come with them from Ce, their detachment was impressive.

"Dunmar occupies a magnificent position, Cam." Elise turned to him, her face flushed from the chilled wind. A thick shawl protected her from the unpredictable autumn weather. He tore his gaze from her and looked up at his inheritance, trying to see it from her eyes.

But all he saw was an ancient, sprawling stone hillfort that lacked every luxury Elise was used to.

"Aye." His agreement was reluctant, but it was the truth. Dunmar did possess a magnificent position, although it was nothing compared to Ce-eviot.

"From what you have said—or rather, what you haven't said—I imagined Dunmar to be little more than a roundhouse." Elise laughed at him, but he couldn't bring himself to laugh back. She sighed and reached for his hand as he gripped the reins. "Truly, Cam. I would be happy to live in a roundhouse if you were there with me."

"It's no Pictish palace."

She squeezed his fingers. "Circinn is not as wealthy as the Kingdom of Ce. I'm not nearly as pampered as you imagine."

He looked at her and as always, her mischievous smile lightened his heart. "You deserve to be pampered." For Elise he would overcome his loathing of all that Dunmar represented to him. He'd ensure his estates prospered now that he had a wife worth providing for.

His steward met them outside the entrance. Thank God for Dugald and his skilled management of the estate for the last nine years. If not for this man's dedication, Cam would have even less to offer Elise in her future home.

"My lord." Dugald bowed and after greeting him, Cam helped Elise from her horse and introduced her. He would never tire of introducing her as his wife.

"My lady." Dugald displayed all the respect due to her status and, as the warriors who had accompanied them made their way to the stables, Cam took her arm and led her inside.

His servants had lined up, clearly eager to meet their new mistress, and Elise greeted them with a fine balance of regal dignity and reserved friendliness. But as he led her through the great hall and pointed out the various chambers, he couldn't help seeing the drab conditions.

Finally, he took her up the curved staircase to the bedchambers. He had instructed his mother's old chamber be readied for

Elise but as he led her into the small antechamber, a suffocating sensation wrapped around his chest.

He ignored it, smiled grimly at Elise's polite exclamations of pleasure, and opened the door to the bedchamber where a fire burned brightly in the fireplace.

No fine tapestries adorned the stone walls, but it was clean, and the fragrant scent of heather dispelled any lingering sense of disuse. The chamber, after all, had not been occupied for twenty years.

"It is beautiful." Elise turned to him and grasped his hands. He shook his head at her exuberance. How easy she was to please.

"I'm glad you like it." He felt a familiar scowl threaten and battled to keep it from his brow. He rarely frowned when with Elise. Now that he thought about it, he rarely scowled even when they were apart. Somehow, her magical touch and the knowledge she truly belonged to him had eased the hollow ache in his heart in a way he had never dreamed could be possible.

But he couldn't quite succeed in keeping his feelings from his face this time. "My chamber is next door." His father's chamber. His gut clenched at the notion of sleeping in it, but he could hardly keep his old chamber. It was at the other end of the passageway, too far away from his tempting bride.

Elise tilted her head to one side, clearly considering the matter. "Perhaps there is no need to be too hasty about our sleeping arrangements, my love. Until we have worked out a suitable compromise, perhaps you should use this chamber as your own. Share with me, I mean."

He laughed. Could not help himself. "A princess share her bedchamber with her husband?" The nobility did no such thing, so he was sure royalty didn't. Not that he found the idea distasteful. Far from it.

It wasn't as if he intended to let Elise sleep alone in any case. But there was a difference between sharing a bed and sharing a bedchamber.

"Why not?" She laughed up at him, and then a shiver chased through her and she glanced over her shoulder toward the fire. A small frown fluttered across her brow, as though something had disturbed her.

He had heard nothing. But he would ensure a few cats were installed to chase out any errant rodent.

Elise shook her head and looked back at him. "As I was saying, why shouldn't I share my bedchamber with my husband? My ladies can take the chamber next door, and you can continue to use your old chamber for your personal business."

He lifted her in his arms and swung her around. "I had no idea you were so fond of issuing orders. This is a revelation to me."

She wound her arms around his neck. "I'm very conversant with giving orders, as you shall soon discover."

He dropped her onto the bed, still holding her, and the sweet scent of heather cocooned them. He gazed into her blue eyes and the sound of her giggles sent glimmers of sunlight into his soul.

"I look forward to it," he growled and tugged at the ties of her bodice.

"It's the middle of the day," she gasped. "What will your servants think?"

"They will think how fortunate their master is." He pulled her gown over her breasts and dragged his thumb over her erect nipples.

She sighed and stirred restlessly. "You delight in torturing me."

"Aye." He grinned down at her. Lovemaking had never been so pleasurable or leisurely a pastime before Elise. "It is my right as your husband."

She laughed and pulled at his shirt. "And it's my right as your wife to see your naked body whenever I command it."

He rolled back onto his knees. "How easy your commands are to obey." He stripped off his shirt and discarded his plaid. He would give Elise anything she asked for if it was within his power. But she asked for so little.

He vowed that one day he would give her the world.

Feverishly she wriggled out of her gown and tossed it onto the floor. She lay back on the furs and gave him a provocative glance from beneath her lashes.

She was beautiful. Perfect. She no longer tried to hide her injured leg from him, and a strange pain drove through his chest at the knowledge of how much she trusted him.

He bent his head and sucked her ripe nipple into his mouth. She threaded her fingers through his hair, pressing him close, and his cock ached for release.

Slowly he kissed his way down her body, his fingers sculpting the curve of her breasts and hips. Her scent ensnared him, drawing him between her thighs.

She opened her legs to accommodate him, her fingers tangling in his hair as her breath became erratic. He caressed her with the pads of his thumbs. She was already wet. For him.

He spread her swollen folds. Mesmerized he gazed at the silken flesh that promised him a taste of paradise. Her clitoris peeked from beneath its hood and he stroked her slit with his fingers, using her juices to coat her sensitive bud.

She clutched his hair, and her gasps of pleasure stoked his lust. She arched into his hand and he pressed a finger against her pearl. She cried, a hoarse, inarticulate sound of passion, and as her liquid heat flooded over him, his control unraveled.

He moved over her and pushed his cock inside her slick crease. She contracted around him, the aftermath of her orgasm driving him to the edge. He tipped his hips forward, so his lower body pressed against her sensitized spot, and felt another wave of ecstasy roll through her.

His wife. For an eternal second, he gazed at her enraptured face. Her cheeks were flushed, her lips parted. He had never seen anything so captivating in his life.

A primal groan scorched his throat as he made her his once again.

~

IT WAS LATE the following afternoon before Cam returned to the hillfort. He'd gone round his estate with Dugald and was satisfied with the progress they had made. He had a list of repairs and renovations he wanted finished before winter set in and intended to make long-term plans in the coming days.

He swept into the great hall and beckoned a servant. "Where is the princess?" He imagined she was in their bedchamber. He would have to arrange for her to have a downstairs chamber for her use. Since they were now sharing, she needed a place for her and her ladies to do… whatever it was ladies did.

"The princess went to the village this morning, my lord."

His serenity shattered. "The village?" Unformed fear gripped his heart. Without waiting for an answer, he stormed back outside, hand clasped around the hilt of his sword.

What was she doing in the village? Why would she even leave the hillfort? For God's sake, was she mad? It had never occurred to him she would take it into her head to wander. But he should have. Elise loved to wander.

Sick terror churned his gut. Had she gone alone?

Even as horrifying scenarios ripped through his mind, he saw a mounted party heading his way. Elise and her ladies and the warriors who had accompanied them from Ce. His heart slowed but the terror mutated into fury. How dare she put herself in danger?

Her bright smile of greeting did little to appease his receding shock. If she noticed his scowl—how could she not notice his scowl?—she chose to ignore it. He helped her dismount.

"My lady. A word if you please."

She walked with him, signaling her ladies to remain behind.

Obviously, she was not as blind to his mood as she pretended. Once they were out of earshot of his household, he turned to her and battled the urge to simply take her in his arms and hold her tight.

"Did your day not go well, Cam?" She frowned up at him and clasped his hand to her breast. Maybe she didn't realize why he was so furious after all.

"I would rather talk about your day." The swell of her breast cushioned his hand. He attempted to ignore the way his body responded. He would not be distracted. She had to learn that she could no longer just wander the countryside as she had when she was in Ce.

It wasn't that he didn't trust his countrymen. Except when it came to Elise and her safety, he didn't damn well trust anyone.

"Oh." Her eyes widened and unless he was mistaken, excitement shone in her eyes. "I had a very productive day. I discovered several village women with admirable skills in both weaving and the needle. And although there is only one healer—*one* Cam, can you imagine?—her knowledge is breathtaking. Alas, she is also quite ancient, but my ladies and I are certain we can find several acolytes among the children who will be willing to learn her secrets."

He stared at her, speechless. Of anything he thought she might have said, none of this came close.

She appeared not to notice his incredulity. "It will take some time, but I promise you I will have our household running efficiently in all aspects. Oh, and I have also arranged for two young girls to come help in the kitchen, although I believe we'll need to expand our servant numbers significantly to cater for the additional workload."

Silence hammered between them. Elise raised her eyebrows, clearly waiting for his response. He cleared his throat. His mind had gone strangely numb.

"I didn't realize you intended to…" His words trailed off. Now he thought about it he realized he had never thought at all about what Elise might do with her time. Was this what royal wives did? He had somehow thought they would delegate all such mundane matters.

"I thought you knew." She paused and then cradled his face with one hand. "You do not mind?"

"Of course not." His voice was gruff. "But when I returned and you weren't here, I was concerned."

She flashed him one of her irresistible smiles. "Ah but I am learning, my dear husband. I took not only my ladies with me but also a contingent of warriors."

"Aye." He let out a ragged breath. Elise was safe. She wouldn't put herself in jeopardy again by roaming the countryside alone. "Go inside. I will join you shortly."

ELISE KEPT the smile on her face until she and her ladies entered the antechamber. Then her smile faded and as her ladies fussed around her, removing her shawl, and tidying her hair, she remembered the look on Cam's face.

He had been more than concerned by her absence. He had feared something had happened to her.

She sighed. He would probably always worry about such things and she couldn't blame him. All she could do was try to reassure him that she'd never willingly put herself at risk.

She glanced toward the bedchamber. There was something about the chamber, but she couldn't quite fathom what. As her ladies busied themselves in arranging for refreshments to be brought up to them, she slowly walked through the opened door.

For a moment, all was well. And then the eerie sensation that she had experienced the day before shivered over her arms.

Once again, she looked over to the fireplace. The fire had not yet been lit and the chamber was chilled. But that wasn't the reason she shivered.

Unable to help herself she knelt before the hearth and leaned over the dead embers. She peered up. The stone was blackened. There was no foul stink to indicate some small creature had become stuck and died.

She reached out and pressed her palm against the stone. She had no idea why. Only that she was compelled to do so.

"Elise." Cam's harsh voice echoed around the chamber and she rolled back on her knees, feeling unaccountably guilty. He was staring at her from the door, a combination of shock and disbelief on his face. "What are you doing?"

She didn't know what she was doing. She pushed herself to her feet and dusted the soot from her hands. The uncanny prickle that had haunted her mind a moment ago had faded.

She turned to her husband and opened her arms. "Waiting for you."

It had been ten days since they had arrived at Dunmar. The days had taken on their own rhythm as Cam tended to his neglected estates and she cultivated the necessary foundation for the running of a productive household. She'd even used a few of the treasures Ferelei had left her, unsure at first as to how Cam would react. But he hadn't seemed to mind the two Persian rugs in their bed and antechambers and so she'd put a few more things around their private chambers to relieve the bareness of the stone.

There was still plenty of treasure left, not only to buy and barter whatever they might need in the future, but also for Droston's freedom.

She felt so guilty that she had not yet secured his release. But since leaving Fortriu, there was a strange certainty in her mind that, when Bride decreed the time was right, everything would fall into place. And somehow it was linked to her cousin Aila.

Bride had never failed her. Elise knew her goddess would not fail her now. She simply had to put her trust in her and wait for the sign she knew was coming.

"My lady, are you certain this is a good idea?" One of her

ladies glanced nervously over her shoulder. The other ladies shuffled uncomfortably as they all stood outside the locked door of the only chamber in the hillfort that Cam had not invited her inside.

It was the chamber next to his old one and Elise knew exactly who this one had belonged to. His sister, Isla's.

She didn't know why the door was kept locked, but she did know that as long as it was, those dark shadows in the depths of Cam's eyes would never fade.

She had sworn to herself she would heal his wounds, and in her heart, she knew opening this door was a vital first step.

"Yes." She took the keys that hung at her waist, the ones Cam had presented to her the day after they'd arrived. With a deep breath, she sorted through them and then inserted one into the lock.

The door swung open, and instinctively she and her ladies retreated at the stale smell that wafted out. Goddess, the room couldn't have been opened in years.

With her hand across her nose and mouth, she crossed the threshold. It was gloomy and damp and she hurried to the window to unlatch the timber shutters and let in some fresh air.

As she turned around, a deep sense of melancholy washed through her and she gripped her hands together at her waist. She had never possessed the gift of communicating directly with those who had passed through the veil, but she had the irrefutable certainty that she and her ladies were not alone in this chamber.

"Lady Isla." Her whisper floated around the chamber, as insubstantial as the dust motes that danced in the pale shafts of sunlight that spilled through the window. Nothing else stirred, save for her ladies who clutched their arms and shivered.

"Elise." Cam's voice echoed along the passageway and her ladies fluttered in alarm, hurrying from the chamber as her husband marched in. The desolation that thickened the air instantly lightened. Elise stared, mesmerized, as a sunlit aura surrounded Cam.

He paused for only a moment before stepping toward her. The illumination around him scattered into countless rainbow fragments that glittered in the shadowy corners of the chamber before slowly fading.

She caught her breath and pressed her hand to the base of her throat. Great goddess. Isla had been trapped in this chamber, snared in the same web of guilt and regret as her brother.

Except for one significant difference.

"Damn it, Elise." Cam grasped her shoulders and shook her. "Speak to me. What is it?"

Only now did she recognize the note of panic in Cam's voice. She blinked rapidly and gripped the front of his shirt.

"Lady Isla." Her throat was raw, and it was hard to speak. But she had to make Cam understand. "She has been unable to pass through the veil. She can't leave you, Cam, until you can forgive yourself."

A spasm twisted his features, and his fingers bit into her shoulders. "Stop this." His voice was harsh, but she heard the heartache beneath. "You're not a witch. Stop speaking like one."

She had no idea what he meant. It didn't matter. "Isla loves you," she said softly. "She has never stopped loving you. You have to let her go."

He glared at her and then thrust her from him and raked his fingers through his hair. "You don't know what you're talking about." He swung on his heel, caught sight of her ladies and clearly the glare on his face was enough to send them scurrying back along the passageway. He heaved in a great breath before once again turning back to her.

Pain engulfed her heart at the look of desolation on his face. If only it was possible for him to see, for even a second, the breath-stealing devotion of his sister. Then, surely, he would understand.

"Isla died more than nine years ago. She's not here, Elise. You don't know anything about her. Don't try to take my guilt away with pretty words. I don't deserve them."

She took his hands and ignored his half-hearted efforts to pull free. She could no longer see the purity of Isla, but she could feel her ethereal presence all around.

"You have no reason to feel guilty." She could understand his sorrow and his regret at losing his sister, especially when Isla had been so young. She could even understand his self-reproach about being unable to save her.

But his self-condemnation had corroded his good sense. Sometimes the gods would accept no sacrifice in return for mercy when they chose a mortal. Death could claim anyone at any time.

Isla's death, no matter how tragic, was not his fault.

He stared at her, his dark eyes filled with so much recrimination his pain ate into her heart. What wasn't he telling her? What terrible secret did this chamber conceal?

"I was in Dunadd when Dunmar was attacked." Bitterness weighed every word. She stiffened in horror. He hadn't told her his hillfort had been attacked. Goddess, was that how Isla had died? Because she had been caught up in the attack?

His fingers tightened around hers. "The Pict leader murdered my father and raped Isla."

Nausea washed through her, twisting with the revulsion that crushed her chest. *The Pict.* A Pict had murdered his beloved sister.

No wonder he had hated her people. There was nothing she could say but she had to say something.

"I am so grieved for you, Cam..." Her voice was hoarse, and she had the alarming notion she might weep. But that wouldn't help him. This was no time for her to show useless feminine weakness.

He swallowed and the terrifying certainty hit her that he hadn't finished.

"Isla was barely eleven. But she conceived that bastard's child. She died trying to birth it six months later."

She died in my arms. His words had always haunted her, but now she knew how Isla had died her heart cracked at how he, at barely sixteen, had tried to comfort his sister in her final hours.

He pulled her hand up to her face, and the rough pad of his thumb tenderly wiped her cheek. She hadn't wanted to cry. Had not even realized a tear had escaped. But he simply rested his forehead against hers and his solid strength seeped into her soul.

Finally, she asked the question to which she was not certain she wished to know the answer.

"Was justice served?"

Silence greeted her and stretched for so long she feared she had been right. Justice had not been served. That was why Cam was so eaten up with guilt. Because he'd been unable to find the one responsible.

But then he spoke. "Aye." He sounded defeated, as though he expected her to disapprove. She straightened and looked him in the eyes.

"Good." Her voice was firm. "Blood for blood. It is done."

A shudder inched over his body and he looked at her in something akin to awe. In that moment, the shimmering aura reappeared around Cam and his tense muscles noticeably relaxed. And then his gaze slid to a point above her head and he froze, as disbelief, shock, and finally wonderment claimed his features.

Elise held her breath as the sparkling illumination once again faded. Cam looked back at her. He didn't say anything, and she knew he would never mention what he had seen. Because she knew, for one precious moment, he *had* seen.

But it didn't matter whether he ever acknowledged it or not. Because for the first time since she had known him, peace finally claimed his battered soul.

~

CAM STRETCHED IN BED, unaware of what had woken him from the depths of sleep. He lay there unmoving trying to define what was different. Slowly the answer washed over him.

He no longer ached with grief and guilt over the violent passing of Isla. He missed her. He would always miss her. But holding Elise's hands in his sister's old chamber, he had thought —for one mad moment—he had sensed Isla's forgiving presence.

It wasn't possible of course. It was Elise herself who had managed to ease his guilt. He didn't know how she did it. He didn't want to know how she did it. Because he had the terrible certainty it was linked to her heathen faith, and deep inside he still harbored the formless fear that her worship of pagan gods drew danger to her.

He could protect her from his fellow man. But how could he protect her against demons?

Instinctively he rolled onto his side to pull her into his arms. She wasn't there. He opened his eyes and at the same time heard a strange scraping sound coming from across the chamber.

He sat up and peered toward the noise. Elise crouched at the hearth and in the low glow from the embers, he saw she was wearing his shirt. His gaze snagged on her as he drank in the astonishing sight. He had never imagined Elise wearing his shirt but with her golden hair tumbling down her back, she looked close to divine.

It took another few seconds for him to drag his lascivious thoughts from taking her where she knelt to the question as to why she was in front of the hearth in the first place.

He pulled a fur around his shoulders as he left the bed and strode over to her. He crouched beside her and she fell back, giving him a startled look.

"I didn't mean to wake you," she whispered.

"What in the name of God are you doing?" He stared at her hands, which she'd wrapped in two of her veils. They were now blackened and ruined.

She clasped her swathed hands on her lap. "I can't explain it." She nibbled her lip and glanced at the hearth. "There is a loosened stone at the back there. It's just difficult to grasp, especially with the heat."

"A loosened stone?" He stared at her and unease licked through his chest. "How did you know there was a loose stone there?"

She shifted on her knees as though she was uncomfortable, either by the hard floor or his question was open to debate.

Finally, she sighed and looked him in the eyes again. "Bride guides me, Cam. I didn't know there was a loose stone until I found it. But I did know there was something there. Now I need to discover what it is my goddess needs me to find."

His chest tightened as the fear gripped his heart. He wanted to forbid her to touch the stone. To promise him she would never follow the voice of her heathen goddess again.

He wanted to remind her that she had promised to obey him as her lord and master, that she was his wife and could no longer follow the pagan ways she had before their marriage.

The words lodged in his throat. He would never utter them. Elise loved her goddess and if he demanded she abandon her faith, he might just as well carve out her heart.

He doubted she would obey him in any case. She would still find a way to worship her gods, and this fragile, glorious connection between them would wither and die.

He would do a great deal to keep this elusive happiness that blessed their union. He would do anything.

Without a word, he unwrapped the flimsy material from Elise's hands and wound them around his own. He knew she stared at him in shock, but he refused to meet her gaze. The fur slipped from his shoulders as he reached across the hearth and tugged at the stone that protruded slightly from the blackened wall.

With a grunt, he pulled it free and dropped it on the floor in front of them. There was nothing special about it. But he knew it wasn't the stone Elise and her cursed goddess were after.

He gritted his teeth and pushed one hand into the cavity beyond. It was no great surprise to discover a small stone casket. He placed it beside the stone on the floor and glared at it.

Elise traced one shaky finger across the top of the filthy casket. "Do you know what this is?" Her voice was hushed.

"I've never seen it before in my life." It was plain, with no encrusted jewels or intricate engravings. It was a practical object that could be used for a multitude of household functions.

There was no earthly reason he could imagine why anyone would have hidden it in such a place.

"Will you open it?" Elise was staring at him but again he refused to meet her eyes. And why would she go to such pains to retrieve this casket and then expect him to open it?

It could have been concealed generations ago. Why did the eerie certainty crawl over him that it should have remained concealed forever?

His reluctance made no sense. Perhaps there was treasure inside, enough treasure to acquire Elise luxurious rugs from Persia so they could sell the ones she had brought with her. He wanted to get rid of all the cursed goods she had brought with her, but how could he deprive her of the few indulgences she had placed around the chambers when he could offer her nothing in exchange?

With a silent oath, he lifted the stone lid and set it on the floor. And then he looked inside.

Lying on top of a soft leather pouch was a small, silver, five-pointed star set within a circle. He stared at it, uncomprehending, as his heart pounded against his ribs and a wild rushing sensation thundered through his mind. From a great distance he heard Elise gasp and was aware she pressed her fingers against her mouth, but he couldn't drag his hypnotized gaze from the ancient pagan symbol before him.

He had seen this silver necklace before.

Buried memories bubbled up from the darkest corners of his mind where they had been imprisoned for twenty years and more. His mother, her hair as black as midnight, had always worn this necklace. She had laughed and she had smiled, and she had always held him close and told him…

Agony speared through his heart. She had told him so many times how much she loved him.

With fingers that shook, he picked up the star. Aye, she had laughed but never when his father was home. Then fear would descend over the hillfort, extinguishing any tiny bud of happiness.

He tore his gaze from the necklace and looked up at Elise. "She was wearing this the day he abducted her." His voice was hoarse. Elise nodded in understanding. "She only wore it when he wasn't around. Thank God he wasn't often around."

As a small child, the pattern had fascinated him. He'd love to play with it. And his mother told him fantastical tales of mythical creatures who lived in trees and water and of gods and goddesses who presided over the lives of man.

"Tell no one, my sweetest boy," she would whisper as she stroked his hair before he went to sleep, and even as young as he was, he knew she meant his father. "This is our secret."

He had told no one. He had kept her secret. He'd kept her secret so well he had forgotten everything she'd ever told him.

He picked up the pouch and unlaced it, but he already knew what he would find. Glittering crystals tumbled onto his open palm and with them, the final, blackened memories escaped their fetid prison.

Terror slammed through him and he reeled back, no longer seeing Elise before him or the chamber around them. He was in the great hall, blood trickling down his face, cowering behind one of the tables where his father had tossed him. All he could see was his mother being dragged by her hair along the floor, as his father cursed her for a witch, a heathen, and worse.

When the beating had started, he'd run to her aid, only to be flung aside like a worthless bone. The next thing he recalled was her hiding her precious things, telling him it was for the best.

She had never worn her necklace or shown him her crystals again.

Only when he felt the heavy drape of furs around his shoulders did the violent memories fade. Elise was before him, holding onto the edges of the fur, as she tried to stem the shudders that racked his body. Still clutching the necklace and crystals, he roughly pulled her close.

Warm. Alive. *His.* He closed his eyes and dragged in a shattered breath. Her scent sank into him, calming the frenzied thud of his heart.

"When she died, my father blamed her." His voice was muffled as he buried his face in Elise's shoulder, her hair a silken sheet against his lips. "He told me God punished her for her pagan beliefs because she was a witch. He tarnished her memory, Elise. And until now I didn't even remember how."

Aye, he'd forgotten the details. But the fear his father had instilled into a grieving, terrified child had remained with him throughout the years.

Elise stirred in his arms. Her breath was a soothing balm against his ear. "But you remember now. That is all that matters."

CHAPTER 25

*E*lise could scarcely believe the difference in Cam during the last two days since he'd discovered his mother's casket. There was still an indefinable trace of something bleak in his soul, but for the most part the darkness that had surrounded him and eaten into the fabric of his being had finally faded away.

Several times, she had hovered on the brink of telling him how dearly she loved him. But each time a foolish sense of not wanting to spoil what they had between them held her back. Suppose he didn't feel the same way? Her heart would break a little if he did not return her love.

This way she could pretend, and it wasn't hard. He only had to smile at her and her day filled with sunshine.

There was another reason she held back too. The glimmering suspicion that Bride had answered her prayers. It was too soon to tell for sure. Her moon time was not yet upon her, but in her heart, she knew.

She had conceived Cam's babe.

And just as she knew that Bride had a plan when it came to Droston, she also knew her goddess would show Elise the right time to share her news. She wouldn't be at all surprised if the catalyst to it all was when Cam held her in his arms and said *I love you.*

She was still daydreaming of that happy moment when Cam marched into the chamber he had allocated for her and her ladies personal use. He didn't smile when he saw her. He had his old familiar scowl on his face, the scowl she hadn't seen for weeks.

"What is it?" She took his arm and peered into his dark eyes.

"MacAlpin has returned to Dal Riada and we have been summoned to Dunadd."

Dunadd, the royal stronghold of Dal Riada. The place where Droston, her father, and all the other hostages were held.

Excitement burned through her at the knowledge Bride had so swiftly answered her. This was the sign she had been waiting for.

"Will my cousin Aila be there?"

He stiffened, and shock flared briefly in his eyes. "How did you know—" He broke off and exhaled a long breath. She knew he was thinking of Bride. He hadn't spoken of her goddess, and on the surface, nothing had changed. But she knew without him having to say, that her beliefs no longer troubled him in the way they once had.

"I don't know," she assured him. "But I have always believed I would see Aila before she gave birth. And time is now running short for I know she wishes to be back in Ce before her babe is due."

Cam looked vaguely uncomfortable by her revelation. "Aye, that's the reason MacAlpin gives for wishing us to make the journey. Connor and your cousin will be in Dunadd in a week for five days before they leave for the Kingdom of Ce. It appears we don't have a choice in this." Once again, a thunderous glare settled over his face.

"But I long to see Aila again, Cam." She couldn't contain her delight any longer and went onto her toes to kiss the scowl from his lips. "And I'm certain I will finally get the chance to speak to your elusive MacAlpin."

There was no mistaking the tension that radiated from Cam's rigid muscles. "Why are you so intent on speaking with him? He won't release your father, Elise. Not until he's certain all of Pictland acknowledges him as the rightful king of Fortriu."

One thing hadn't changed. Cam was still as tactless as ever.

Not that she wanted him to change. His forthrightness enchanted her, even when it irritated her.

"I know that." She couldn't help the acid note in her voice because did Cam truly think her so clueless of politics? "I wouldn't give him the satisfaction of requesting something he would never entertain. I wish to broach the possibility of paying a ransom for the freedom of my dear Droston."

Cam's glower darkened further. It was obvious the thought of her requesting anything from MacAlpin sat very badly with him. But there was nothing she could do about that. MacAlpin was the only one who possessed the power to free Droston. Therefore, MacAlpin was the one she needed to see. However much the prospect disgusted her.

DUNADD WAS SITUATED on top of a mighty hill on the west coast of Pictland. Its location was admirable, but nothing when compared to Fortriu. Elise took a deep breath as they rode toward the stronghold and tried to calm her thoughts. Becoming agitated over the upstart MacAlpin's betrayal would do her no good at all. Especially when she needed to mask her true feelings toward him and flatter him so he might grant her request.

The chamber they were allocated was small but adequate. As her ladies fluttered around whispering about the primitive conditions and wild location, she watched Cam. Arms folded, grim expression on his face, he glared through the narrow window.

She went to him and slid her arm through his. "It's only for five days," she reminded him. "Then we can return home." It was strange how at home she felt at Dunmar. While she had fallen in love with the hillfort soon after crossing its threshold, she'd known it had been hard for Cam to be there. But since opening Isla's chamber and the discovery of his mother's possessions, she'd sensed a change in Cam's feelings. He no longer flung furtive glances into dark corners when he thought she wasn't looking. The evil of his father had been exposed and the poison was leaking away.

When they returned to Dunmar she intended to have his father's old chamber stripped bare. She would have everything from that chamber burned. It was the only way to cleanse and purify. Only then would the last lingering shadow that she sensed still lurked within Cam's soul be vanquished.

Cam wound his arm around her and gave her a hard hug. "Aye." He released her and stepped back. "I'm going to find Connor. I'll get someone to take you to Lady Aila."

AILA'S CHAMBER was somewhat grander than the one Elise and Cam had been given. Her cousin, blooming with good health, took Elise's hands and hastily pulled her from the small antechamber into her bedchamber and shut the door on all their ladies.

"How wonderful it is to see you again." Aila smiled but tears shimmered in her eyes.

Elise laughed and kissed her cousin's cheek. "You are fairly glowing, my love," she said. "Don't spoil it by weeping because you're so happy to see me."

"I *am* happy to see you." Despite the tears that Aila appeared unable to help trickling down her cheeks, she peered at Elise in clear anxiety. "But what of you? You seem well and happy but…" Her voice trailed away, and she frowned and bit her lip.

Elise led Aila to the bed and they sat, still holding hands. "I'm very well and very happy."

"And wed to Cameron MacNeil." There was no disguising the concern in Aila's voice. "We heard this news only very recently. I insisted we had to stop here on our way to Ce, under the pretext that I had to see you. I knew MacAlpin would make sure you were here for me. He cannot do enough to ensure my wellbeing while I am with child."

"Aila, I know this is all very strange, especially when you know how I avoided Cam back in the spring. But he is truly the bravest and most honorable man I have ever met. I'm proud to be his wife."

Aila opened her mouth, hesitated, and then pressed her lips together. She appeared stunned by Elise's confession, and fiddled with the edges of her shawl. Finally, she took a deep breath.

"You love him." It wasn't a question. Elise didn't bother to answer, since she was sure the besotted smile on her face told her cousin everything she needed to know. "I'm so delighted for you, Elise." Aila sniffed and another tear escaped. She brushed it away and smiled. "I know your first marriage was difficult. Bride works in mysterious ways, to be sure, but my heart is light once again to know you're with a man you truly care for."

Bride did work in the most mysterious of ways and for a moment, a ripple of unease marred her happiness.

For years, she had begged her goddess for Ferelei's ship to be lost at sea, or for him to be delayed indefinitely on his countless journeys. But a missing husband was not a dead husband. If no body was ever found, Elise would never have been free to wed another.

Until she met Cam, she had never wanted to wed another.

Bride had heard Elise's prayers and, when the time was right, had taken Ferelei in a way that irrefutably gave Elise her freedom.

But what price would Bride demand in return? During the last few weeks, Elise had pushed the thought to the back of her mind, not wishing to dwell on the intricate manipulations of the gods.

A tempting thought surfaced. Perhaps Bride's price was nothing more than Elise having helped Cam to face the shadowed truths of his past?

After all, his mother had been a true believer of the old ways. Surely that was what Bride had wanted in return?

She clung onto that notion and returned her attention to Aila. "You have no need to concern yourself with my wellbeing, Aila." And then something occurred to her and she frowned. "What did you mean when you said you insisted you stop here under the pretext of seeing me? Why is this a pretext?" It made no sense. She must have misunderstood Aila.

Her cousin blinked and for an odd moment Elise got the impression Aila was concealing something of shattering importance. But then Aila squeezed her fingers and she pushed the feeling aside.

"No pretext. Merely a figure of speech. Now, do you feel up for a stroll? I confess being inside the oppressive walls of Dunadd is not something I enjoy."

"Of course." Elise stood and then could contain herself no longer. "Aila, I must share my secret with you. I believe I am with child."

For a heartbeat Aila looked stricken, but before Elise could comprehend why her cousin should be devastated at such wonderful news Aila hugged her, and the uneasy suspicion that she was hiding something vanished.

~

THE CONFRONTATION with Connor MacKenzie was not going well. After a terse greeting Connor suggested they go for a ride, and while climbing back in the saddle after the journey to Dunadd was the last thing Cam felt like doing, it wasn't a request.

After a strangely circular gallop across the surrounding countryside where they ended up within a stone's throw of where they started, Connor pulled to a halt.

"You wed Lady Elise." It was not said by way of congratulations.

"Aye." Cam narrowed his eyes and glowered across their mighty hill toward the western ocean. He could guess where this conversation was leading.

"After her husband, Ferelei mac Uurguist, conveniently died in a drunken fall."

Cam tensed, waiting for the familiar black rage to consume him at the mention of that cursed Pict's name. But only a strangely muted sense of regret at Isla's stolen life washed through him.

Isla. His beloved sister. Who had never blamed him for not being there when she had needed him the most.

"God's death, Cam." Connor glowered at him as though something in his expression had touched a nerve, before glaring toward the distant Firth. "If not for this alliance I would be the first one behind you in your thirst for vengeance. The bastard deserved it. I don't presume to pretend to know how you feel. I only know we need to preserve this alliance at all costs."

Cam had sworn to Ross that he would never divulge the truth of what had happened. He would keep Ross' part out of it. But Connor was his superior officer. And it belatedly occurred to him that through their wives, they were now related.

Connor deserved to know the truth.

"It was self-defense."

Connor rounded on him. "Self-defense?" It was obvious he doubted it.

"Aye. I won't deny it. I confronted him, Connor. I would have severed his damn head from his shriveled body and taken the consequences. I owed that to my sister. I gave her my word long before I swore fealty to you."

Connor looked murderous. "Call yourself a warrior? I could still have your head for this insubordination."

"I didn't touch him. I turned my back and he attacked. The bastard slipped and cracked his skull open." Even now that injustice burned but not with the same ferocity as it had before.

He took a deep breath. He would never be able to think or speak of mac Uurguist with a clear mind, but it was a relief to no longer feel the ravenous talons of vengeance rip through his every thought.

Connor's knuckles were white as he gripped his reins. "And then you took his widow as compensation."

Cam bared his teeth. "Beware how you speak of my wife, MacKenzie."

Connor's eyes narrowed a fraction. It was clear he hadn't expected such a reaction. "She is also the cousin of my wife."

It was none of Connor's business why he had taken Elise as his bride. But he didn't want the other man thinking he'd taken her as some form of continuing retribution. "I wed her because she's the only woman I want in my life. God knows why she said yes. She could have chosen anyone. You can assure your lady wife I'll do everything in my power to make her cousin happy."

Connor grunted. It was clear he was enjoying this conversation as little as Cam. Why then did he continue? Was it because he had promised Lady Aila?

The thought darkly amused him. He was only being civil in response to Connor's interrogation because of Elise and her connection to Lady Aila.

It appeared they were both in thrall to their royal wives.

"You should know there are rumors about, Cam." Connor slung him a sideways glance. The anger had gone. "Rumors that

MacAlpin was behind the wedding, to add another Pictish princess to his bow. Aila was," he swallowed and took a deep breath. "She was distraught when she heard. It doesn't look good. You must admit to that. But if you and Lady Elise are happy that's all that matters to us."

It had been a long time since Cam had been happy. The concept was foreign to him. Yet with Elise he had found a peace and contentment he'd never imagined could exist for him. Happy? Aye, he was happier than he could ever recall being.

Was Elise happy? He believed so. She was like a beam of sunlight that illuminated Dunmar. She didn't complain and her ready laugh warmed his heart.

But did she love him? Sometimes in the dead of night, he would gaze down at her, this golden bride of his, and wish he could see inside her heart. She had married him, but did she secretly wish she had married her dear Droston?

"We are happy." It was a growl because the thought of Droston reminded him of why Elise was so determined to speak with MacAlpin. It had nothing to do with her wanting to negotiate her father's release. She wanted Droston freed. What then? Did she think to take him as her lover?

He'd kill the bastard before he allowed the Pict to lay hands on his wife.

"MacNeil." Connor's voice was sharp. Clearly Cam had missed whatever Connor had been saying to him. "I asked you if Lady Elise is aware of the rumors. She knows of your connection with mac Uurguist?"

Shit, the rumors. How could Elise believe anything but the worst if she heard the truth? This was why he hadn't wanted to come to Dunadd. Why he wanted to keep her ensconced at Dunmar where nobody would ever tell her anything to disturb her peace of mind.

His peace of mind.

Aye, and did he really believe he could keep Elise secluded

from the rest of the world forever? It was a good dream, but a dream nonetheless.

He simply didn't want this dream to shatter.

Connor cursed, disgust evident in his voice. "You have to tell her, man. She can't find out from anyone else. Tell her the truth and all will be well."

CHAPTER 26

*E*lise and Aila took a sedate walk away from the looming presence of Dunadd. Although both her and Aila's ladies accompanied them, as well as their bodyguards, they still had enough privacy to catch up on gossip.

She hadn't realized how much she had missed her cousin. According to Aila the physicians of Dal Riada were primitive barbarians she refused to allow near her. She trusted only the healers of Pictland and her own relatives to tend her when she gave birth.

The knowledge gnawed into Elise's mind. She had no experience of the medical expertise of Dal Riada, but she trusted the healers of Pictland with her life. With the blessing of Bride, they had once *saved* her life. Would Cam agree to take her back to Pictland so her grandmother could assist when their babe was due?

A smile warmed her. She couldn't wait to share the news with him. Perhaps she would wait until they returned to Dunmar. Too much blood and betrayal stained the walls of Dunadd to share such a precious moment with her husband.

As they approached a gentle slope, a couple of warriors

appeared on the ridge. Elise frowned as they approached but there was no mistake. One of the Scots was MacAllister.

Bride could not have been clearer in her message. She had ensured MacAlpin's mouthpiece directly crossed her path for one reason only. Elise squeezed Aila's fingers. "One moment. I must speak with MacAllister."

"I do not trust him." Aila's voice was pure ice.

"Of course not." As far as Elise was concerned, that went without saying. There were few Scots she trusted. "But nevertheless, I must speak to him." She didn't wait for her cousin's permission and stepped toward the two men.

They bowed. "My lady," MacAllister said. Elise was not fooled for a second by his show of respect. But two could play that game.

"MacAllister." She inclined her head.

"I trust you have everything you require, my lady?"

"Indeed. But I am grieved I have not yet had the opportunity to make closer acquaintance of your king."

An oddly blank look washed across MacAllister's face. Why was he pretending to have no idea what she was talking about? She knew quite well he was MacAlpin's closest confidant.

"I will tell the king you wish to speak with him, my lady."

Elise gave a brittle smile. "If you would be so kind. Perhaps your king will be able to accommodate my request here in Dunadd. I appreciate our time was somewhat curtailed in Fortriu." *While that cursed upstart defiled our Supreme Kingdom.* She hoped her thought didn't show on her face.

"Had the king been aware of your wish to see him, I know he would have gone to great lengths in order to accommodate your request." MacAllister offered another half-bow. "He wishes only peace and prosperity between our two lands."

Elise could feel disgust radiating from Aila who stood by her side. Truly, the arrogance of both MacAllister and his king was breathtaking. But she couldn't afford to tell him what she really thought of him. Not when Droston's life hung in the balance.

"Perhaps your king did not receive my previous communications," she said graciously. Of course he had received them. Cam had asked the king personally on more than one occasion.

"I fear this is true. I'll make certain to convey your wishes to him directly, my lady. Thank you for bringing this oversight to my attention." With a final bow, he continued back to Dunadd and Elise let out an infuriated breath.

"Curse their lying tongues." It was the politest thing she could manage.

"Do not distress yourself." Aila took her arm. "Think of your babe. Why do you wish to speak with that upstart king? Do you wish to see your father?"

Guilt threaded through her. She did wish to see her father, but it was more important to gain Droston's freedom. Her father was valuable. MacAlpin would allow no harm to befall him. But Droston, in the eyes of the world, was nobody. If relations between Pictland and Dal Riada degenerated further, Droston was expendable.

"Yes." But that wouldn't be the first thing she asked.

"He will allow it." Contempt wove through Aila's words. "I've seen my brother and he is well, as are all hostages with royal blood."

"What of our nobles?"

"I haven't seen any of them, but I'm told they are accorded the respect their status deserves. A few of them have been ransomed and returned to their kingdoms."

That was good news. Elise focused on that and pushed the hint of unease her conversation with MacAllister had provoked to the back of her mind.

ELISE SAT in the bed her arms clasped around her knees and watched Cam pace the chamber. Every now and then, he slung a sideways glance at her ladies, who were settling down for the night at the other end of the chamber.

It was a most primitive arrangement. Although another chamber had been offered for their comfort, neither they nor she had wanted to accept the offer. There might be an alliance in place, and she might be married to a Scot, but here in Dunadd, they were surrounded by enemies. She would keep her ladies close, for safety and peace of mind.

"What troubles you, my lord?" She knew he had seen Connor MacKenzie earlier while she and Aila had been together. Cam had been surly since his return, but she hadn't had the chance to ask him what had transpired. She hadn't felt inclined to discuss personal matters during the feast, especially when she was aware that both MacAllister and MacAlpin gave her speculative glances throughout the evening.

She tried to ignore it but as each hour passed, the uneasy knot in her chest tightened. Damn MacAllister and his blatant lies. She would not allow his sly insinuations to tarnish the bond she and Cam had forged.

CAM STARED at his wife as she sat on the bed, her hair in a long braid over her shoulder. Connor's words rang in his ears. *You have to tell her.*

That was easy for Connor to say. But how could he tell Elise the truth when she gazed at him with those innocent blue eyes? How would she react? Would she understand? Or would his confession tear apart this fragile web of peace she had woven around them?

Once again, he glanced at her ladies across the chamber. He understood Elise's reluctance to allow them to sleep so far away from her but hell. This arrangement was barbaric. His plan of making love to Elise until she was spent and pliable in his arms and then revealing the truth withered. He would not perform to an audience. And they had four more nights after this one.

He let out a pained breath. Four more nights. He would tell Elise the truth about mac Uurguist when they returned to Dunmar.

"Cam?" There was an edge to Elise's voice, and he dragged his mind back to the present.

"Nothing troubles me." He knew he was glowering at her. He hadn't glowered in weeks, but the stone walls of Dunadd were oppressive in a way he had never found before.

But he hadn't known of the bloodied betrayal before.

After their tortured exchange regarding the wellbeing of Elise, Cam had asked Connor what he knew of the night the nine Pictish lords had died. He thought Connor wasn't going to answer. But then he did.

The Picts hadn't turned on their hosts. They had been brutally slaughtered by order of MacAlpin, to eliminate any threat on his claim to the Kingdom of Fortriu.

Connor had ordered him to never breathe a word of it to anyone. As if he needed to be told. Even knowing this information was tantamount to treason.

But he and Connor were both married to Pictish princesses. To women who had personally been affected by MacAlpin's actions. If the day ever came to question his loyalty, would he choose his king? Or would he choose his wife?

Against his better judgment, he once again looked at Elise. He couldn't help himself. Whenever they were together, no matter what else was happening around them, his gaze always returned to her. She was, and would always be, the light that guided his battered heart.

There was no question to answer. His loyalty was to Elise. God help him if MacAlpin ever discovered it.

"Your meeting with Connor MacKenzie went well?"

He could feel his frown darkening, despite his best attempts to halt it. "Aye." What else could he say? That MacKenzie and Elise's own cousin had feared Cam had abducted and raped her by order of MacAlpin?

She took a deep breath, obviously not satisfied by his response but unwilling to press the issue in front of her ladies. For that at least, he could be thankful for their unwelcome presence.

"I've been wondering," Elise said, as she fiddled with the end of her plait as though it fascinated her. "Back in Fortriu was it MacAllister or MacAlpin himself you spoke to with regard my request for an audience?"

"What?" How had they got onto this subject? He didn't want to speak of this. Not ever, but especially not now when he needed to tell her of mac Uurguist.

Four more nights.

"If it was MacAllister," Elise persisted, still not looking at him, "I wouldn't be surprised if he didn't pass on the message to his king at all."

Sweat trickled along the back of Cam's neck. He couldn't lie to her. But he couldn't tell her that he had never passed on her message either.

Not until he had sorted everything else out with her.

And so he gave an uncommunicative grunt that might have conveyed anything.

Elise pressed her lips together. He couldn't tell whether she had discarded this line of conversation or whether she was preparing another question that would twist his long dormant conscience inside out.

He couldn't risk it. He strode across the chamber and only when he reached the door, did he pause and glance over his shoulder. Elise was staring at him, a bemused expression on her face.

Four more nights. "Forgive me, my lady. There are matters I must attend to." He gave an inelegant bow and hastily left the chamber.

⁓

THE FOLLOWING morning as her ladies readied her for the day, Elise attempted to hide her growing unease. She'd had a restless night and what little sleep she had managed had been filled with ominous dreams.

But it wasn't her lack of sleep that caused the unformed dread that lurked in her breast. It was because for the first time since they had wed, Cam had not shared her bed.

It had nothing to do with the question she'd asked him concerning MacAllister. Of that, she was absolutely convinced, and ruthlessly squashed the tiny sliver of doubt that refused to believe.

It was because, as Aila had told her the day before, the walls of Dunadd bled evil. No matter how delighted she was at seeing her cousin again, she couldn't wait to leave this royal stronghold and return home.

As she and her ladies left the hillfort to wait for Aila, Cam strode toward her. As always when she saw him, a pleasurable pain squeezed her heart.

Of course he hadn't lied to her.

"My lady." He took her hand and kissed her knuckles. He continued to hold her hand as he stared at her and she resisted the urge to pull him into her arms. He looked as though he hadn't slept at all, with shadows under his eyes and the previous day's stubble darkening his jaw.

"You didn't come to bed." Her voice was low. She wanted no one to overhear their exchange.

"Forgive me." His thumb caressed her fingers, such a light touch yet it reminded her of all the other times he caressed her, and desire stirred. "I didn't want to wake you. And," he hesitated and slung her ladies a furtive glance. "I'm not comfortable sharing the chamber with your ladies."

She laughed and tugged him close. Curse etiquette. "Will you avoid my bed for four more nights, my love?"

A pained expression crossed his face. "Don't torment me, Elise. Promise me you'll wait four more nights until we leave this wretched stronghold."

She smiled, but even as he once again kissed her knuckles and left, his final words echoed in her mind.

He might have been referring to the fact it would be four more nights before he shared her bed, or before they made love. But she couldn't shift the certainty he had meant something else entirely. What that might be, she could not imagine.

"My lady." The sound of MacAllister's voice shattered her thoughts and she turned to give him a cool look. "The king will see you at the tenth hour today, if that is acceptable to you."

She stared at him in shocked disbelief. He didn't move and she realized he was waiting for her approval or otherwise. She inclined her head and brutally reeled in her scattered thoughts.

"That will be acceptable."

"I'll send a messenger for your convenience, my lady." He bowed and strolled off and Elise took a few deep breaths to calm her racing heart.

It would not be calmed. All she managed was to make herself lightheaded.

It was sheer coincidence that MacAlpin had agreed to see her, barely a day since she had requested audience with him. He had agreed because it pleased him to do so. It had nothing to do with the fact that until now he'd been unaware of her wish to speak with him.

"Elise, are you well?" Aila's concerned whisper pulled her back to the present and she forced a smile for her cousin. Her thoughts were too tangled to share with Aila. She needed time to process them. What she really needed was to talk to Cam and ask him outright. It couldn't be denied that his response to her question last night had been unsatisfactory to say the least.

"Quite well." She took another deep breath and dizziness spun through her. "You're right about Dunadd. Even its shadow makes me ill."

"Come." Aila linked arms. "Let us walk to the monastery. Its library is not nearly as magnificent as the one in Ce, but the Dal Riadans are immensely proud of it."

While Elise had never felt the need to take advantage of the services of the monks in Ce she had to agree. The library there was breathtaking.

Under the watchful eye of a monk who made no secret of his disapproval of their invading his domain, Elise, Aila and their ladies explored the library. It was quite fascinating, but Elise found something else far more intriguing.

When the monk finally stopped glowering at her from across the chamber to focus on one of Aila's ladies who had dared to open a book, she clasped Aila's hand and pulled her into a side passageway.

"Do you feel it?" Her voice was low, but it seemed to echo along the passageway and a shiver whispered across her arms. There was great power here, the kind of power she always felt at the standing stones of both Ce and Circinn.

"Yes." Aila glanced over her shoulder and then led Elise farther along the passageway where it opened out into a large chamber. They remained in the shadows as Elise frowned at the far end of the chamber at the chancel, where the altar stood. It was uncannily similar to the layout of the monastery in Ce. "The old gods do not rest easy here. But I've discovered the Scots have taken many of the ancient places of worship in Dal Riada for their own." Then she sighed. "But so have the Picts. It seems all gods gravitate to the same sacred ground."

Before Elise could answer, two warriors entered the chamber from behind the chancel.

"… if all the princesses of Pictland are as fuckable?" said one with a leer. Elise glanced at Aila and without a word, they stealthily retreated into the shadows of the passageway.

"I would have no objection if MacAlpin ordered me to wed one to strengthen the alliance." The second warrior laughed and made an obscene gesture. Elise ignored Aila's tug on her hand to return to the library, even though she knew if she remained, she would end up offended by the Scots lewd talk. But something stopped her.

"Aye. But why choose MacNeil? He hates the Picts. Surely MacAlpin could have found another willing warrior to bed such a luscious prize."

Elise pressed her hand against her aching thigh. It was no great revelation. She knew Cam hated the Picts, and she knew why he did. She also knew he did not hate all Picts.

He couldn't look at her the way he did if he loathed the very sight of her.

"MacNeil is the one who snared this princess from the start. Don't you know who her former husband was? The bastard he's been hunting for the last nine years. What better revenge can you think of than to take his widow and have her every night?"

No. *No.* She ground her hand against the rough stone wall to clear her head. She had misunderstood. This wasn't true. Ferelei wasn't the Pict Cam had told her about. Even the thought of it churned her stomach. Of course he hadn't planned to snare her from the first moment they had met. Cam wasn't devious. He was honorable and noble.

As the two Scots left the chamber, she heard the first one give an incredulous laugh. "MacNeil's a sly bastard. So he was the one who killed mac Uurguist after all…"

"Lies." The hoarse word scraped her throat and she roughly pulled free of Aila's grip and stumbled into the chamber. "I will have their heads for such slander. How dare they…" The words lodged in her throat as the chamber closed in on her. Goddess help her. She would not faint.

She swung about as Aila once again gripped her hand. Her frenzied thoughts froze at the look of wretched sympathy on her cousin's face.

No. Aila didn't know Cam. She wouldn't believe it. She wouldn't. But even as the denial thundered through her mind, she slowly lifted her hand.

Her palm was bloodied from where she had ground it against the stone wall. The same hand where only weeks ago her crystal had grazed her skin. Terror and denial warred within her heart, but it was a futile battle.

As with a sickening sense of inevitability, she watched a single drop of blood roll from her palm and splash on the unforgiving ground.

CHAPTER 27

ila wrapped her arm around Elise's shoulders and forced her back along the passageway. With every thud of her heart, Elise's denials grew fainter.

It wasn't true. But Bride had spoken in blood.

This was the price her goddess demanded for ridding Elise of Ferelei mac Uurguist.

As they entered the library, her chest grew tight and lungs contracted. A wild rushing sensation filled her head and she pushed Aila away and hurried to the door.

Outside she gasped in the brisk autumn air, but it did nothing to allay the terror snaking through her. She had prayed, *begged*, for her goddess to intervene so she would be free of Ferelei. Bride had put Cameron MacNeil in her path, the one man who wanted Ferelei dead even more than she did herself.

Her stomach heaved. Ferelei had been the one who had raped Isla and caused her death. From a thousand miles away, she heard her ladies flutter behind her, asking her what was wrong. She picked up her skirts and ran across the rutted ground, not knowing where she headed. Not caring.

What did it matter where she ran? She could never escape the sordid truth that polluted her heart.

She had fallen in love with the one man in the world who could never love her in return.

Had he truly planned this from the start? He had sought her out the day after Ferelei had died. Only now did she recall the fresh wound on his face and how relieved she had been that it looked clean.

The wound he must have received before killing his worst enemy.

She pulled up short by the side of the forge, sagged against the stone wall and lost the contents of her stomach. Eyes squeezed shut, sweat trickling along her neck, she ignored the anxious murmuring of her ladies who had followed her. She couldn't face them. She couldn't face anyone. She had been the instrument of Cameron MacNeil's vengeance. And she couldn't even truly blame him for it.

"God damn it, Elise. What ails you?" The voice of Cam, the only man she had ever wanted, smashed through her head and she flinched closer to the wall. "Lady Aila sent a messenger and said you were unwell."

No, she was not unwell. All that ailed her was that her heart had broken beyond repair.

With a muffled curse, he grasped her shoulders and turned her about. She buried her face in her hands. He might despise her, but she still didn't want him to witness the aftermath of her sickness. The evidence on the ground was humiliating enough.

Before she realized his intention, he swept her into his arms. For one weak moment, she longed to curl into his strong embrace and press her hot face against his muscled chest. His familiar scent weaved a false cocoon of comfort around her, an illusion of safety and protection she had fallen for so easily. But it was all a shallow masquerade.

With a sense of dread, she realized he was marching toward

Dunadd. Panic twisted through her. Dunadd was the last place she wanted to be.

"Put me down." Her voice was muffled through her fingers and Cam ignored her. She stiffened and glanced wildly around. People stared, clearly enthralled at the spectacle of one of their Scots warriors manhandling a Pictish princess, even if she was his wife.

His wife. The words were a hollow mockery that seared her heart.

Mortified she looked down at her lap. She would not make a scene. But she couldn't go back into the stifling stronghold.

"I need air."

He hesitated and then swung around and marched away from the stronghold until they reached a small copse. With apparent reluctance, he lowered her to the ground and then held onto her arms as though concerned she might fall.

She edged away from his embrace. She couldn't bear to have his hands on her when she knew how he must disdain her.

The ferocious frown was back on his face and she looked away from him. She had to speak. But she had no words. And she was terribly afraid if she tried to ask him for the truth her fragile façade would crumble to dust.

He snatched the gold circlet from her head and before she had time to react, he pulled her veil from her head. Frozen by such indignity she glared at him as humiliating visions pounded through her mind.

Would he take her here, now, simply to prove he had the right? But she didn't believe he would ever do such a thing. It wasn't in Cam's nature. But what did she know of his nature? Perhaps everything she thought she knew of him had been nothing more than a cruel disguise.

He screwed her delicate veil into a wad, pulled his water bag from his belt and wet the material. "Here." He thrust the crumpled veil back at her. "To refresh yourself."

She stared at the sodden veil and felt blood heat her cheeks. While she had been thinking odious thoughts of her husband, he had merely been trying to ease her discomfort.

Without a word, she took the material and wiped her face. Why was he being kind to her? But she already knew the answer. It was because he didn't realize she knew the truth.

But Cam had never treated her with disrespect. He didn't flatter but he had never given her any reason to doubt his motives. An insubstantial thread of hope flickered to life.

The warriors had been wrong. Ferelei had died as they had been informed—in a drunken accident due to the foul weather.

He was not the despicable Pict Cam had told her about.

She took a deep breath. She would ask him. He would allay her fears. All would be well.

"Cam." Her voice was husky, but she couldn't help it. He still glowered at her, but it wasn't a fierce glare. It was filled with concern. She swallowed. Perhaps she could pretend she hadn't overheard that conversation. Simply continue her life with Cam, and the babe they had created.

But she knew in her heart, the suspicion would never truly die. The last thing she wanted was for it to fester and corrupt what they might build together. It didn't matter whether Aila believed Cam capable of such duplicity. Elise should never for a second have imagined the worst of him.

There was a simple explanation and he would share it with her.

"Aye?" His voice was guarded and the way he'd folded his arms across his chest, her circlet hanging from one wrist, didn't inspire her with confidence. But she wouldn't take the coward's way out.

"I have heard vicious rumors." She licked her lips, but Cam's expression didn't alter. "That Ferelei mac Uurguist," her voice faltered. Goddess, she couldn't say the words. They were too foul.

But they had to be said. "That he was the Pict who attacked Dunmar nine years ago."

She held her breath as she waited for Cam's vehement denial. The silence screamed in her ears. And the way Cam's expression turned granite hard and unforgiving told her so much more than an overheard conversation.

"Cam?" Her voice was sharper than she intended. Trepidation fluttered through her breast, making it hard to breathe. "It's not true, is it?"

She didn't think he was going to answer. Then his eyes narrowed. "It's true."

What? No, he hadn't just confirmed it. He must have misunderstood her question. "But…" she floundered before brutally reeling in her scattered thoughts. "No, that cannot be. Ferelei surely was not the Pict you told me who—who so cruelly treated your sister."

Except she could believe it. Goddess help her.

"It was Ferelei mac Uurguist." His voice sounded oddly remote, as though only a small section of his mind was focused on this moment.

She let out a jagged breath. "Did you kill him?"

"I was responsible for his death." The words were curt and reeked of bitterness.

Of course he was. He had spent more than a third of his life plotting such a fitting retribution. "Why didn't you tell me?"

His lips curled in an unmistakable gesture of contempt. Her heart shriveled. Finally, she was seeing what he truly thought of her, and it was so much worse than she had feared.

"Why would I tell you that, my lady?" The contempt she saw in his face dripped with deadly intent from every word. "Even I know that is not conversation fit for the ears of a princess."

A princess. *My princess*. The words he had whispered to her so often in the past came back to haunt her. He might not embrace his own royal heritage, but he had always appeared fascinated by hers.

My princess. Far from being a tender endearment as she had so foolishly imagined, had he called her that with deliberate intent?

Had he really planned to make her his, right from the very start? To secure another Princess of Pictland through marriage to strengthen MacAlpin's claim on her beloved land?

She clutched her veil in her hands and watched water drip onto the ground. It reminded her of her blood that had splashed onto the floor of the monastery.

The gods gave nothing without great sacrifice. Her foolish dreams of a love-filled future with Cameron MacNeil was the sacrifice Bride demanded.

"Why did you marry me?" Her voice was low but somehow she kept the tremble from it.

"I had no choice."

His words couldn't have hurt more if he had plunged his dagger into her chest with every heartless syllable. She tensed her muscles and straightened her spine. She would not crumple at his feet. She was a Princess of Pictland with a thousand-year heritage, and she would not disgrace her foremothers by showing any weakness.

"By MacAlpin's order." Contempt wove through her accusation.

His jaw clenched. "Aye." It was little more than a ferocious growl.

She had been wrong. He hadn't intended to make her his bride. He had been forced into it by his king.

How noble she had once thought Cam because he didn't flatter her with pretty words or shower her with extravagant compliments. Naively she'd believed it was because he was different to other men.

Other men would say anything to get a woman to lift her skirts. She had never fallen for any of their silken tongues.

But how fatally she had fallen for Cam. He had never attempted to impress her because he had never wanted to impress her. He had pursued her only because his king had commanded it. How blithely she had told him that a man could say anything, but all that counted were his actions.

Today she saw the result of Cameron MacNeil's actions, and they were devastating.

She offered him a brittle smile. "Did you ever have any intention of delivering me to Fib?" Just because Fib had never been her real destination didn't matter. All that mattered was Cam's reply.

She saw his fists clench although his arms remained folded across his chest. "If you left the Kingdom of Ce you were to be taken to Fortriu."

Dal Riada had never been the Scots intended destination. Cam had known before they left Ce that they were traveling to Fortriu and he had never told her.

"I see." Her voice was chilled, in stark contrast to the turmoil tearing her heart to shreds. "It appears there is nothing further to be said. When my cousin leaves Dunadd I shall return to the Kingdom of Ce with her."

The rigid mask cracked, and Cam loomed over her, a dark shadow pulsing malevolence. He gripped her arms and glared into her face.

"You will remain here by my side, where you belong."

She laughed, a scornful sound that scraped along her nerves. "I don't belong by your side, Cameron MacNeil. I belong in Pictland among my own people whom I can trust."

His face twisted. Anyone would think her words wounded him. But she was past believing anything she might say could touch him. He despised her, had always despised her, and while she understood why he could never love her, it didn't make her pain any less.

"You're my wife." His dark eyes raked over her face as though he was committing every feature to memory. "I'll never set you free, Elise, do you understand? I'll never let you be with your dear Droston." He spat the last words at her as though they were a curse.

"Unhand me." It was an icy whisper and when he didn't immediately comply, she pulled back. She knew her strength was nothing compared to his, but for some reason he chose to release her and then stood glaring at her, the way he'd glared at her back in the spring whenever their paths had crossed.

Great goddess, this price was too high to bear. She had been married to a man she hated and feared and thought nothing could be worse. But now she was married to a man she loved more than anyone or anything in the world. A man she had thought admired and respected her, even if he hadn't loved her in the way she secretly craved.

But a life with Cameron MacNeil would destroy her. She would die slowly from the inside, until her heart and soul were nothing but empty husks.

She wouldn't do that to her child. Not even for her goddess.

CHAPTER 28

As Elise turned from him and walked away, Cam battled the savage urge to swing her around, pull her into his arms and make good his threat to never let her go.

But it was no threat. He would never let her go. She was his wife. *His.* She was his reason for rising in the morning, the reason he'd made plans to improve his estates, the reason why he no longer saw shadows lurking in every corner of Dunmar.

When she reached her ladies, who had been waiting for her, they surrounded her like a rainbow cloud. He clenched his fist around her circlet and the gold bit into his hand.

He should have found the time last night to tell her the truth. Now the rumors had poisoned her mind against him, and he couldn't blame her. Every question she had asked him had carved through his chest. And every time he answered, the pain in her eyes had struck another fatal blow to his unprotected heart.

With a violent curse, he marched in the opposite direction of Dunadd. He was in no fit state to meet anyone, least of all his wife. Rage boiled his reason and despair knotted his guts. Only a good fight would ease the torment firing his blood.

But hours later, drenched in sweat and body aching from

fighting four warriors in a merciless training session, he was no closer to seeing clearly. Doubled over, hands on his knees as he tried to catch his breath, he ignored the friendly punches on his shoulders from those who had watched his marathon workout.

All he could see in his mind's eye was the look of contempt on Elise's face when she had told him she belonged in Pictland among those she could trust.

He caught sight of her circlet, fastened to his belt. The inkling of a plan slithered through his mind. He would go to MacAlpin and request permission to leave Dunadd this day. The king after all owed him a boon. Once they were back in Dunmar, away from all outside influence, he'd work day and night to earn back Elise's trust.

He would find a way to grant anything her heart desired.

Anything but her freedom.

In time, she would forgive him. She had to. The thought of never seeing her smile his way again or hear her carefree laugh echo through the hall of Dunmar chilled his blood.

She wasn't a captive bride as his mother had been. Elise had made a choice, and she had chosen him.

But she no longer wanted him. Would he keep her at Dunmar against her will? Suppose she never forgave him for killing mac Uurguist, deceiving her about their journey to Fortriu and the way MacAlpin had forced his hand into taking her as his bride to protect her?

What then?

He straightened and speared his fingers through his matted hair. He wasn't his father. He hadn't abducted and raped Elise and coerced her into marriage. But what of the future? What if she never wanted him to touch her again? Could he bear to live with her, share her bed, and never again know the searing bliss of her welcoming body?

The prospect caused his gut to clench in denial. To live in

such a way would be hell. To watch her light slowly diminish would kill him.

But to let her go would destroy him.

~

ELISE and her ladies had not long returned to her chamber in Dunadd when Aila arrived. Her ladies discreetly left them alone and Elise went to her cousin's comforting embrace.

She squeezed her eyes shut and a bone deep shudder racked her body. "I have made a terrible mistake," she whispered against Aila's shoulder. "I can't stay here, Aila. I have to return to Pictland."

Aila didn't say anything for a few moments, simply held her close and rubbed her back. Finally, she stepped back and held onto Elise's hands. Sorrow filled her eyes.

"I'm so grieved for you, my love," she said. "I was delighted we were wrong when I saw how happy you were. But if you've discovered the truth..." Her voice trailed away but Elise knew what she meant.

She had finally seen the truth that everyone else had seen from the start, except she had been too enchanted by Cameron MacNeil's manner to look for hidden motives.

"It's partly my own fault." She shook her head when Aila frowned in clear disagreement. "No, it's true. I begged Bride to keep Ferelei far from me, and although I never prayed to her for his death, she knew what was in my heart. And this... this is the price I must pay."

"Don't say that." Aila sounded uncharacteristically fierce. "Bride is not cruel or vindictive, Elise. There's always a reason for what she does. Do not think this is merely a punishment for wishing to be free of an evil man. Remember she has blessed you with a child."

Of course she remembered that. The thought of her child was

the single flicker of light in the bleakness of her future. But what was her cousin suggesting? "You would have me stay?" Elise stared at Aila in disbelief.

"Of course not. I had a plan in place to rescue you and return you to Ce with me before we ever entered Dunadd. It was the sole reason I insisted we all meet here."

So that was what Aila had meant by *under the pretext that I had to see you.*

She only half listened as her cousin explained the details of her plan. It involved giving Cam a draught that would make him listless and sick and, apparently, susceptible to manipulation. Elise would insist they take him to her Pictish healers thereby raising no alarm that she was, in reality, escaping.

The thought of deliberately making him sick brought her no pleasure at all. Was this truly the only way she could be free of him? Why was it that, even now, a part of her wanted nothing more than to stay with him for the rest of their lives?

"It cannot be done until tomorrow," she interrupted Aila, who appeared convinced they should put her plan into action instantly. "I have an audience with MacAlpin this afternoon to negotiate a ransom for the release of Droston."

She may have failed in her marriage, but she would not fail Droston.

Aila stared at her blankly. It appeared Elise's remark had rendered her speechless.

"Droston?" she said at last.

"Yes. He saved my life and I will not leave him here to rot." Perhaps, aside from her babe, this was the only reason Bride had secured her marriage to Cam. To ensure Elise would reach Dunadd and finally procure Droston's release.

ELISE FORCED herself to remain still on the stool as her ladies continued to fuss over her hair and veil. It was lucky she had brought two circlets with her to Dunadd, as Cam had kept the one he'd snatched off her head earlier that day.

But she couldn't think of Cam. Not now when she was preparing to meet with MacAlpin.

Aila sat on the bed. Elise knew her cousin wasn't happy about the upcoming meeting, but she had long since stopped trying to convince Elise against it. Elise knew it was only because she had evoked Bride's name that Aila had finally fallen silent on the subject. It certainly wasn't because she agreed that Elise owed Droston for that long-ago debt.

There was a knock on the door and when Connor MacKenzie entered, Aila leaped to her feet and went to him. "Is something wrong?"

He wrapped his arm around her. "No, nothing is wrong." But the way he then glanced at Elise belied his words. He looked back at his wife. "I need you and Lady Elise to return with me to our chamber, Aila. Alone."

Elise swallowed her impatience. "Could this wait, Connor?" To be sure, there was an hour before she was due to meet with MacAlpin, but the last thing she felt like doing was socializing.

"Forgive me." Connor bowed her way as best he could, seeing as he was still holding Aila. "But it cannot wait, my lady."

She took a deep breath and stood up. "Very well." She motioned her ladies to remain behind and followed Connor and Aila to their chamber.

Connor opened the door to their antechamber and against protocol indicated Elise should precede Aila. Frowning, Elise entered the chamber. And stopped dead as Droston turned toward her.

"My lady." His familiar grin pierced her heart and with a choked sob, she ran to him and flung herself in his arms. He held her tight, patting her back and eventually she pulled free so she could look into his blue eyes, so similar to her own.

"You are well?" Her voice was husky. From the corner of her eyes, she was aware of Aila's anxious glances toward her husband, but she ignored her cousin. She didn't care what Aila or Connor thought.

"Well enough." He squeezed her hand. "And apparently I'm also free to return to Circinn."

"MacAlpin has freed you? But why—has a ransom been paid for you?" His mother and her husband were nobles, to be sure, but they were far from wealthy. The news that they had managed to raise a ransom enough to entice MacAlpin staggered her.

Connor cleared his throat. "My lady." There was an oddly reluctant note in his voice that managed to drag her attention from Droston. "MacAlpin released this Pict at the request of your husband, Cameron MacNeil."

"Cam?" She stared at Connor, hearing his words but they made no sense. "Why would he ask MacAlpin such a thing?" Cam didn't even know Droston, except for the fact that he had once saved her life.

But the last time they'd spoken, he had spat Droston's name at her, as though he hated the very sound of it. Now she thought about it, that hadn't made any sense either.

"MacNeil has entrusted your safety to me, my lady. I'm to ensure you and your friend Droston are safely delivered back into Pictland."

Cam had asked Connor to take her and Droston back to Pictland? But why? Only hours ago, he stood in front of her and snarled how he would never let her go. That she belonged to him.

I will never let you be with your dear Droston.

A shiver chased over her arms as she recalled the savage look in his eyes as he'd thrown those words at her.

No. Surely not. Surely Cam didn't believe she was in love with Droston.

"Goddess." Aila pressed her hand to her breast and looked between Elise and Droston. It was glaringly obvious what she was thinking. "Cameron MacNeil has set you both free."

"Droston saved my life." She pressed her lips together before she spilled the secret that could never be revealed. But if Aila, her own cousin, believed she was in love with Droston then why was it so difficult to believe Cam had drawn the same conclusion?

Heat washed through her as she remembered the times she had mentioned Droston's name to him. She had desperately tried to convey she loved Droston as a brother, but it seemed she'd failed.

But why would he care who she loved, if the only reason he wanted her in his life was because of her royal Pictish blood? If he chose to, there was nothing to stop him from keeping her captive in Dunmar, just as his father had kept his mother.

But Cam would never do that. Despite everything he had done, at his core he was still the honorable, noble man she had always believed.

"MacNeil said he will ensure all the treasure you brought into Dal Riada is returned to you." Connor was scowling at a point above her head, as though this conversation deeply offended him. It probably did. Cam was a fellow Scots warrior who had snared another Pictish princess. Of course Connor wouldn't be pleased to see her slip through MacAlpin's grasping fingers.

But even as the thought formed, she knew it wasn't true. Connor would think no such thing and as for Cam…

Her thoughts shifted and fragments of their conversations haunted the corners of her mind.

The day she had waited for him by the sacred stones, when she had no longer needed to coerce Cam into helping her free Droston, he had warned her of coming danger.

It might be wise if you remain in Ce, where you are safe.

Why would he say that to her, if his sole objective was delivering her to his king? If his only motive was snaring a Pictish princess of his own?

I will do everything within my power to protect you.

Perhaps he had never intended to make her his bride, but what if marrying her was the only way he knew how to protect her from the machinations of his king?

Yes, he had deceived her and deliberately kept the truth from her. But why had he? Was it because, as he'd told her earlier today, he'd had no choice?

"Where is he?"

Connor finally refocused on her. "I don't think that's—"

"I need to know where he is." Her voice was regal and booked no argument. Connor looked at Aila who shrugged in clear confusion.

"He was on his way to the docks."

"The docks?" That was the last place she had imagined, and unease flickered through her breast. She would march through the mud of the training fields to confront him but the thought of getting so close to the vast expanse of gray sea was another matter entirely. "Why would he go there?"

Connor gave her a calculating look. "I believe he intends to sail to the Isle of Iona."

Disbelief speared through her. Cam couldn't go to Iona. The Vikings were forever attempting to gain a foothold on that isle, and she knew the Scots kept a contingent of warriors there as a deterrent. But if the Vikings attacked unexpectedly, what chance did a small band of warriors stand against the brutal onslaught of barbarians?

"I must speak with him. I need to go to the docks now."

"Elise," Aila stepped toward her. "The docks are no place for you. Let Connor send a messenger. It will reach Cameron MacNeil faster than if you—"

"No. I must see him." It wasn't up for negotiation. "Although I would be greatly obliged, Connor, if you could arrange a small contingent of warriors to accompany me."

"I'll go with you." Droston squeezed her fingers. "I want to meet this husband of yours, my lady, and thank him for my freedom."

~

THE DOCKS WERE A NOISY, bustling place, with ramshackle buildings overflowing with the stink of ale and poverty and sex for sale. Droston helped her dismount and Connor, who had insisted on accompanying her along with three of his most trusted compatriots, marched up to her.

"Wait here, my lady. I'll be back as soon as I discover where Cam is."

As Connor disappeared into the crowd, Droston pulled her back from the other three warriors. "I saw your father several times, Elise. He is well and misses you greatly."

How good it was to hear Droston call her by her name. He always did when they were alone, a shared reminder of the carefree times they had enjoyed while children.

"I am glad. I miss him, too." But her priority had always been Droston. "I pray MacAlpin will soon release all his hostages." Even as she said it, she knew it was a hollow wish. Pictland would never bow to the upstart king and therefore he would always keep some royal blood as security.

Droston glanced around as though ensuring they had privacy. "We got to know each other during those times. A few days ago, he told me who my real father is."

Elise stared at him as his words thundered through her mind. "He told you?" Her voice was scarcely above a whisper. She had kept the secret for so long even now she couldn't say the words.

Droston shrugged one shoulder and squinted into the crowd. "He said he had always wanted to acknowledge me, but events proved that to be impossible." He looked back at her and gave her a wry smile. "He also said you've known for many years and he grieved for the burden you were forced to bear because of it."

"Oh." Elise flapped her hand at him and forced back the irrational tears that threatened. "I've always loved you as my brother, Droston. When I discovered you truly were, it was a bittersweet revelation knowing I could never openly claim you."

Droston's gaze slid over her shoulder. "The Scot returns." He looked down at Elise. "Alone."

Elise swung on her heel and watched Connor approach. Where was Cam? A terrible thought assailed her. Had Connor found her husband enmeshed in one of the countless brothels?

Other unsavory thoughts hit her. Was Cam drunk in a side alley? Embroiled in a street fight?

Connor stopped before her. "I've discovered his whereabouts." He turned and Elise followed his gaze. To the massive ship moored a frightening distance from shore.

CHAPTER 29

The tiny rowing boat was half-aground, and Elise clenched her sweaty hands a few times in a vain effort to still her nerves. Droston was already in the boat, arms outstretched to assist her, but she was frozen in place.

"Come, my lady," Droston coaxed. "Do you wish me to carry you onboard?"

What a fine spectacle that would make. Without warning, she was catapulted back in time, to that terrifying moment when she'd lost her footing on the slippery crag and plunged into the raging river. The icy water had filled her mouth and nose and clutched greedily at her gown, trying to suck her under. Shock and terror so utterly consumed her that it had been several seconds before the agony of her shattered leg engulfed her.

She couldn't think of that now. There wasn't time to indulge her old nightmares of drowning and pain so intense she begged for oblivion. She took a deep breath, but the salty air only reminded her of the terrifying expanse of water she was about to willingly risk her life on.

But there was no other way if she wished to speak to Cam. She swallowed, mouth dry, and stepped off the edge of the world.

Droston caught her. She was safe. She opened her eyes, unaware until that moment that she had even squeezed them shut, and let out a ragged breath. She sat on the timber plank as the men began to row toward the open sea.

Waves lapped against the side of the boat. It swayed alarmingly and her stomach heaved in erratic tandem. Sweat trickled along the back of her neck and her hands, clasped on her lap, were clammy.

"Almost there," Droston said with a reassuring smile although it was blatantly obvious there was still a huge distance to go. She licked her dry lips, but it did no good. She gripped the side of the boat, hung over the edge, and retched violently.

Goddess. How mortifying. She kept her eyes shut but somehow that made the boat lurch all the more. How much farther? She only hoped Cam had not witnessed her humiliating upset.

"Here." Droston passed her a length of material and she pressed it against her lips. Gingerly she sat back on the plank and focused on the curved bottom of the boat. She would not think of the swirling water or the treacherous rocks that lurked beneath. All that mattered was she saw Cam before he set sail to Iona.

CAM GRIPPED a length of rope between his hands and glared in disbelief as Elise boarded the ship. What was she doing here? He had resigned himself to never seeing her again. Except he knew he would never be resigned to such a fate and seeing her now only reinforced that fact with mocking contempt.

As she swayed on the deck, her face as white as the snow-capped mountains in winter, she clutched onto a man. With damning reluctance, Cam tore his mesmerized gaze from her and focused on the one who held her with such insulting care.

A cursed Pict. With blond hair tied back from his aristocratic face, the tall, lithe bastard looked a fitting consort for a princess. His gut clenched and the rope burned his palms. He had never seen the man before but knew who he was.

Her dear Droston.

"MacNeil, a word if you please."

Connor MacKenzie's sharp command bit through the crimson fog clouding his vision. He hadn't even known Connor was there. What in the name of God was going on? Women didn't set foot on a war vessel and his wife most certainly did not belong on this ship, where she was currently the focus of every man with eyes in his head.

He rounded on the spectators and the ferocious glower he arrowed their way caused them to shuffle backwards, although they didn't immediately return to their tasks.

It would have to do. He turned back to Elise and saw how she had straightened from her beloved Droston, and how her hands now grasped the skirt of her gown in clear distress.

She was terrified of a fast-flowing stream. What had possessed her to climb into a boat and face the open sea?

He crushed the overpowering urge to wrap her in his arms and reassure her she was safe, that all was well. He had lost that right when he'd asked MacAlpin to release the Pict as his boon the king had promised.

Cam had vowed to give Elise the world. How bitter to discover that her world was Droston.

He ignored Connor. "What are you doing here?" He sounded feral but Elise didn't flinch before his voice or his furious glare. But then if she had his withered heart would have died a little more.

She stepped toward him, lurching inelegantly as her leg gave way. He dropped the rope and caught her arm, and then could not release her.

"Thank you." Her breathy whisper tore through his chest. She didn't pull free from his grasp, but it had to be his wretched imagination that her fingers tightened around his forearm. "I have to speak with you, Cam."

He tried not to lose his soul in her spellbinding blue eyes, but he had lost his soul to her months ago. "I believe we have said everything to each other, my lady."

Aye, they had said everything, and he had told her nothing. But how could he tell her what she meant to him, when she had given her heart to Droston so many years ago? He knew she had once cared for him as her husband. Maybe in time she would forgive him enough to care for him again. But he wanted more than that. He wanted it all, and that was why he had set her free.

She had already been trapped in a loveless marriage. He would not trap her in another. It didn't matter that she was his sun and moon, or that the stars in the sky could not compare to the light she had brought into his bleak existence.

Elise deserved more than that. She deserved to be with the man she loved.

"We have said a great deal." Elise gazed at him as though she was trying to impart a hidden message. God, this was torture. Every second he looked at her, every second he touched her, made it harder to cut her from his life. "But we can say anything. It's our actions that truly count."

An eerie shudder inched over his arms. She had said something similar weeks ago. Words had never come easily to him, and to know a princess like Elise was not concerned by this lack had torn him up inside. Because if she knew all the things he'd concealed from her, contempt would replace the admiration illuminating her lovely face.

"Leave now." His cursed actions belied his words as his fingers tightened around her arm. "While you still have the chance."

The tip of her tongue moistened her lips. Didn't she know how close he was to reclaiming his rights as her husband? How easy it would be for him to sweep her into his arms and confine her in Dunmar, where she would never see her Pictish lover again?

"There is someone I wish you to meet." Her voice was husky, and he glared at her, unable to believe she wanted him to meet the man who aroused such conflicting emotions. Hatred because he held Elise's heart. And gratitude, because without Droston Elise would have died that day in the river.

The Pict stepped forward and appeared unconcerned by the deadly intent Cam directed his way.

"Cameron MacNeil." He spoke in Gaelic, his accent similar to Elise's as though to underscore how far more suited to her he was than Cam. "I offer you my thanks for securing my release. You have my loyalty for this."

Cam's lip curled. "I care nothing for your loyalty. I did it for the princess."

Droston glanced at Elise. It appeared to be strangely calculating and a surge of protectiveness rushed through him. How dare the Pict look at his wife in such a manner?

God help him. Elise had to leave now, before he lost his mind.

The Pict looked back at him. And then, unbelievably, took a step toward him. "The princess is bound by a blood oath to silence, but I'm tethered by no such bonds." His voice was low. It was obvious he wanted no one else to overhear. Elise took a sharp intake of breath and shot her Pict a shocked look.

"Droston."

"No. I will speak the truth this once, Elise, to clear the air between us three."

To hear the Pict call Elise by her given name ripped through Cam's guts. Only by sheer force of will did he stop himself from gripping the hilt of his sword.

That, and the fact Elise was still clinging to his other arm. God damn it, why did she have to stand so close to him? Why did she have to look at him in that beseeching manner?

"I've loved the princess since we were children," Droston said, staring him down, daring him to retaliate. Cam's fingers curled around his hilt. He might have been instrumental in freeing this man, but he'd be damned if he'd stand by and let the bastard rub his nose in the fact Elise had chosen him over her own husband.

Except deep in his heart, he knew he would. He'd do anything to try and make up for the way he'd deceived her and coerced her into marriage.

"So I've heard." He raked his gaze over the Pict. "You saved her life. For that you have my thanks and now we are even."

"No." To Cam's incredulous disbelief the Pict leaned in closer until he was almost level with Elise. "You're wrong. Elise and I love each other but not in the way you think. She is my half-sister."

The ship lurched beneath his feet and the world reeled, as Droston's words echoed through his mind. He slowly dragged his gaze from the Pict to Elise, and then back again. Shock stabbed through his heart.

On the journey to Fortriu, Elise had said *some things can never be discussed, no matter how dearly one might wish it*. He'd thought she was trying to give him a hidden message. But he'd imagined she referred to her first unhappy marriage.

She hadn't. She'd been speaking of Droston, of the blood oath that prevented her from ever confiding in anyone.

Even him.

Droston bowed, a mocking smile on his lips before he retreated, leaving him and Elise with a semblance of privacy.

"Forgive me," she whispered. "I wanted to confide in you, but I am unable to ever speak of this matter."

She asked for his forgiveness? She had done nothing wrong. It was he who had lied to her, who had jumped to conclusions and thought to treat her as despicably as his father had treated his mother.

He didn't deserve her. But he had never deserved her.

"There's nothing to forgive. I also have been bound by unwanted oaths." It was a growl and he knew his old familiar glare was back on his face. It was the only way he could function. If he let his guard down for an instant, he knew he'd carry out his earlier desperate thought.

To take Elise back to Dunmar, whether she wanted to or not.

"I asked you back in Dunadd why you married me." Her voice was soft, but her gaze was penetrating. "I stand before you now to ask you the same question. Why did you marry me, Cameron MacNeil of Dunmar?"

He felt his scowl slip as her words hammered through his mind. She had faced her deepest fear of the sea because she wanted to know why he had married her?

He'd told her the truth before. He'd had no choice. But God, that wasn't the whole truth. Did she truly want him to lay his battered heart at her feet and risk having the slender thread of hope that she might one day love him in return severed for all time?

It wasn't his imagination. Her fingers dug into his forearm, as though she had no intention of letting him go until he'd answered her question.

She would not have crossed the harbor simply to tell him she was leaving him. Would she?

In the depths of his soul, the flicker of hope stirred. He took a deep breath. Facing the Norse in battle was less torturous than this.

"MacAlpin threatened to have you compromised if I didn't take you as my bride." Even saying the words now, weeks later, caused black rage to coil through his gut. But before his fury could fully get hold, he saw the light diminish from Elise's eyes.

"So you married me to protect me." She smiled, but it didn't reach her eyes and a deep sense of sorrow radiated from her. "As you promised you would do anything to protect me while we were in Ce."

"Aye." He frowned, unsure why his disclosure appeared to grieve her. It hadn't been his intention or his hope. "It was the only way to keep you safe from his further machinations, Elise. I don't know why you agreed to become my wife but," he grimaced, fighting for the right words. Why was it so hard to tell her how he felt about her? Why could they not drip easily from his tongue, as such flattery did from every other man he knew?

Except he didn't want to flatter her. He just wanted to tell her the truth.

"But?"

Was it his imagination or was there a fragile thread of hope in that one word? Could he risk Elise leaving now, with her brother, simply because he found it so hard to spit out a few goddamn words?

He trailed a finger along the line of her face, only realizing what he was doing when she caught her breath. Would she be here if she despised him? If she hated him for everything he had put her through? Was she here because she wanted to give them another chance?

There was only one thing he could say. "But I'd dreamed of making you my bride since the moment I first saw you. I knew it was an impossible dream. I fought against it. And then circumstances thrust us together and I was lost."

Her bottom lip trembled but she smiled, and the indefinable sense of sorrow faded. "You married me because you wanted to."

"Aye." Hadn't he made that plain? "The thought of another man touching you caused murder to fill my heart. I would never let you be so used, Elise. Not even to please MacAlpin."

"I know." Her whisper was so low he had to strain to hear it above the sound of the waves lapping against the ship and the gulls screeching overhead. "You are truly the most honorable man I have ever met."

Her simple praise cut like a blade through his chest. He could ignore it. He knew Elise herself would never raise the question of what had happened to mac Uurguist. But she would always wonder, and it would hover between them like a specter.

He gripped her free hand, as though that might make the words come more easily.

"I sought out mac Uurguist that night to seek vengeance for Isla." Shit, did he always have to be so blunt? Couldn't he have found a way to soften his words? He sounded as though he accused her of something, when that was the last thing he wanted her to assume.

"I know. Please, Cam." Distress threaded through her voice. "You weren't the only one who wished him dead, although your cause was greater."

And now she was shouldering blame for the bastard's death. "But vengeance eluded me. It was no lie, how he died. He did fall and crack open his skull, although if I hadn't been there, he would likely never have fallen in the first place."

"You did not kill him?" Her voice was oddly hushed.

Had he? Maybe, but not in the way he had always envisaged. "In the end—no."

"I thought Bride had guided your hand."

Instead of unease at how she invoked her goddess, a strange sense of calm descended over him. "Perhaps Bride stayed my hand."

She stared at him, a look of wonder on her face. "Justice was served for Isla and my darkest prayers answered. But perhaps, after all, Bride had her own reasons for the ignoble way Ferelei ended his journey."

Perhaps she had. Who was he to argue with powers he knew nothing about? Isla had been avenged. Elise had been freed. And he was not left with blood on his hands that could, even unintentionally, come between him and Elise.

He pressed his forehead against hers and ignored the distant good-natured jeers of his countrymen. There was something he had to ask her.

"If we were not wed, and knowing everything you now know about me, if I asked you to be my wife now—how would you answer?"

She didn't even give him time to hold his breath. Her gentle laugh and the way her fingers squeezed his gave him hope before she even spoke.

"I would say yes, Cameron MacNeil. I would be honored to be your wife."

It seemed his heart expanded inside his chest. A foolish notion, but he relished the warmth that flooded his veins and the light that suddenly filled the world. He wrapped his arms around his bride, heedless of their bawdy audience. What did he care for others' opinions? Elise knew the worst of him and still consented to be his wife.

"But I have a stipulation," she gasped against his ear, and he froze.

"A stipulation?"

"Yes. I know it's my dowry, but we must strip Dunmar of every item I brought with me. We can sell it, Cam. It will fetch a good price. But I want no reminder of my former husband in my future home."

He didn't care about her dowry. He had never cared for what riches Elise might bring to their marriage. He had only suffered mac Uurguist's treasure because of the luxury it brought his princess.

"If that is your wish." His voice was husky.

"Yes. And I have another wish. Please, Cam. Please do not sail to Iona."

He looked at her and saw the concern in her eyes. Concern for him. "I'm not going to Iona." He had come onboard to help and sailing to Iona had been only a notion in the back of his mind. Something to consider once Elise had left for Pictland.

But Elise was not leaving for Pictland. Not unless he accompanied her as her husband.

She let out a relieved breath. "Thank goddess."

For the second time within minutes, he found himself agreeing with her heathen sentiments. And for the second time he questioned his convictions when it came to higher powers.

He didn't know the truth of such things. Perhaps he never would. But he could respect Elise's beliefs.

God knows, they had been the same as his mother's.

He reached for a pouch on his belt, and his hand knocked Elise's circlet. He would return it to her later, now he no longer needed to keep it as a solitary reminder of her.

With infinite care, he pulled out the precious treasure from his pouch and offered it to Elise on the palm of his hand.

"Would you take this as a token of our marriage?"

He heard her sharp gasp as she tentatively traced her finger over his mother's pagan necklace. The necklace he had so loved as a child. That, damn it, he still loved.

"I will treasure it always." She looked up at him, and tears sparkled in her eyes. "Why, Cam? Why do you want me to have this?"

How could she even ask that question? Wasn't it glaringly obvious?

He leaned in close so there was no possibility of even an errant goddess overhearing him. "Because I love you Elise, Princess Clodrah of Circinn. You gave me back my life. I want to share it with none other but you."

She pulled back, just enough so she could look him in the eyes. "My noble Scot warrior." There was a catch in her voice. "I married you because I loved you and I will always love you, Cameron MacNeil of Dunmar."

Fierce love, pride and protectiveness surged through him. "We'll leave Dunadd this day and return home." Relief and wonder spiked through him that he could so easily refer to Dunmar as his home now. But it was only because Elise also thought of it as her home. Hell, he'd be happy living in a cave, if it pleased her.

"There is one more thing, my lord." A spark of mischief lit her eyes. "We will not be returning to Dunmar alone."

He knew she wasn't referring to the warriors or her ladies who would accompany them. Did she mean her cousin and Connor would be visiting? He thought they were on their way to the Kingdom of Ce.

"Your cousin and all your relatives are always welcome in our home, my lady."

She gave a small laugh. "Indeed, that is very generous of you. I don't believe we need worry that my mother will visit us any time soon, although we will need to visit her in the spring. But I wasn't referring to that." She paused and he attempted to work out what she was talking about. And failed. She rose onto her toes and her lips all but brushed his. "I'm speaking of our babe, Cam. It's very early, but I am certain Bride has blessed us."

A baby. Elise had conceived his child. A sense of awe engulfed him, and his gaze slid to her belly. He had never really thought about having a family with Elise. Just having her in his life had filled his thoughts.

But a child. Their child. The final shadow slipped free from his soul, releasing him from the darkness of his past.

With a laugh, he picked her up and swung her around. To hell with his surly reputation and the unrelenting mockery he would receive from his countrymen for displaying such unseemly behavior in public.

His wife loved him. They were going to have a child. For a hazy second, he thought he saw an ethereal rainbow shimmer around Elise and the strangest sense of peace wrapped around him.

Isla. Their mother.

And Elise. Always Elise. She had opened his eyes and his mind, and she had filled his heart. He realized he hadn't answered her, and even though her smile told him she had no need for his words, that his reaction told her everything she needed to know, sometimes words were simply needed.

He took a deep breath. "You were worth waiting for." It was not eloquent. It was blunt. And from his heart.

She cradled his face, his beautiful princess, and whispered words he never thought to hear. "And so were you."

HER BASEBORN SCOT

THE HIGHLAND WARRIOR CHRONICLES
BOOK 3

A warrior with cursed royal blood...

Commanded by his king to hunt down and marry the elusive Princess of Pictland, Finn Braeson is captivated by a mysterious Pict lady with secrets in her eyes. If only he were free to make her his.

A princess who must hide her identity...

Determined to avenge her people against the upstart king, Mairi cannot fall for the silken charms of a Scots warrior. Yet despite the dangers, she cannot resist his allure.

First love, only love...

But when betrayal rocks their fragile alliance, they must fight the political intrigues that surround them and put their trust in each other – or risk being torn apart forever.

HER WICKED SCOT

THE HIGHLAND WARRIOR CHRONICLES
BOOK 4

A warrior rumored to have no heart...

Sent into Pictland to discover the identity of a desperate assassin, Ewan MacKinnon fights his fascination with the aloof princess, Briana. Although he wants nothing more than to take her into his arms, he won't taint her with the curse that has blighted him all his life.

An ice princess, who has vowed never to love again...

After her first disastrous marriage, Briana is determined to dedicate her life in service to Pictland and her beloved goddess. But her goddess is elusive, sending only visions of a splintered future–a future that is tied irrevocably to the one man she fears could shatter her heart forever. The enemy of her people, Scots warrior Ewan MacKinnon.

A forced marriage that could break them both...

As Briana and Ewan battle both duty and desire, political intrigue tightens its noose around them. But with the assassin edging ever closer they must forsake the shackles of their past and risk their fragile love for a chance of surviving an ultimate betrayal.

288

ABOUT THE AUTHOR

Christina Phillips is an ex-pat Brit who now lives in sunny Western Australia with her high school sweetheart and their family. She enjoys writing paranormal, historical fantasy, and contemporary romance where the stories sizzle and the heroine brings her hero to his knees.

She is addicted to good coffee, expensive chocolate, and bad boy heroes. She is also owned by three gorgeous cats who are convinced the universe revolves around their needs. They are not wrong.

Discover all of Christina's books on her website ChristinaPhillips.com

ACKNOWLEDGMENTS

A big thank you and squishy hugs go to my long-suffering husband Mark and our children. You guys rock! For Amanda Ashby and Sally Rigby, thank you for always helping me to see the light at the end of the tunnel! And Mel Teshco and Cathleen Ross, for all the support and cyber chocolate over the last few years. What would we do without email?

AUTHOR'S NOTE

Although this is a work of fiction, Kenneth MacAlpin, king of the Scots of Dal Riada, did become king of all Pictland in 843 or thereabouts. How he achieved this is open to speculation and I've based my interpretation of events on myths and legends and my own imagination.

www.ingramcontent.com/pod-product-compliance
Lightning Source LLC
Chambersburg PA
CBHW050143120726
47903CB00002B/467